About the Author

Leon Gray was born in the north of England and has worked throughout the UK in finance and taught for many years in a number of state high schools in Newcastle Upon Tyne and County Durham. He has written extensively in the fields of education and philosophy.

Leon Gray

In the Stars

A Novel of Wych Elm

AUSTIN MACAULEY PUBLISHERS™

LONDON • CAMBRIDGE • NEW YORK • SHARJAH

A CIP catalogue record for this title is available from the British Library.

ISBN 978-1-78693-054-5 (Paperback)
ISBN 978-1-78693-055-2 (Hardback)
ISBN 978-1-78693-056-9 (eBook)

www.austinmacauley.com

First Published (2017)
Austin Macauley Publishers Ltd.
25 Canada Square
Canary Wharf
London
E14 5LQ

There seem to be a hundred reasons to account for every act. Finally one hesitates to ascribe any one of them to the act. Life gets more and more mysterious, not less.

Lawrence Durrell, Tunc, 1968

Chapter One

"Have you heard? He's in the stars..." said Sandra, in her light singing voice, coupled with a beaming smile. Some 20 odd years ago she might have made it, a sort of stardom, with some encouragement and training. Stamina wasn't an issue and neither were her looks; high cheek bones and big hazel eyes that had a tendency to flicker in artificial light. Even 20 years ago he may have chanced his arm with this one – supple curvature and fine legs, coupled with a visible bust which was ever present but not in earth-mother excess.

Even just some years the wrong side of forty, with a son soon to graduate from Manchester in one of the sciences and a daughter training to be a 'proper' nurse, as Sandra regularly expressed it, Danny had often noted an altogether attractive persona who could have gone far. Would she have wanted it? Really wanted it? There he detected some doubts in the scenarios he thought up for her and he always placed her in his mid-60s heydays, three years, at least, before she was even born. But scenarios, or memories, were the things that kept him going now, living a version of the past in the present. He would not see eighty-seven again. The party they gave him to celebrate this rather dubious event, shortly after his arrival here, a little over two years ago, remained in his memory akin to a bout of dysentery. His body may be elderly; his mind was not.

His fame helped. But even that could be a double edged sword. A persistent journalist wanted to interview him for a second time later today. Though female, with a sort of fame and notoriety which would normally attract him, he discerned trouble from this one. Though originally local, she had made her name in London. He felt he was being used, mechanically manipulated for a purpose he couldn't immediately identify. The targets are there in anyone who has really lived and had the material success which he had grafted for since the end of the war. However, it takes one to know one and Jan Dale, at sixty, still attractive at distance, or in half-light, did give him the continuing mental stimulation he craved.

Sandra had arrived with his mid-morning coffee. She was ideal as one of his dedicated carers here in the *Sunny Brook Home*, owned by a private company where Danny held half the shares. There was another, *Sunny Acres*, occupying what had once been a farm house over in Aspen Hill, five miles distant over the ridge way. Both care homes were for the elderly who could either pay a bit or who qualified, through residence in Wych Elm or

Aspen Hill, for grants Danny had made available in trusts where a few million pounds had been deposited in the mid-80s. It had saved him a fortune in tax liabilities and given him a new type of publicity to die for, thus assisting his progress in areas outside pop music and television.

Both homes eschewed the smell of urine covered by scented cleaning materials. Residents were given a hotel type of experience – regular bathing and daily changes of one's clothing and a laundry service that returned material in good condition rather than boiled into the consistency of cheese cloth. In some of the other places clothing came back as if boiled in a central heating system. Staff were carefully selected, paid well and expected to maintain the highest standards. Any hint of coldness toward the elderly and even previous experience in care homes was looked on with a sceptical eye; there were no barking nurses' who gave the impression their earlier career in the torturing profession had been terminated due to excessive cruelty.

As far as he could be, Danny was settled here. His past career had established him. His continued local residence, a long ownership within his family of a stone quarry employing generations in Wych Elm, and the fact that there were still people around who remembered him opening *Danny's Place* in what had been a tin-roofed shack of a cinema way back in the 40s. It had served to make him a quietly approved celebrity. The venue had been a relatively inexpensive place to dance with six nights and three lunch sessions per week, a youngsters' dance club on Saturday mornings, and the first known use of twin-deck record players in this part of the north. It was *the* place to be and, later, saw Danny Hird as a professional disc jockey, television host, pop promoter and all round media personality. Indeed, it had been Sandra's mother who had told her to use Danny's intro from the late 50s, *Have you heard?* It was loosely based on the Frank Sinatra/Bing Crosby number from *High Society* and was a play on Danny's surname, Hird. Sandra said her mother had once been one of the trio of girls selected to sing this ditty back in 1958 or maybe 1959, at the beginning of the Saturday evening session. Danny selected three girls at random to come up to the small stage and warble down the microphone while he clowned behind them. He could not remember Sandra's mum but pretended he did. There were some girls he could recall for an assortment of reasons and he could have missed her, being occasionally absent on other business at that time. Maybe Cliff Hindle or Tommy Edwards had chosen her when he was away.

Danny put his finger to his mouth with a grin, cupped his ear and nodded toward the open door which Sandra had almost sashayed through. She put the cup on the small table where Danny was sitting and listened with him. Across the corridor another resident, Mary Hobson, was in full flow. Her son had plucked up the courage to visit her again after a fairly tense visit the evening before. Mary was ninety-five. Her son, Henry, was sixty-seven, a retired merchant banker who still sat on various boards of leading financial institutions in the city of London and locally on regional boards based in

Manchester. He had won arguments with government ministers, senior bankers at home and abroad, and negotiated two of the biggest industrial mergers of 1975 and 1982. However, he could never win an argument with his mother. This morning was no better and typical of these politely grinding encounters.

Mary had arrived a year ago. She had suffered two bad falls at home and the home-based care had proved inadequate. Danny spoke to her from time to time. She had come to Wych Elm in 1946, originally of Irish heritage, from a small town on the Scottish border. She had retained her Scottish accent, often saying the Lancashire accent of her husband "was no' polished" and "gave a bad impression." Her husband had inherited the family iron monger's business off the high street. He had met Mary at a dance in Trowbridge, Wiltshire, when he was serving in the Royal Army Service Corps and where she had escaped small-town Scotland to work in England – which she described as "much more polished" – in the war department which eventually merged into the Ministry of Agriculture.

She had hankered after Wiltshire or, frankly, any southern rural English county ever since and had spent a quarter of a century of marriage "shipwrecked," as she put it, in Wych Elm among Lancastrians whom she felt it her duty to look down on from an ever-increasing height. Her husband had died following a severe bout of pneumonia in 1971, with Henry having finished an Oxford degree and working in London and her daughter Lucinda recently engaged to a dentist from Sussex.

Having sold the shop, yard and small smithy, everyone who knew her assumed she would move south "for the better weather" or the "much more pleasant people." But no. She seemed to thrive in her dark moods, her sense of superiority, her careful charitable giving and only went away to spread her discontent with either of her children or, for one week a year, at an inexpensive hotel in Worthing.

Henry's choice of bride was deemed positive. She was Catholic, could cook in the French style and was privately educated. Lucinda's husband failed the religious test, being firmly Church of England, but as the son of a vicar and therefore "polished," he was considered adequate enough for her daughter. Henry divorced in 1988, much to Mary's chagrin, his wife taking their child to live in Spain. Lucinda stayed married and her two boys seemed to fit some, albeit a small minority, of Grandma's exacting requirements. While attending Mass regularly, Mary rarely spoke to the priest except to criticise something or other and remained the type of faithful Catholic who could cheerfully light the faggots under remarried divorcees or anyone badly dressed in the pews. It was a simple faith which made stern demands and Mary felt it her duty to pass on those demands with interest. She was kind in her own way but expected deference for showing her charitable side to "those in genuine need."

Mary would also tell anyone how she had been permanently ill for years, poorly treated by doctors and not being listened to – especially by her children. They had dumped her in this place full of old people, some of them gaga and so few of them capable of a conversation.

"I start to talk to people and they fall asleep or they walk away!"

Mary made it clear that she had children all those years ago to look after her. It was a form of biological insurance and a source of permanent deference.

"I'm their mother. It's their duty."

"They should be looking after me! They've sold my bungalow, left me here and are getting on with their lives! Sheer selfishness, that's what it is!"

Mary would not acknowledge to anyone that Lucinda had been diagnosed with multiple sclerosis at the age of thirty-seven, nor would she discuss, except in passing, Henry's ongoing problems with stomach ulcers.

"You should eat properly. Not that spicy foreign food you serve up when I come to your house. And I haven't had a proper invitation for years!"

Danny had explained the real issue to Sandra months before. Mary, like a lot of women of her time, felt liberated by the war and had enjoyed every minute of it. The return to peacetime conditions and expectations, then the rationing, lack of opportunity and the utter dreariness of the early 50s had put her into a depression from which she had never fully recovered. Now, Danny had stated, with a certainty Sandra had rarely seen since his arrival in the home, Mary resents anyone enjoying themselves even in the most innocuous ways. She wants

11

to root out happiness wherever she sees it; even its remote possibility in herself.

Danny was sitting, almost entranced, listening to Mary's voice and Henry's firm yet diplomatic responses. It could be experienced from the outside as tragedy or as comedy. From the inside the experience was one both Danny and Sandra would happily want to avoid. Henry possessed an inner toleration the size of Everest but that was insufficient for his mother's needs.

"Henry, why can't I stay with you? I'd be no trouble."

Danny smiled and held Sandra round the waist as they awaited Henry's reply.

"Mum, that's all very well. But my flat in London would need a lot of changes. It would be impossible to adapt it for you."

"You can afford it."

"But, Mum, what if I went first?"

"What do you mean?"

"What if I died before you?"

Mary considered carefully.

"Well, I'd be no worse off than I am the now"

At this point Danny doubled up, stifling a laugh, while Sandra almost collapsed on top of him. As they recovered some composure they heard Henry respond more sharply than usual.

"Mum, your sight is going, you could fall anytime without the constant care and supervision you get here. They check your hearing aid and change the batteries. You are fed from a menu of the widest choice and, as far as humanly possible, the staff attempt to fulfil your every need. Yet nothing is ever good enough, nothing at all. Mum, have you ever been happy?"

Mary pondered a moment before replying thoughtfully and with a hint of nostalgia for a memory which clearly warmed her heart.

"I was once, in the summer of 1944, after D-Day and I was living and working in the County Hotel. It was really nice"

"Well, Mum, I think that about says it all. Before you had children, before you were even married, with your future husband on active service in France. That well and truly says it all."

"Well, you did ask."

At that point Sandra closed the door over and asked Danny what his mother had been like. Danny, even approaching ninety, felt a lump in his throat. His mother, Maman, had been regarded as exotic in Wych Elm. They spoke a good deal of French at home and he was fluent in the language by the time he went to the local grammar school and, once there, picked up Latin and Italian quite easily. He was regarded at school as a great academic prospect but his interests were practical, a part of his nature inherited from his father's side of the family – quarry owners, stone masons and, in the more distant past, clay pipe manufacturers. William Harold Hird had married Catherine Madeleine Verrier in December 1918 in Amiens Cathedral. The marriage had been quickly arranged after the Armistice at the earliest opportunity, Billy having converted to the Roman faith, courtesy of his regimental Padre. He and Catherine were established in Wych Elm late in 1919. Helene Beatrice was born in November 1920, with himself, Daniel Jacques Hird, following on 14th October 1922.

It was a wonderful home life, comfortable rather than overtly rich, with four weeks every summer spent in Amiens with his mother, his elder sister and the Verrier family. Billy would join them for the final week and the of outdoor fun – book-ended by railway and ferry travel – and a night in London seeing someone like Bert Ambrose or Jack Hylton provide the entertainment in one of the better hotels. That was a time Danny viewed as more than idyllic. For him any popularly held aspect of heaven was essentially second best compared with those continental summers in Picardy.

His French grandparents, Jacques and Jeanne, were slightly aloof with their grandchildren. They were not the type to join in with fun and games like his English pair, Harold and Evelyn, back home in Wych Elm. However, Catherine's sister, just ten years' his senior, provided the entertainment, care and attention which made the annual holiday what it was for both Danny and Helene. For Danny, not that he would ever have confessed it, his aunt Therese – dark haired, ever smiling and possessing dancing, mischievous eyes – created a blueprint within his mind and emotions for a *real* woman which had stayed with him to this day.

Danny told Sandra of the sheer incongruity of eating French style in 1930s Wych Elm and about his mother's carefree attitude regarding his upbringing. She had been more careful with Helene but Danny was mixing with the men in the quarry very early on, could handle a pickaxe at ten, explosives shortly afterwards, drive a small van at 13 and shoot his father's single-barrel 12-bore shot gun before his fifteenth birthday. He and his Grandad Hird regularly provided the local butcher with a selection of game birds in season, shot on the moorland behind Angle Pike, the Pennine peak which overlooked Wych Elm, a mound positively brooding during a sleet-lined winter, and a green heathery backdrop in a cloudy summer.

Wych Elm, then and to a smaller extent now, was rather a one-off in this part of Lancashire. It was originally a small collection of cottages, a few small mills making towelling and some small farms around Angle Pike which made a living from sheep and pigs. The arrival of the Lancashire and Yorkshire's railway works and foundry at the end of the last century had changed all of that poor, inward looking 'scratch a living' village and produced a small town where work was hard, apprenticeships long and pay was on the low side. There was also an attitude of slight hostility to management, posh voices or any knowledge worn on the sleeve and promenaded regularly.

The linguistic style of Wych Elm was an assertion, delivered in a nasal Lancastrian way – similar to that of Bolton – and followed by the phrase 'tell um' because the locals had lots of 'ums' whom they viewed with, at least, suspicion. They had a very. empirical view of the world. Religion was social and not at all mystical. Life was hard and designed that way. They appreciated the beauty of their countryside, be it Rovington village or the higher moors. Education was appreciated provided it was maths or the sciences. Foreign languages could be useful, selling to or telling foreigners what to do. Fancy stuff, literature, history and the rest were for retirement, not for life.

Even the countryside was enhanced by a chain of well-sited reservoirs which provided the city of Liverpool with water. Trees planted around the waters' edges masked the spiked railings which protected the drinking water from intruders, dog walkers and casual urinators. The reservoirs had the appearance of real lakes and even sported a folly of Liverpool Castle on one shore. In all, Wych Elm appeared to be pretty, with a sharp and jagged edge.

Religion was more a matter of identity and while the family attended the small Catholic chapel, neither Catherine nor Billy had any interest in overt display nor any Irish sentimentality involving 'them and us,' especially as Billy's family were 'them' – undemonstrative Church of England people, quiet in charitable giving, gossip, hymns and with an understated charm. The national church tradition in Wych Elm was decidedly 'low' and fripperies like candles and any form of elaborate vestments were entirely absent.

"Most of Wych Elm looked at my mother as though she had dropped from Mars. She wore good, well cut clothes, not expensive but *different,* and she often bought material from Bolton market and made up her own. She insisted Dad and I had decent haircuts with, at the weekend, slightly perfumed dressing. That was expensive. Grandad reckoned he could smell my Dad from the other side of Wych Elm on Sundays."

"By the time I was 16, fully matriculated and school wanting me to apply for their Cambridge Scholarship – 'Your boy is certain to get it, Mr Hird, the money is substantial and no one has used it since 1899' – my father sent me to work in the office at the railway works to get some business experience and perhaps get qualified in engineering. He was well aware war was coming, again, and I'm sure he wanted to slip me into a reserved occupation."

"Mother would have been happier with me sailing a punt on the Cam but realised the family firm would claim me at some time. Helen married in the summer of 1939 and became a widow in 1941. Bob, her husband, son of Brown the grocer was killed in North Africa. She remarried just after the war and moved to Newcastle shortly afterwards with her husband. He was a Geordie. They had two girls. She passed away some years ago, within a year of Nichol her second hubby. Mother outlived both of them."

Sandra was listening in some fascination as she tidied up the room and turned to ask Danny how his Mum had coped in the war with her family in France. That was a good question and one for which Danny would have to exercise some care in his reply. She saw the slight flicker of emotion slip across his face and added,

"Sorry, Danny, I don't mean to upset you. I just find it so interesting."

"It was difficult, as though part of the world had been taken away."

As he said it, Danny's mind drifted off to the time he had enlisted at Jericho Barracks over in Bury. That was a name that would crop up again. Basic training and long trips to Catterick, then various locations and interviews all regarding his linguistic skill, his proven ability with rifle and handgun, his physical fitness and what a certain Major Gorringe described as, well, in the words he used following a couple of interviews.

"That boy has an instinct, a sharp instinct. He's a survivor. It's not that he couldn't give a damn — he could. For himself, that is. He is useful. Especially useful in front and behind the line ways."

"His record so far is exemplary," commented the army medical officer across the table. "Are you recommending special training?"

"Without a doubt," replied Gorringe. "Get him up to Scotland without delay."

Delay? Wartime railways were all about delay, crowding and sheer boredom. Danny had seen the chaos around Manchester's Victoria station following the 1940 air raid which destroyed half the platforms and the roof. Using the adjoining Exchange station simply created a bottleneck in what was already a restricted area. Nearly three years on the position was still bad. Twice he had endured five-hour trips to Glasgow, bumpy truck rides to Hebridean training locations and special training at Arisaig House. Other young men came and went, got injured, or proved themselves at one thing and not the others.

The conversation varied around music, food, family and sex. Danny had often, in later years, marvelled at how many young men died on active service while still virgins. The conversation and the jokes often betrayed their condition. Some paid for sex –the equivalent of half a crown up Bradshawgate. The military warnings, given regularly, he could still recall, some of them word for word.

"Beware the easy lay. There are lots of willing amateurs about."

"Put it about, syph will have you."

"Keep out of other men's beds – bad for you, bad for him, bad for morale and against the bloody law."

Danny listened. His experience was rather different. At 14 he had embraced his willing language teacher at Wych Elm Grammar School – newly engaged, pretty, somewhat controlling and, Danny now realised, curious.

A walk from school one sunny lunchtime shortly afterwards led to a more compelling experience in the soft grass well away from prying eyes and, especially, ears. Her squeal of delight coupled with his groan of pleasure would have registered quite a few yards away. It had the effect of making him very specific as to his own needs but made him, especially in later years emotionally distant even when aroused. But he was way ahead of his comrades-in-arms in this respect, even some of the married ones.

What happened to Miss Baines? She became Mrs James, left and had a baby. He still thought about her during quiet moments in the early hours when sleep can occasionally be a stranger. In our thoughts, people stay as they were. The advance of time ceases. The memory becomes aspic.

Danny learnt to embrace two particular weapons well outside the standard military issue. The De Lisle Carbine was a new specialist silenced rifle, bolt action, low maintenance and inaudible at fifty yards. There was no visible muzzle flash and, when handled properly, it was incredibly accurate. He had been shown one of the early examples while parachute training at Ringway aerodrome in Manchester and test fired one during similar training in Scotland. Danny impressed the instructor by immediately pointing out that it was low maintenance, useful away from close support and its only weakness was the noise of the bolt click when reloading after the first shot.

"The first shot has to be good," Danny said, on hearing the click at night.

"Otherwise you have a choice of lying doggo, hoping the bastards don't spot you or causing a fire fight that negates the De Lisle's whole raison d'etre."

"Quite so, my son," the moustachioed trainer replied. "You are less valuable than the bloody gun. We don't want Jerry getting his hands on one of these. Christ knows what he'd do with it."

Soon afterwards Danny was introduced to the Welrod, a silenced pistol, again a bolt action gun, with its magazine in a removable grip making it easy to conceal. This was a close-range assassination weapon used by specialist units and supplied to resistance forces in occupied Europe. Danny clearly saw its potential, but quickly discovered it needed maintenance after five shots and was pretty useless beyond thirty yards, no matter how good your aim. Ideally your victim should be right next to you. It was good for sending sentries to their maker but problematical if surrounded and fighting for your life.

Danny was given a sort of military treat early in 1944. He was sent up to Station IX, at Welwyn, to have intensive training using the De Lisle and its use of .45 ACP rounds – a subsonic bullet which contributed to its lethal silence. It was there that he received a summons to London to discuss an impending birthday party. One visiting Colonel had taken him aside and remarked, with a faux casualness,

"I hear you've been selected to celebrate alone."

"Well, Sir," Danny replied blandly, "if that is the case, it means I get all the cake, Sir."

"Enjoy your cake."

Danny did. He attended two local military dances involving local girls and entertained two of them, al fresco, on successive nights. He introduced some American airmen to bar billiards and demolished a bottle of whisky with them in less than 20 minutes. A week's leave was spent back in Wych Elm. The town was dark in aspect and mood. Two of his former school friends were dead in action, three missing, presumed dead, and one was known to be in German captivity. The mills were working at full capacity, one given over to making parachute webbing; while the railway works were doing necessary repairs on steam locomotives at the same time as producing light armoured vehicles on a 24-hour production line. The outside brick walls were painted in a camouflage pattern to match the surrounding flat moss land. The pattern was still visible thirty years later.

The pubs were busy and the food basic. – Even so, his mother seemed to acquire her own supplies of better fare when the occasion demanded it; he ate steak for the first time in a year, accompanied by a vegetable selection he had rarely seen since joining up. Neither parent asked about his next posting. An unspoken presumption prevailed. Danny engaged in a good deal of conversation with mum, in French. Dad persevered in the quarry and commanded the local Home Guard unit. Their principle remit was to keep an eye on the local reservoirs, protecting the source of the water supply for Liverpool. Liverpool itself had suffered quite a bit of aerial bombing. Logs were floated on the water surface, but there remained a fear of poisoning or aerial damage. Essentially it was a case of hours in the dark looking at expanses of still water. Wartime – waiting and watching.

****

The Lysander aircraft bumped down into the narrow grass tufted field. The air was damp. Danny said long afterwards that he thought they'd taken a detour and landed in Wych Elm. It was typical Lancashire weather. Just two bicycle lamps guided them in. This was very much a one-off from a one-off organisation. They weren't called the Baker Street Irregulars for nothing. The Special Operations Executive specialised in one-offs. Danny wore specially produced French clothing, worn but the better side of shabby. His official papers were immaculate. The aircraft left. Pierre Manon extinguished the lights. In a brusque French idiom, he wished Danny well, checked his contact details and nodded him toward the back road to Amiens. Once there, Danny assured him, he knew his way around. Pierre looked closely into his face. There was little moonlight. Danny had the aspect of a grey wraith, with a canvas fishing rod bag across his back and a small holdall in his left hand. The Frenchman could barely hide the sceptical tone in his voice – the gendarmerie were out searching for the escapees with German Gestapo officers established in the main police building. German military vehicles were on most roads, patrols were frequent but irregular in timing. One mistake and you would be dead or worse: captured, tortured, interrogated and, if you were lucky, a quick death.

Pierre did not doubt the bravery of the Royal Air Force pilots, attacking the prison from a low level – and yes, they had breached the wall, and yes, resistance prisoners had escaped. Some were recaptured within a week and some were dead. Very few of the prisoners remained at large and the German determination get them was not in doubt. But, he had poked Danny hard in the chest to emphasise his point, Amiens had suffered air raids, occupation and a good deal of collaboration, with little help from the English. It was your idea to launch *Operation Jericho* and breach the walls of the prison. The population had suffered for *that*. One of the imprisoned leaders had refused to escape, knowing the consequences for his family had he done so. So, Monsieur Jacques was wished a hearty *Bon Chance* and a large index finger pointed out the route to Amiens with the assessment he should be fine once there. But he had to get there first.

Pierre melted into the darkness. Danny turned smartly away and cut across the fields running parallel to the road, walking quickly but with a stiffened wariness as his shield. As dawn approached he could see the northern district of the city in the middle distance, slowly coming to life. He hid himself behind a close boarded wooden fence and awaited his chance to merge in with the populace and eventually make an unexpected call on the family. What a surprise for them.

This, as far as SOE were concerned, was the weak spot in the exercise. Were his relatives reliable? The family had received just one letter in May 1940 and nothing since. Almost four years had gone by. The local resistance had confirmed his aunt's presence and that of his grandfather some three months before. But there was a nagging suspicion in SOE that their local network was compromised and the aftermath of *Operation Jericho* had increased the doubts among SOE controllers. Danny was confident in himself and his equipment. Everything else was suspect. It was far simpler to think in that way.

Danny had walked among the people with his head down at first, stopping every so often to get his bearings and gradually adopting a gait suited to the surroundings. Saint Leu was the poorer quarter of the city, crossed by canals, and parts of it could have passed for Manchester were it not for the number of wooden houses on the roadside. The effects of bomb damage and bits of shrapnel were the same anywhere. Danny knew the geography of the area and made for Henriville, a much more prosperous neighbourhood, and he found himself laying low behind a shack of a summer house in the long garden behind the family home. He had approached from the rear through an old gap in the fence, easily recollected from previous visits and totally untouched over the years. He felt a little chilled and carefully picked the padlock on the wooden shed door, using a hair pin brought especially for the purpose, and was soon able to sit on the wooden floor among some musty old sticks of furniture that had seen better days.

The canvas fishing bag was laid carefully aside with his holdall beside it. It was then he noticed the rather untidy appearance of the garden and the obvious attempt to grow vegetables along the far edge of the land which sloped, less steeply than Danny remembered, toward the house. Three apple trees remained in evidence which shaded the area around the back door, a solid nineteenth-century timber object which Danny recalled as well varnished but was now rather flaky with a few chunks out of the frame.

Danny saw some shadowy appearances in the kitchen area and hands drew the blinds in an upper room, but otherwise no one made an exit at the back. He could hear children's voices from the garden behind him and later the voice of a firm mother calling them in. Danny recalled two toddlers in that house five years before – the father had an office job of some kind on the railway, the mother, dark haired with sharp features, according to Therese came from a prominent local farming family and aspired to open a restaurant once the children were older.

Therese, where was she?

As the evening drew in Danny saw the blinds being systematically drawn shut in the house and only then did he see his aunt Therese's unmistakeable features at a ground floor window, her hair drawn back in a pleat and her eyes fixed into the middle distance beyond the garden, her mouth in motion as though speaking but, in all probability, singing. Looking left, right, above and behind, Danny moved in a half sprint to the back door, glanced back again and tapped on the wood. He called to Therese, using her name and following it with his pet name for her, "my little kitten." She opened the door warily, peering into the grey of the evening and Danny's face appeared around the door. The shock of him standing there, smiling, trying to ease the moment with a whispered "C'est moi," only added to her elated confusion. She waved her hands for him to come in and then, as she closed the door, he noticed the tears dropping from her eyes. Danny discarded his bags and held her softly, then as she shook in his arms, held her more firmly, kissing both sides of her face more than once and then gripping her body so as neither to let her go, nor fall apart.

Therese was not one for explicit language but her whispered demand to know what he was doing here, a sob, how did he get here, another sob, and who knows you are here, were all accompanied by diabolical references usually used of Satan himself. Danny could not resist referring to himself as her nephew from hell, at which point, with the hint of a smile covering her utter confusion, Therese pushed him away and looked him up and down. She clasped both his hands and repeated her questions, again adopting a whisper that betrayed not only confusion but, quite explicitly, fear. She repeated the questions. Who had seen him? Had anyone seen him? She spoke with an urgency that went beyond fear and crossed the border into terror. Danny realised he had been completely off-guard for quite some minutes and the maxim that 'just one of these lapses is enough to kill you' fronted his mind with a vengeance. The nephew from hell stepped back into his dark comfort zone and began to ask his own questions instead.

Grandma had died last year from a combination of the flu and pneumonia. Grandpa was suffering from a fever, coughs and general malaise, having taken to his bed three weeks earlier and refusing what little food was available, confining himself to sips of water and warm milk during the night. The food situation was far worse than Danny had been led to believe and he vowed to Therese he would do something about it. She had boiled some potatoes and sprinkled them with a few herbs and a little oil. Over this meal he explained that he had been sent on a specific mission and she examined his identity papers carefully, remarking on their authenticity and the choice of name, his own middle name with the maternal surname. He was purported to be a cousin recently released from labour in Germany due to a serious illness. Danny told her she need not risk him staying in the house, but she would hear no more. He was staying. She warned of Boche activity following the air raid on the prison, arrests of escapees, their families and the rest. But far worse was the recent arrival of the Miliciens: patriotic Frenchmen who supported Vichy, avoided forced labour in German factories, were mostly local and aware of their area and had been successful in the south against resistance groups. The Malice had recently been trusted enough to work in the occupied north and west, acting as a paramilitary force against the resistance. They were effectively a law to themselves, operating as a parallel body alongside the local police and not subject to the civil, or for that matter, any military law. They were feared, wearing the gamma insignia badge on a uniform consisting of a brown shirt, blue jacket and a wide blue beret hat.

Danny wanted to know if she or anyone she knew had any details about the local group. They were based in the main police station she confirmed, with a nod in the direction of the city centre, and they used torture as a regular part of their interrogation of suspects. Therese said that they were rumoured to be rounding up Jews in Paris, the gang here having been moved from that duty to deal with the situation here. She had heard two of them talking in the past week, in a city café. Both had local accents. The man in charge was rumoured to be a close relative of Joseph Darnand, a member of the Vichy government and an alleged friend of Marshall Petain. Grandpa was pro Petain, had favoured *Action Francais*, hated Communists but had his memories of the Great War which had resisted any attempt, in his weaker moments, to be pro-Nazi. He represented much that was France at the time, essentially patriotic and feeling that allies of any kind compromised the type of patriotism that saw France as a civilising imperialism, good for the country and good for the world.

Therese simply hated the fear, deprivation and negativity she associated with the occupation and wanted to live again. The feeling of dread, a dark awareness that things would never quite be the same, and seeing herself being manipulated toward a future of dull recrimination and an even duller hypocrisy, were totally at odds with her emotional attachment to the world.

The same thoughts hovered around Britain but found expression in a more direct way, a way more hedonistic than Therese would subscribe to, an urban rather than a rural response, a 'sod the lot mentality' which never quite left the British consciousness either immediately after or, for that matter, in the present day.

Maybe it was the wartime effect, but that very evening Danny was sharing Therese's bed without much guilt on either part. Grandpa remained beached in his room, responding to Danny's arrival with just a spark of interest accompanying a cynical laugh that perhaps he was here to kill the Boche. Danny simply said he'd come for the summer, like the old days. Grandpa said nothing.

After three days, with Therese's help, Danny had established how the black market operated in and around Amiens. Farmers were generally doing quite well. The poorest were not. Informers, needing money or favours for loved ones, were common. Few were doing anything for an ideological motive. It was deemed enough to survive. Danny's wodge of French currency allowed Therese to replenish a largely empty larder. Danny risked a couple of outings with her to local cafés, where he observed German soldiers in twos and threes, Gestapo types speaking to the owners and eying everyone else with clear suspicion. Then there was a Milice raid on a house two streets away where a woman, two children and an old man were taken away in a German truck. Six, almost certainly the entire Amiens squad, were involved, quietly, efficiently and without fuss removing people to God knows where or what. Danny noticed that two of them carried British Sten guns, more than likely taken from resistance fighters, while the man in charge held a Walther pistol. The others had standard-issue French rifles.

It was after this incident that Therese, aware that the light baggage Danny kept in the attic were fire arms and that he had, in the kitchen, near a waste pipe and among earthenware bottles, the barrel of what he later revealed as a Welrod pistol; the magazine-cum-handle was either with him or constantly moved elsewhere in the house.

Therese led him to the contents of an old wooden trunk in her mother's dressing room. Some discarded clothes covered what Therese described as a gun, given to Grandpa by a close friend whose son had been captured in the 1940 debacle by the Germans. It was a gun all right. Danny had seen one before. It was a Boys' anti-tank rifle, useless against proper armour but good if used accurately against other vehicles. Danny could see it had been fired once, if at all, and there was even a pouch containing an oil can and a cleaning kit. He looked at Therese in amazement, told her it was dangerous and said he would get rid of it. This was said as he checked the magazine, in place, with five of the large high-velocity rounds. Danny had fired one of these in his earliest training and immediately remembered the volcanic noise and the fearsome recoil. One recruit had broken his collarbone firing one of these guns. The French had not been supplied with them. The gun had obviously been discarded by a British unit and somehow made its way here. Danny began to redefine his plan. This brute of a weapon could be useful.

The Welrod accompanied him that night, where, as for a few nights before, he risked the dangers of the curfew. He took a circuitous back-lane route to the rear of the raided house. Two policemen were searching inside and one of the Miliciens, in full uniform, was standing sentinel at the back, near to the path and smoking. Danny was in the hedge alongside and the tall bereted man paced a little and stepped back to look up toward a shape on the upper floor. His back touched the Welrod, Danny pulled the trigger and the muffled discharge caused the guard to fall forward across the path, his lit cigarette burning a mark on his cheek as it crumpled against the weight of his face on the grass. The Milicien felt nothing, his spine broken, dead before he hit the ground. The fear, the elation, the sheer satisfaction were held in check. This was easier than Danny had thought. Now he could develop a plan and really make the risks taken by those who brought him here worthwhile.

No one had heard the shot. Danny waited a good three minutes before engaging in the cumbersome process of manually reloading the weapon and slowly heading back to whence he came. It was almost an hour before the search team realised they were a man down. Danny was, by this time, engaged in vigorous congress with Therese, she biting on his shoulder, unaware of his deed that night. He had broken curfew before to see, as he put it in English, to see for himself how things worked. Now he was doing the work with not even a little abandon. Danny was certain that humanity consisted of risk-takers and diffident souls. He was one of the former. No pride was taken in this. It was a kind of determinism. Some naturally would keep the law, others break it or find a way around its strictures. Some were sympathetic, some were not. Some were fearful, some showed a calculated courage. Danny felt he knew himself.

The real difficulty for Danny was how far he should confide in Therese, this trusting, warm, brown haired beauty that he spoke to as another person, rather than as his aunt. She went along with the pretence, never asking too much but showing her willingness to help. The searches, enquiries – the police were knocking on doors very early that morning – were ongoing for days. Therese spoke to two of the local police at the door, inviting them in for a warm drink, but they declined and left asking as to the health of her father. She shook her head, saying her mother's death had left him almost senseless. The elder of the two commiserated and they moved on. Danny was upstairs during this episode and admired her style. Perhaps he took after her, rather than she learning from him. Therese explained that the older one knew her father from their army service in the early part of the Great War. Both of them – Jacques commanding an artillery unit at Verdun, which had the young Georges Ferrer loading shells – had survived against staggering odds. Georges had not seen Jacques for some time, but on hearing of Jeanne's demise had enquired of him when his path had crossed with Therese in local shops or in the street. Danny's cover story would not have run well with him. He knew something of the family.

The black market for food was a way of life and anyone with access to anything edible would try to work it to their advantage. Amiens was like Wych Elm – nods and winks indicating where meat was available today, fat tomorrow and a variety of fowl the day after. Therese had made it clear early on that Maurice Malin operated on a different level. His farm provided the German military with pork of the highest quality and his cured hams, legendary before the war, now had mythical status. It was also generally accepted he was an informer. Danny and Therese had cycled to his farm: an old, large building with two curing sheds and three pig sties. All of the site was protected by Malin's rather deficient son – mongol would have described him then, although his large ponderous nature, allied to a disorientated wit and trust in an old shotgun might have produced a varying diagnosis and description today – and his rotund wife. On seeing her for the first time, Danny thought she had a stunning resemblance to one of Wych Elm's formidable pub landladies. She weighed at least 16 stones, a round chubby face surmounting a ponderous body, her small eyes moving around in a reptilian way.

Therese had done the buying, Danny staying in the background at first and varying his appearance, all the while watching the Malins and their environment, fairly certain, in short order, that there was a real opportunity here.

Maurice, unlike his wife and son, was stick thin, originally tall but now somewhat stooped in a gangly sort of way. All of them had a Picard patois, one which Danny could understand but not emulate. When he did speak to him, Danny stuck to his formal pronunciation, using local dialect only in passing when he was confident of the context – a method he adopted generally in those weeks and from then on embedded in his very being.

There were two concrete garages joined together to the right of the farmhouse frontage. They had housed two cars before the war but Maurice claimed to have sold them or, at other times, claimed the Boche had requisitioned them. They were padlocked and no one was sure what was inside. The rooves were covered with loose sheets of tarred felt, with a large tarpaulin slung haphazardly, hanging to one side, and a ladder handily leaning between the two apexes at the back.

Danny immediately saw the point between the two apexes as a first-class lair, high enough with a straight view of the dirt road leading into the farm. He walked a rambling route on field pathways from the edge of town twice, to check timings, possible observation points and alternative rat runs in the event of trouble. He cycled alone a few days after the preparatory missions, offering to buy a full ham and showing Maurice one of his 20 gold sovereigns, which had been given in England for just this type of eventuality. Maurice did not react, save to say he would want four of these and, in any event, could only provide a suitable ham the following morning at, say, nine and could he bring a suitable bag or sack to carry it away. This was agreed. Danny was amused by his cheek – four gold ones for a ham – and the utter insincerity of the deal.

That night Danny carried the Boys rifle in sacking to the back of the Malin's property and climbed a perimeter fence, eventually hauling himself and his weapon up the ladder and laying it, on its small bipod, beneath the apexes of the garages, covered with felt and he himself beneath the cold tarpaulin sheet. At first light, he had checked his sites down the approach road and while immobile, in position, had allowed his mind to wander, thinking of the reassurance he had given to Therese. He would be back soon, not to worry, he was on operational duty and on his return, they would celebrate.

The son appeared, with his gun, slouching toward the pig pens at the rear. Pigs began to squeal as they were let out into the fresh air. Maurice stood outside the front door briefly, peering down the road. He returned inside and immediately a car approached along the bumpy track, quite a pretty black Citroen saloon. Only later did Danny discover that this *Traction 15G saloon* was the pride and joy of Louis Darnand himself, commander of the local Milice; he was driving with Hans Dietrich Held – second man in the Gestapo, over from Paris – in the rear. One of Darnand's men in the front passenger seat said nothing as they drove along for what would be an easy arrest of someone with resistance connections and, from what Malin had said, with possible direct British links. Malin had never been wrong before and Darnand saw this as a way of impressing the Gestapo, especially after losing one of their own in circumstances defying all reason; a man, a patriot, murdered while searching the house of a traitor.

Danny only discovered the details later. He braced himself for the recoil, firing his first shot at eye level through the windscreen and immediately rattled through the bolt action to fire a second shot through the shattered glass into the passenger side. Only then, did he deliver a third shot into the engine via the front grill, the vehicle lurching and the stopping in the centre of the road.

The noise of the three reports would have been audible miles away.

The recoils led Danny to think he'd done a ten-round stint against a heavier opponent in the boxing ring.

The first shot split Darnand's skull like a water melon, the bullet passing on into Held's mouth and finally exiting from the back of his neck into the leather upholstery. Momentum and reaction caused the third man to lean right, opening the door as the second bullet passed through and removed most of his left shoulder. He crashed onto the ground in utter shock, clutching his Sten gun in his right hand. Maurice and his son, disorientated by the shots, simply ran toward the car, black smoke now emanating from the bonnet grills. The young Malicien, mortally wounded with the remains of his blue jacket soaking black through the loss of blood, simply saw two men running toward him and fired at them from his prone position. Both of them fell as they ran.

"Well done sunshine!" said Danny aloud.

Then, in more of a whisper to himself, "That saves me a couple of jobs."

He descended the ladder, adrenalin pumping, and tried to breathe slowly. He ran to the front of the garages, pulling out his small pistol, a *Webley Bulldog*, a vintage but easily concealed weapon. Speed was now essential. The two male Malins were still; there was no movement from the car. Sprinting forward he grabbed the Sten from a dying hand and returned through the main door of the house. He found Madame Malin on her knees behind an armchair. He used the Sten to shoot her in the head. Like a trained automaton he returned the Sten gun to a now dead hand and only then slowed his pace, walking to the back, entering a curing shed to discover a host of hung meats finished and in preparation. He bagged one ham on the bone and headed back whence he came, slowing even more after the first half mile. Eventually he entered town with a ham under his jacket, strolling as army vehicles sprung into action and the local gendarmerie appeared to be running around every street.

Within a day, intercepted radio traffic was deciphered in London. Danny's controller read the reports with some incredulity. Reporting up, he advised that not only was Darnand dead but so was Held, and between them they realised an event of such enormity would leave the Gestapo no alternative but to throw everything into getting the assassin and taking terrible revenge on anyone remotely connected with an incident like this.

"I hope he moves out as planned and heads for Paris," said one.

"Or that he isn't picked up," said the other.

"Hird could just as easily head for Berlin and take Hitler himself. How did he manage the two of them?"

"Ambush, apparently."

"Ambush? I cannot see it, just using a silenced rifle and a couple of pistols? Mustn't have been alone, eh?"

Therese looked askance at the ham as Danny sat at the kitchen table. She knew where it had come from. Her attitude was one of relief and, for the first time, a genuinely darkening mood involving a nagging realisation he would soon have to move on. Danny told her as much, but reassured her he would be back in a few weeks. He left a note in his dead letterbox arrangement, a wall cleft near the cathedral, and using one of the old family cycles took the back roads toward Paris. He followed orders to the letter. Therese quickly realised why. She was left, as before, in something worse than limbo, fearing for herself, her father and, despite everything, for Danny.

Had this been a theatrical play or a cinematic film, he would have suffered checkpoints, escapades and searches en-route, as well as perhaps a romantic interlude in a barn. He simply cycled, slept once within a field and was bitten by some insect or other. He made contact with the Paris resistance, as arranged, within a suburban café using a series of passwords and phrases. He organised a coded message to be sent to his control that night. After a night in a narrow bed, but at least in clean sheets, he awoke in the tiny flat above a baker's shop to find a familiar figure sitting in the next room. Pierre Manon, the one who had greeted him on landing in Picardy weeks before, had come to debrief him and give him some further news.

Pierre confirmed the Milice were finished in Amiens and, following Danny's handiwork, they were very jumpy in the capital. The Gestapo blamed the Milice for Held's death in Amiens but quickly discounted the idea that Maurice had double-crossed them. They knew a British man was involved, probably Kommando, connecting him to the death of a young Milicien days before the farm ambush. The Gestapo had not worked it out themselves, not entirely anyway. The Boys rifle proved the key in a way Danny could never have expected and in a way, he could not have foreseen.

The Gestapo quickly fixed their investigation on the anti-tank rifle and the local police were able to identify its origin. They raided the Verrier home the following morning and took Grandpa and Therese for questioning. Later in the evening Therese was taken to Paris, to Gestapo premises on *rue de saussaiens* or possibly *Avenue Foche*. Danny was immediately demanding to be shown where these places were, but Manon handled him gently, while informing him that his weaponry was somewhere safe. He could retain his pistol for his own protection – the *Bulldog* was easily concealed – but information was patchy and a one-man assault on Gestapo HQ was out of the question. Therese could easily be in the women's prison at *Fresnes* and the various resistance groups had people on the inside, including staff, making an attempt at rescue a far more viable proposition.

Danny simply observed that Therese would be in prison only if she had talked, and he was certain she had not. Pierre shrugged. When Danny asked about torture, another more awkward shrug emanated from Manon's frame and he said he would let him know any definite news. In the following weeks Danny got to know the various resistance groups in his area. Most were men and women whose adherence to communism was essentially romantic. He learnt from them ways of acquiring information from simply listening in a bread queue or a café. He learnt to sing to accordion and piano, dance in Latin style and was shown ways to coordinate two record players to give continuous but changing musical tempo in small cafés.

Therese never left his mind, yet a young dark-haired Jewish teenager showed her dancing skills to perfection during several long evenings and nights. Danny saw the Paris situation as a stand-off between enthusiastic and committed resistance brigades, ill coordinated and lacking heavy weapons and ammunition against an occupying force which was heavily armed but relied essentially on the local police to control the city. German military were few in number but had artillery. A simple rising could never work. As anticipation of the allied landings approached, Danny was able to make radio contact with his own controller in London. His instructions were to stay, assist and await further orders.

Manon's group employed him and his carbine directly, taking out two known informers in broad daylight, one a dental surgeon who was taking his regular lunchtime drink at a pavement café and the other on the street by the Gestapo HQ. He was a co-owner of a restaurant which catered exclusively for the German military. Both operations were conducted from rooftops with carefully rehearsed escape routes. The second assassination took place on Tuesday 6th June.

The following weeks were the worst of all. Allied progress was slow. The military governor of Paris, von Choltitz, prepared himself to do just enough to justify himself to Berlin while preparing a case for his humanitarian guise as saviour of Paris. Danny was finally told of Therese's fate at the hands of the Gestapo torturers and her death at *Fort de Romainville* prison on the outskirts of the city. Her body was found there when a resistance group stormed the gates during the uprising. The city was virtually strikebound from 15th August and at a standstill on 18th. Danny watched resistance street barricades destroyed by German artillery, individual German soldiers shot and their weapons grabbed for immediate use in street battles. There were instances of summary executions on both sides.

The first Free French armoured column reached Paris on 24th and the following day Danny was instructed to report to them. The city was surrendered on 25th and Danny saw De Gaulle's arrival and parade on 26th August. Manon, wearing the uniform of Free French colonel directed Danny to a vantage point close to Notre Dame to take out two snipers of interest to his people, who, with a few Germans, were shooting at the crowd and De Gaulle below. As each one fell, Manon was making some reference to what Danny thought was something like ducks in a row. He may have been mistaken, but getting a slap on the back was the only time Danny had seen any real emotion in Pierre Manon.

The city emerged like a butterfly from a chrysalis and for a few days sleep was a stranger, drink a danger and no one   an enemy. One resistance party found a Gestapo employee hiding in a city cellar and Danny's little dark-haired girl was quick to let him know. They had him tied into a chair when Danny arrived and he spoke to this wretched man quietly, almost confessional in tone. He confirmed Therese had been hung by her thumbs, whipped at least once and submerged in an ice water bath. The latter had caused what appeared to be a stroke. She was sent, half dead already, to die at *Fort de Romainville*. Danny asked the others to leave. When alone he produced his knife from inside his uniform coat and calmly made an incision in the jugular area of the prisoner's throat, despite his pleas that he had not done the deed. Danny was emotionless, left the room and told his captors to leave him a half hour or so and prepare a grave rather than a rope. They did. Danny kissed his little Jewish girl goodbye, never to see her again.

Through Manon's offices he obtained permission to make a trip to Amiens. He had been instructed to re-join British forces and return to England. XXX Corps had entered Amiens on 18th August and was already heading into Belgium. The Free French commander, General Leclerc, was the Comte de Hauteclocque and was aware of Danny's role in getting the Milice out of Picardy. Danny was given a jeep, spare fuel, his carbine and the *Welrod* expecting to travel alone. However, a major in the Intelligence Corps, an Oxbridge professorial type, was going with him, and while providing company on the circuitous journey, he seemed far more interested in Danny's position in society, his circle, his family and other social scale indicators, all the while contrasting them with his own. This small, elfin character managed to annoy him more than anyone in the past few months. He was sharp, clever even, but seemed to give the impression of having had an easy war.

When they reported to the small British base – more like a checkpoint at Amiens – Danny was glad to rid of him while he went about making enquiries in the city. At least it seemed in no worse condition than when he had left a few months before. In any event, earlier that day

Manon had finally given him the details of the aftermath of his little job in the town and, more to the point, what had happened to Therese and Grandad. How long Manon had held onto this information, Danny could only guess. Perhaps he thought Danny may go on a rampage, putting other lives at risk. Manon did not know him well enough to make such a judgement. Not well enough at all. All the city needed was food, time and a slow recovery. There was only a little desire for recrimination and it was directed sparingly to specific individuals who remained stoic in their attitude, convinced they had made the right decisions.

Manon's attitude was a version of this. Clear the wreckage and allow an open route forward. France could not remain Germany's enemy forever. After all, they were permanent neighbours.

Manon had taken him aside and made it beyond contradiction that the information he had given him was both accurate and required no further action on his part. Any subsequent action would be purely a French affair and one that Danny should accept as final. Manon's eyes gave nothing away. It was a feeling of inevitability rather than coldness that swept over Danny's frame and probably contributed to his irritation and passivity in the jeep.

Danny was given the news in the neutral, clipped tone of a country undertaker and it was only afterwards that he reflected this was the outcome of living for four years under an occupation where such events were commonplace. Manon had certainly given similar news many times before. The very morning of Danny's action the Gestapo and the local Gendarmerie had raided his grandfather's house, the focus of attention being the Boys gun. Grandpa and Therese had been taken away for interrogation and, while nothing was known for certain, there were clear indications that Therese was in Paris within a day, either at Gestapo HQ, *11 rue de Saussaies* or *84, Avenue Foch,* or perhaps in the women's prison *Fresnes.*

Manon waived away Danny's agitation and told him that was why his arsenal of weapons had been temporarily moved elsewhere, for his *own* safety. He had kept his pistol for his own protection and if any firm news arose, he would have been told. Danny knew Manon was right. His running around Paris with a *De LISLE* or the *Welrod* would lead to a total disaster for him and everyone else. The Germans and the whole of Paris were expecting an allied landing soon and who could guess what effect that may have. He had contented himself, meeting other members of his resistance group, male and female. He was brave to a fault and burning with the socialist desire only a true romantic communist could engender or possess.

Perhaps it was the end of an adrenalin-fuelled episode, weeks in the making, that caused Danny's sudden discomfort. How could things be the same again for him and his family? Of all the people he had killed, most were detritus, people on the wrong side at the time, forgiven now they were dead. Therese's death was rather different, in the sense that *he* had caused it, leaving her as an unsung heroine dragged into a process not of her own making.

And then there was Jacques, bereft at the death of Jeanne, holding onto a British weapon. Why? Did he intend to use it sometime? His mother would find much of this story difficult to absorb. What should he tell? What should he miss out? Revenge, as Manon had made clear, was out of the question. France would struggle once this war was over. Not economically – they built good cars, had lots of prime agricultural land and the basis of a fine fishing fleet. No, it was more of how the aftermath was handled personally. Informers? Half of Wych Elm would have informed on the other had Britain been occupied. Danny began to take the view that he should push his immediate past back, tell Maman the bare minimum, go forward and *forget*. There was still a war to be won. Perhaps France should also forget and move ahead. The past is, after all, past and nothing will change it. What would be the point of arguing over presentation? He showed himself a true child of Wych Elm – no mysteries, just the bald facts and the devil may care about the rest.

Soon he would be back on home territory. What would be expected of him there? Danny stopped trying to apologise to himself. It was not necessary and the mean could take advantage of such a trait. Onward, ever onward, became a sort of motto for him – a lasting legacy of the war.

It also occurred to him that, despite the odd fear and trembling, it had never crossed his mind that he may not survive. Mortality was an aspect of life reserved for others. He retained an adolescent sense of indestructibility, which he maintained even now, approaching his 90s. He had sufficient contempt for the enemy, any enemy, to hold that approach to life.

Chapter Two

The 'lads,' as Danny called them, were busying themselves in his room, cleaning his en suite bathroom facilities with a speedy and efficient effect. Marcus was a huge, beaming Nigerian man in his mid-20s. He was an enthusiastic evangelical Christian, forever singing hymns as he worked and always wearing his faith with a smile. Petro, on the other hand, was a little older and from Poland. He wore his Catholicism like a national badge. His English was grammatically perfect and when at rest in conversation he sounded like a civil servant of the old school. Both were married with children, eking out an existence on low wages but enhanced by tips and gifts from their appreciative clientele. Mary Hobson liked both of them, Marcus because he made her laugh and Petro because of his willingness to listen to her and appear, at least, to support her grievances.

Petro was taller than Marcus but not so broad. Between them they were the home's heavy lifting team.

Each of them was known to be voluble and amusing in their own distinctive way. Danny encouraged them. Marcus in his singing and Petro in his willingness to bring in a couple of cans of Polish-branded beer occasionally, as Danny had taken a partiality to its taste and strength.

They did the clean-up and wipe-down in under ten minutes, doing a theatrical wave as they left, and Danny was left wondering why Petro in particular should link his last mind journey to the past with *enemies.* How did that come about? His brain function was a source of worry to him and he dreaded losing his faculties. He did quite a bit of speech analysis, checking for anything worse than the usual absent-mindedness of the elderly or the loss of names.

Then it came to him, in a flash of instant recognition. Petro bore a striking resemblance to Arthur Thompson, a pub landlord in Manchester. Thompson was not an enemy. But in 1952 their paths happened to cross, permanently in Thompson's case, with someone who was. Suddenly Danny had left 1944 and here he was, eight years on, his memory clear and bearing down on Bert Harrison, an accountant in Wych Elm and would-be beau of Danny's widowed mother. Hubert Harrison was fairly typical of success in Wych Elm at that time –he owned a sound business, was comfortably Masonic, a proponent of the idea shared with Geoffrey Fisher, Archbishop of Canterbury, that there had to be a return to pre-war standards. and the laxity in behaviour, built up in wartime, had to go. Harrison spoke in committee and in public about moral laxity, exemplifying it with unsuitable cinema films and the beginnings of what became teenage culture. He had asked Catherine to accompany him to a Masonic charity ball the year before. She had accepted and enjoyed some of the company and the dancing. Quite a few of the guests were familiar with the Hird side of the family. She did say, on her return, that the meal had been a travesty of the culinary art – undercooked stringy lamb and in contrast, vegetables boiled within an inch of their existence.

Danny knew of Harrison but did not know him personally. He could be seen strutting around Wych Elm in a three-piece suit with a gold watch chain on prominent display. A widower since 1939, his wife Elsie had contracted peritonitis following a minor operation and they had produced one son, George, who was in his mid-20s, qualified and working in his father's office on a small salary. He was obliged to live with his father in the family home, the largest Victorian terraced house in Bridge Street. There were rumours of tension between father and son. The young Harrison had been at the grammar school and made his mark as a mathematician. The father would not contemplate university in 1945, insisting George took the professional route into accountancy and financial control. He qualified in 1949 and became a Chartered Secretary two years later. Father controlled the purse strings and made sure George knew it.

Bert visited Catherine at home, rarely when Danny was there and rarely by invitation. Danny said little to

Maman but his demeanour showed his distaste for his mother's suitor, venturing once the comment that, of all the fish in the town pond, he was the worst of the species available. Catherine told him not to be so silly, but Danny took the precaution of having one of his quiet words with his police contacts. To his own surprise he was directed to see Fred Mullings, a newly appointed detective based in Bolton. They met by arrangement at the *Hen and Chickens* pub one Tuesday lunchtime.

Over a pint of bitter Mullings explained that, in his professional capacity, Harrison was beyond reproach. His private life was rather different and even within Masonic circles there was some concern at his attitude both to brothers' wives and attached ladies outside. He had suffered an assault by an enraged husband on two occasions in the last year and caused one poor wife to try to gas herself as a direct result of his activities three years before. Danny could have said it takes one to know one, but didn't, and simply assimilated the information for future use. Maman was, after all, fifty-two and could make her own mind up, provided she had all the information. Even then, Danny reflected that she may *be* fifty-two but her grooming and appearance made her look at least ten years younger. How to reveal this information was the question. Openly? Or push it, perhaps, from – to use an American phrase he picked up – left-field?

It was then that Mullings revealed a couple of gems. Police interest in Wych Elm surrounded an affair he had started with one of the serving officers. They had been caught, coupling vigorously, on the open moor behind Angle Pike. The report had come from young children running around their mother and their two dogs. They only had to walk down to the farm below the watch tower and make a telephone call to the local station. The constable sent to investigate, driving the station's new black Wolseley for the first time, found his sergeant's wife and Harrison "… still at it, stark naked, in the grass."

"As you can imagine, that went down like a lead balloon."

"At the lodge as well as the station, eh?" replied Danny.

Mullings nodded and then went on to say that Harrison visited a pub in a Manchester suburb every Saturday afternoon when the landlord practised his snooker skills down the road. He carefully related the details, roads, times and names.

"The landlord is, I understand, a big lad, ex-Royal Marine. Now, if he found out what's been going on for 12 months and more, it might be a good move for all of us. Do you get my drift?"

It was Danny's turn to nod. He then thanked him for his company and dwelt on how to proceed with minimum damage to Maman. His thoughts were to coalesce in a way he could never have imagined just a few months later. Using the detailed information Mullings had provided, he followed Harrison a fortnight down the line. He took the tram into Bolton and walked to Great Moor Street terminus. He caught the 1.20pm local train – they were all local from Great Moor Street – and the four elderly carriages, non-corridor stock, were propelled by a tank engine, stopping at each station as far as Manchester Exchange.

Danny was in the last compartment of the train and, sitting by the window to the left, was able to observe every stop as they made stately progress at 20mph. The procession of small, suburban stations, generally tidy but positively shrouded in sooty icing, scrolled through *Plodder Lane, Little Hulton, Walkden Low Level, Worsley and Monton Green* until the little train wheezed into *Eccles* where Harrison got off walked briskly to the exit and showed his return ticket. Danny followed behind a woman with her elderly father. Their breadth and slow pace masked him perfectly. Once outside, diagonally to the left he could see the *Bridgewater Arms,* a substantial public house with bay windows. Diagonally to his right he saw the *Central Snooker Club* again a substantial purpose-built single-storey property of pre-war vintage.

He walked to the pub, noting the large front entrance, double doors with a lobby, and a small side entrance with a gate to the delivery yard at the back.

Danny slipped into the side entrance and found groups of men, newspapers open at the racing pages, speaking directly to one another, and others laughing at some blue joke at the far end of the bar. Harrison was talking to a small dark-haired woman, well-dressed and well-groomed, who emerged from behind the bar and guided him toward a door marked *private* just beyond the lavatories. As the door briefly opened he could see they were ascending carpeted stairs.

He approached the bar and ordered a glass of mild. The stout barmaid looked him up and down.

"You're not from these parts, are you?"

"No, love, I'm in Eccles on business," he answered. "Was that the landlord?"

Danny was nodding toward the door.

"No, he's out Saturday afternoons. That was the landlady. The bloke helps with the books," she replied, giving a narrow look.

He finished his drink, walked around the block and approached the building from the rear. The green double gates were locked, but the small gate at the side was on the latch and Danny entered. The paved yard had a pair of outside lavatories against the curtain wall to his left. These abutted a storeroom which adjoined the main pub building. Immediately above were two large second-floor windows. The one above the store had the blinds closed.

He looked around, swung himself up on the tiles of the urinals and, wearing his best rubber soles, walked up onto the store roof. Another quick survey and a shimmy up the drainpipe placed his ear by the window. The sounds from within were unmistakable, unless of course they were keeping pigs and other grunting livestock in the back bedroom. Harrison was, very enthusiastically, helping with the books.

Danny caught a bus into Manchester and returned to Bolton by the more direct rail route into Trinity Street station. This operation would need careful timing. He had no wish to upset Maman and decided to bide his time before sorting out this particular example of moral rectitude. It was a combination of his mother, her wellbeing and Harrison's sheer hypocrisy that motivated him – at least, that is what he told himself. In other circumstances, he may have wished Harrison well. The landlady did look a desirable piece. But circumstances were as they were. Danny would well and truly sort him.

A few weeks elapsed. Danny noticed Harrison sometimes arriving unannounced around lunchtime, suggesting a drive here or a drive there. Maman went along with this at times, but more often than not she made a light lunch and, as Danny saw it, Harrison was not only getting his feet under the table but bringing his slippers as well. It was a Friday early in December when *Danny's Place* was quieter than usual. The weather was rather inclement and people were saving their spare cash for Christmas. Danny drove home and was approaching the unmade driveway before 11.30am, when it would normally, on Friday, be at least an hour later. He saw Harrison's Rover 75 parked up, distinctive with its third centre headlight, the *Cyclops* model.

He avoided blocking Harrison's car in the drive and parked in the quarry yard, waiting a moment before entering through the back kitchen door. The kitchen was illuminated, the lounge was dark and, walking into the hallway, he could hear his mother's voice, very much in a higher pitch, and the sound of physical activity from her bedroom. Danny burned with fierce indignation, finding himself momentarily confused and unsure whether to announce his presence. He retraced his steps and sat in his car – windows steaming, rain showers pattering – in an angry silence for the better part of an hour. Then he stalked to the front door, rattling his key, and entered to find his mother about to see her companion out. She was a little discomfited at Danny's arrival, mentioning she had lost track of time and wondering what people might think.

Danny's eyes bore into Harrison, who retaliated with a gimlet eye and an attempt at an apparently light-hearted comment.

"It doesn't matter what anyone thinks, Catherine, no one at all. We make our own minds up, don't we?"

Catherine did not reply directly and insisted Danny see 'Mr Harrison' to his car. As the two walked in darkness, Harrison said, to no one in particular, as though to the night air, "I'm not after her money, I've plenty of that. Anybody who thinks otherwise is a fool. There's plenty of them about!"

"I look after my mother," Danny replied, staring ahead. "Whether they are crooks, spivs or old lechers, I'll be there. I can be anywhere."

Harrison drove off into the night. Danny was seething.

Maman simply wished him a good night before retiring. At breakfast, the following morning she intimated that her beau was becoming too close, taking liberties, "… and he could never replace your dear Papa."

Danny said he was happy to hear it.

"There is something of the *Marquis de Sade* about him," she went on, casually.

"He hasn't hurt you, has he?"

"Oh no," she smiled. "He cannot mention children, young criminals or young wives without reference to a bloody good hiding."

Maman was smiling wistfully, whereas Danny decided it was time for a bloody good hiding to come Harrison's way. The temptation he had felt the night before to take him out permanently had given way to, as he saw it, a much more subtle approach. Wait till Saturday, old Hubert. I'll have you.

The pattern was the same – Great Moor Street station on a freezing, damp and morbidly grey afternoon. Danny wore an old army greatcoat, black boots and a black woollen hat which covered his hair and ears. The train consisted of four old carriages, one containing locked first-class compartments, obliging Danny to travel in the second carriage while Hubert sat in the coach nearest the locomotive. The train clanked away on time and en-route there were no delays and few passengers due, probably to the bone-aching weather.

At Eccles station Harrison was quickly away. Danny waited and stood for some time by the road. He walked slowly to the right and approached the snooker hall. At the entrance a well-rounded doorman enquired if he was a member. Danny replied in the negative.

"Can you pass a message, an urgent message, to Arthur Thompson? He needs to see his wife in the back bedroom of the pub. Can you tell him that?"

"Aye. Alright. Has she sent you? Is she ill or something?"

"Just give him the message, would you?"

Danny walked off, stood in a nearby side alley and watched what, in the army, he would have called a big happy lad emerge from the club. He looked somewhat nonplussed and scanned the road before striding toward the pub. He stood about six foot in height and weighed in at about 16 stones. Danny did not follow but saw him go through the front entrance at a fair pace. He then walked away to a bus stop and within minutes was heading into Manchester, certain Harrison would be paying for his actions.

In fact the subsequent trial established that bar staff, Thompson's own employees, tried to dissuade him from going up to his own living quarters. He burst up the stairs and into the back bedroom and found his wife facedown, half stripped, on the bed and Harrison removing his trousers. She screamed, Harrison said he didn't want any trouble and Thompson exploded in fury.

He grabbed Harrison by the throat and lifted him off his feet.

"Cheerio!" yelled Thompson, as he punched him full in the face. Harrison's body crumpled against the bedroom fireplace.

"And as for you," he yelled, grabbing his dainty wife by the arms. He threw her on the landing outside the open door.

Harrison stirred and gave a groan. He began to lift himself uncertainly using the mantelpiece as a support. Thompson was distracted. He turned back on him and hit Henderson with a ferocious haymaker of a punch that would have won an average heavyweight boxing tournament. Shaking with anger he then pulled Harrison's body down the stairs, past a transfixed group of customers and slung it out of the front door. The body bounced into the road, where a passing van drove over its head and shoulders. The driver pulled over, tyres screeching and, jumping out of the vehicle, proceeded to be sick on the kerb.

By this time the commotion had led to the police being called and two constables arrived to find six erstwhile drinkers holding Thompson down on the floor of the bar area, a dead body outside and a totally hysterical wife in the living quarters, hunched on the floor and convulsing in terror.

It took over three months to come to trial and the police investigation proved highly complex, especially trying to establish at what point Harrison had actually died. The local police in Wych Elm were indirectly involved and appraised Manchester colleagues of the deceased's background and reputation. Young George, his son, was subject to some formal questioning. Was he the stranger at the snooker club? Eventually, a murder charge was brought and Arthur Thompson was convicted at Manchester Crown Court. The death sentence was expected to be commuted on appeal. It wasn't. In March 1953, the sentence was carried out at the local Strangeways Prison. The number one executioner was a local man. Pierrepoint and his assistant dispatched him, condemned cell to drop in ten seconds.

The rubric and ritual of the execution were followed meticulously, especially as Thompson appeared to say something as the noose was fixed by his jaw. The chaplain and governor spoke about it later, but no formal report was made. This was subject to a further enquiry before being dropped.

In all the proceedings, bearing in mind Wych Elm was initially abuzz with comment and speculation, Maman kept a detached air, making little direct comment other than to express some sympathy for Thompson, none for his wife and to show some concern for young George Harrison. On the latter account she need not have worried. He inherited the practice and lived, happily ever after. He had his father's remains interred in a new grave in the parish church yard, not in his mother's resting place. Arthur Thompson rested in the prison precincts. George reserved his mother's grave for himself, taking occupation forty-two years, three marriages and two children later.

Enemies require careful handling; how much better if others work on them for you, Danny thought; in any other circumstances, the whole episode could have been amusing. As it was, he would settle for a good measure of personal satisfaction. After a year had passed the pubs of Wych Elm – smelling of damp overcoats and Woodbines – discussed other local indiscretions, horse-racing or football. The tale of 'Bert Harrison' dissolved into the realm of mere comparison or jocular warning. It was like the birds flying in the sky, parting the air as they progressed, only to have it re-form at the end of their tails, leaving not a trace of their passing.

Maman carried on much as before. Danny could not recall her mentioning Harrison again, except when discussion surrounded his son. There was more than a hint of satisfaction among the local constabulary but it was never publicly expressed. A new almoner took over at the lodge. Life went on, for some.

Danny found it strange just how many memories from the 40s and 50s formed and coalesced in his mind on a daily basis. The weeks and months leading to him arriving here were vague, dreamlike in their quality and lacking any hard grounding. Danny wondered whether the pub was still open and as for the snooker hall, he had a tiny recollection of it becoming a bingo hall around 1960 and being demolished in the early 80s, making way for a private housing development.

Life did go on, for some.

Chapter Three

Danny found himself walking outside of the city of Amiens – his mind was now timed into 1944 – and he could smell that unmistakeable stench of death. A group of German motor cycle troops, mustering on the road, unaware of the approaching allied armour, had been caught in the open. The lead Sherman tank had fired machine gun bursts into them and some had scattered, a few escaping and others picked off in the fields. Some of the bodies remained unburied, XXX corps having pushed on toward the Belgian border and the remaining MPs and RCT soldiers tasked with keeping the roads open. Amiens was a major traffic conduit to the front. He spotted three British Tank Corps men smoking by the roadside and asked if they were responsible for the aroma from the fields.

"No, son," replied one of them in a distinct Liverpool accent. "They were shot. We fry 'em."

He pointed down the road where the outline of a Churchill Crocodile tank could be seen, mechanics banging around its left -side track. It towed an armoured trailer containing old engine oil, and fired this stuff, ignited, through a tube in the turret, incinerating anything within range. It was ideal for clearing dug-in and entrenched troops and the Wehrmacht in France had grown to fear and loathe these machines, targeting them and the Sherman Firefly in combat. Hard experience had taught them that these mobile weapons were capable of severe damage on their own, as opposed to mass attacks by standard allied armour. In the right circumstances, the latter could be picked off at will but a Firefly could take out the best of German tanks, including the Tiger, and a well-aimed spurt from a Crocodile could see whole platoons of men cremated in prepared defensive positions.

"It's still an infantry tank after all, four mile an hour and a sitter from side on." The Scouser continued his monologue. "We managed to lose a track on cobbles. The rest of the brigade will be in Berlin before we start again."

"Let them," said one of the others. "It's a damned sight safer here."

"You can do the odd trade here," said the third. The second had introduced himself as Brian from Pinner. The first, Paddy from Bootle, pointed to the third man, Arnold from Bolton. "The locals have no petrol, oil or paraffin. A quart of paraffin got us this lot."

He pointed to half a dozen wine bottles in a basket beside them. Danny inspected the bottles and judged it a fine bargain. The conversation drifted onto their experiences in Normandy, Paddy describing it as a "balls up" while both Paddy and Arnold counted off the number of dead in their own group. No one wanted to die so close to victory and the Normandy battles were grinding affairs costing far more than anyone had envisaged in the ranks.

"Around Caen and on to Falaise it was just a mincing machine," said Arnold. "It was like being in a slaughterhouse where you're the damned beast."

Danny observed how pale the men were, sweating round the brow, eyes moving left and right – men who had clearly seen combat. They appeared to be relaxed, said all the right things and adopted casual attitudes but their fear came through, even in their northern humour.

"And if the Germans hit a Sherman with a frying pan, it would set alight," continued Paddy with an attempt at a smile. "The Cromwell *is* a bloody pan. My mother has one like it at home for boiling potatoes. Try getting out of one quickly. It would be easier to jump out of the pan."

A shout from down the road ended their conversation. The vehicle was fixed and transport would be along in an hour.

"Is that today?" Paddy yelled back.

The response was a waved two-fingered salute. Danny wished them all the best and doubled back into the city. He checked around the old family neighbourhood but did not want to make his presence felt. Perhaps he was avoiding uncomfortable memories of his own. Instead he ambled down to the river waterfront where a sort of organised chaos seemed to prevail. He saw a British Army chaplain, head in hands, with a coffee cup in front of him at a table in a café. It was an establishment favoured by the German military in its time. There was some damage, but clearly business of a sort continued. The padre was little older than Danny, easily distinguished by his badge and collar. He represented the Church of England before it succumbed to being the moth-eaten musical brocade of poetic reality. His appearance conformed to that of the military congregation – short for the most part, tired but physically fit, brown matted hair, and teeth that had all the effects of smoking and lack of dental care, above which opaque eyes spotted rather than observed.

Danny sat by him and introduced himself. The exhaustion radiated from the young clergyman. His name was Alban Brooks and 18 months earlier he had been a curate in Carlisle, had joined up and found himself in Normandy on day four of the invasion. He had been given the burial duties for servicemen in this patch but he had performed the rites for dead Wehrmacht and some French civilians as well.

"This was supposed to be a rest," he explained. He began to laugh quietly. "It was supposed to be an adventure. Hardly that!"

"Has it affected your faith?" Danny asked, somewhat bluntly.

"No more than dealing with drunk munitions workers at home, illegitimate babies and man's general inhumanity to man," he replied. "How about you?"

"Me?" Danny replied. "I'm Catholic. Our lot assume squalor, so nothing really surprises us. The devil is real - a real and present danger."

Danny gave a selective overview of his service in France and his family connections to Amiens. Alban listened intently and when he described his erstwhile companion on his drive down from Paris he guessed it was one of the tutors at his old Oxford college.

"I could have sworn I saw Carew across the square earlier on," he replied. "But dismissed it as wishful thinking – you know the sort of thing, mind focused on better things."

"Is that exercise to be part and parcel of your job?" said Danny, without a hint of malice. "Won't you be preaching better things?"

"After this lot," replied Alban firmly, "people will demand better things. They won't put up with the old ways. Relationships, fairness, medical access and schooling will all be under scrutiny. But we have to get there yet and I for one am far from convinced that our betters know what they're doing. The strategy Montgomery is following looks fine on paper. In reality it's a combination of Heath Robinson and Fred Kano's circus."

"With people dying," said Danny.

They walked down the road chatting in general terms about possible futures, with Alban describing some of the bombed-out scenes in Hull, Portsmouth and Plymouth and the awful social conditions endured by some of the families caught up in it. The press had tried to report the truth, but in such a jingoistic way that the truth was hidden, if not lost altogether, except from those who experienced it.

"Money will have to be found," he said. "If it means taking it from old institutions then we'll have to do it."

"Or," Danny suggested, "put more of it in the ordinary man or woman's pocket. It will reach the right place, eventually."

Alban asked Danny about his training. He knew something of special operations and from Danny's gait, attitude and evasiveness in terms of detail, suspected his true role. This presented a bit of a dilemma for Danny. He did talk of the survival training in Scotland and some aspects of unarmed combat. Alban refrained from digging deeper, simply asking how long he'd been in France.

"Six months," Danny replied. "It feels longer."

They parted amicably and Danny went toward the pre-arranged rendezvous to discuss arrangements for a flight back to "dear old Blighty" as the air reconnaissance officer consistently added to virtually every sentence. As he remembered the past, picturing the scene, a rough grass strip, medical staff and their transport, men drinking tea from flasks seated under hedgerows and sergeants bawling instructions some details seemed to blur. It was frustrating. Danny pondered in his chair as Sandra breezed into the room again.

"Do you want a pillow behind you, Danny?"

"No, I'm fine – just thinking," he replied with a wan smile. "You do a lot of it when you're older."

"I bet you are thinking of all the pretty girls you've known."

"That's beyond my ability to count," said Danny. "However, I do know one here." He patted her affectionately.

"Who are you thinking of?" Sandra asked, slightly intrigued at his frown of concentration.

"Just someone I met during the war."

"I bet she was gorgeous," laughed Sandra.

Danny just smiled in a non-committal way. Somehow her questions had opened a torrent of memories, accurate in themselves, but flooding outward in a haphazard fashion; he was trying to control them just to make sense of the past. The Major who accompanied him on the drive down to Amiens was no problem – Danny eventually grew to respect him in the years that followed. Perhaps it was more the self-censorship he imposed on the fate of his mother's family in Amiens. It suited him to imply his knowledge of events was defective and that Pierre Manon had kept the truth from him. That was not the case then and nor was it now. He clearly recalled being overwhelmed by the enormity of it in the course of the afternoon. Alban Brooks perhaps had seen it in him. It was making a return now.

Therese was an icon still. She promenaded within his mind and sometimes without, the feeling he had seen her from the corner of his eye. His adolescent *joi de vivre* had left him then. She perhaps retained it, in his thoughts and dreams, kept close, for another day.

Chapter Four

Only when they shared a meal in the dilapidated hotel that night did the Major actually converse with Danny. He was impressed by Danny's French conversation and realised from the talk Danny had with the waitress that he really did have family in Amiens, and it was not just some fleeting holiday abode. When the two discussed the Gendarme, who had arranged Grandpa Verrier's burial in the family tomb, some semblance of an understanding grew between them. The details came clearer during the securing of the Verrier family house. It contributed to the guilt Danny felt and was soon able to express over the use Boys gun – the Gendarme's brother had picked it up at St Valery in 1940 and given it to Jacques Verrier for safekeeping just before he had been sent into Germany as forced labour, spending nearly three years in the Reich somewhere in the Ruhr. He had been killed in an RAF air raid in 1943. Grandpa had apparently called the Gestapo "silly dogs" when questioned and his ill demeanour made him untypically raucous toward his captors. The missing gun had flown to England; his nephew would use it on them; they would not survive long, little did they know.

He had been shot in the yard, summarily and without ceremony. Hundreds of German troops were pouring into Amiens with the aim of securing the Somme bridges. A silly old man was just a nuisance in the wider scheme of things. Therese was unaware of her father's fate. They felt she could say far more than the old man and needed time to work on her. The neighbour had mentioned a male visitor, a stranger. Danny felt that pursuing the lady next door was something he may have done a month ago, but not now. What was the point? Amiens had suffered enough, as a city and as a community.

Basil Kenneth Carew, always known as Baz, was a philosophy don at Oxford, married to the daughter of a baronet. Alban Brooks had been right but Danny did not mention him. Baz, tried to charm the waitress into an after-hours binge in the bedroom and her rebuff surprised him.

"Better in Paris, what!" he directed a glance to Danny with an exaggerated wink.

Baz began to relate a particularly memorable meeting with a resistance lady who had offered none.

"She was only too willing, what! "he continued, in the heaviest of irony.

Danny affected an interest before retiring to a cold but tolerably clean bed. The waitress joined him later, just before midnight, for two hours' vivid conversation, animating an otherwise cold room. Danny remembered her clearly but was hazy concerning her name. He thought it may be Aurore but it could have been Annette.

Baz and Danny left at mid-morning, in an American light aircraft from a prepared grass strip. By 6pm Danny was in London, briefed and debriefed, promoted to Captain and allocated training duties at some stately pile in Hampshire. The first news he was given came as a greater shock than anything he had experienced to date: his father had been killed in one of the bizarre German air raids, which the text books rarely mention today. Small groups of roaming craft were hedge-hopping the eastern approaches and, in this instance, dropping a parachute mine aimed rather generally over Wych Elm. The target may have been the reservoirs but it could just as easily have been the railway works. In the event it had detonated in the air near the Home Guard hut by the lower reservoir, killing Billy and his companion that night, Joe Gardiner, a retired shunter. The only damage was a few bricks from the facing wall by water's edge and the hut itself. Both bodies were recovered.

Danny was given a fortnight's leave before taking up his new duties. He travelled north knowing he had to cope with the family's loss and dreading having to break the news to the Verrier branch of the family. The irony was in the fact that Dad had died the night before his departure from Amiens, as though the Gods conspired to decimate his clan as an act of atonement for his deeds in war. 'Quid pro quo,' thought Danny, 'was very much a game for two.' He would learn to live by that.

A foul railway journey up to Wigan, five hours to cover two-hundred miles, was followed by a fifty-minute bus trip to Wych Elm, chugging through New Springs, Aspen Hill, Whitestick and eventually down into Wych Elm. For the first time, he noticed the run-down nature of the town. It had suffered little war damage but the effects of five years without décor, paint nor basic maintenance had taken its toll. This was a feature of the whole country for 10 years and of the north for much longer. Rebuilding would neither be quick nor easy. Money would be scarce, especially in a country that had bankrupted itself to win a war.

Baz Carew had talked of shortages in the push to Berlin. For the Americans, it was the adequate supply of petrol; for us it was more a shortage of everything, including men. Recruits were now having to go into the mines as." Bevin Boys". Dozens of them had got on the bus at New Springs after a shift in one of the pits. The accents and body shape betrayed their alien origin. Lancashire miners were short and wiry; when relaxed, they generally sat on their haunches. These young lads, while they had northern accents for the most part, were positively posh. All of them were over five-foot-10 in height.

Danny's arrival home was bittersweet. His mother looked gaunt and, while trying hard to keep on top of things, appeared to be giving up the ghost. She related his father's demise in the finest detail and praised his family for rallying round.

The quarry was being maintained by a previously retired employee with Grandad Hird doing the accounts and wages. The ministry had bought a lot of stone for sea defences as well as the trimmings at the newer local airfields. Helene was working as an auxiliary nurse, had been traumatised by the loss of her husband three years before and now had simply continued in her work through her father's death, as though in a daze. Mother used the word *reverie* to describe it and when Danny eventually spoke to her, he agreed. His sister had become a different person, lacking the spark that he always associated with her.

It was little different when he told both of them what had happened in Amiens. Helene absorbed the details and gave little away, other than to ask him whether he blamed himself. His mother was quick to defend him, guessing which local policeman had been involved. She was right. Danny said it was a lame excuse to cite the war but without it none of this would have happened. He disabused them, in passing, of any notion of it being 'over by Christmas' and said that they should stick together to see it through.

Catherine slept little that night. Having played the role of Danny's mother, she engaged in her identity of sister to Therese, daughter of Jacques *et* Jeanne, and comforted herself with the thought that they were at least together, *en famille*. Danny slept but dreamt vivid dreams of what might have been, what should have been; but woke to what actually *was*. He got up early, preparing no breakfast and walking up to the church graveyard to view the freshly cut headstone of his father's plot. *Killed in the service of his country.* He returned home and from then on tended to refer to his mother as Dauphine or Princess, a name or title she never dissuaded him from using. His letters home began *Dear Princess* and this affectation was to last her lifetime. Verbally he referred to her as *Maman*.

A few days were spent looking over the quarry, talking with Grandad Hird and trying to catch up on news of old school friends. Most of the men were in the forces: two were in Belgium with the Royal Artillery one was in the Navy on anti-submarine work based in Liverpool, one was a POW captured during the retreat to Dunkirk and one was missing in action in Burma. American military had been a common sight in Wigan and Chorley but since D-Day there were fewer around. Helene did see many American airmen, taken to local hospitals; many, as she put it, "Shot in half" during bomber raids over Germany. They were flown into aerodromes in transport planes – less than an easy journey when fully fit, excruciating in the condition some of them were in.

All the youngsters and those on leave simply wanted to dance. There was a black market for almost everything. Grandad Hird told him that these days there was no such thing as rubbish: *whatever you plan to throw away, don't. Somebody, somewhere, will give you something for it.* Danny agreed, saying when the war eventually finished things could get very interesting. During the Great War Grandad Hird took the old liberal, capital view, common in Lancashire at the time – *kill a German, you kill a customer.* His views now were a pale echo of that same sentiment.

The dances were a bit shambolic at times, relying on old record players and even older records, or a scratch band trying to do their musical bit. When a recording of contemporary big band music came available, word spread like wildfire. Danny noted that pleasure, whatever the price, was a price always paid. Would that attitude prevail in the future? Danny wondered and watched.

Back in Hampshire, in apparent luxury, tormented by awful army rations and constantly changing orders, Danny set about training potential marksmen for active service. He was part of a selection team that included doctors, a psychiatrist as well as army personnel whose expertise ranged from promoting vigorous physical training to recounting hard, recent experience. He got to hear of the shambles officially known as Operation Market Garden, but generally referred to as Arnhem. There seemed to follow a lack of momentum and in January 1945 this particular training programme, the one on which he was working, was run down and Danny was told to expect a move to active work in Germany. He did some more work at Welwyn again to develop his own skills and in March was asked to attend a meeting at one of the better London hotels to be briefed on a new project.

More cake, anyone? No one was joking anymore.

Tea, in Edwardian china, was taken in one of the chandeliered lounges. He was left in no doubt as to the importance of this operation. Danny was specifically told to keep to the plan – No anti-tank rifles, however pleasing the outcome. It was a straightforward assassination of a French national, a Nazi collaborator, currently developing a group of like-minded souls intent on waving the Cross of Lorraine to electoral effect. He was living in a large house close to Marseille and Danny would be going on a camping holiday, cycling all the way, accompanied from Cherbourg by a colleague who would secure "some documents important to us" from the house, once its owner and his bodyguard were eliminated.

He would have the same French identity and cover story as before, but would arrive in Cherbourg as Captain Hird, Intelligence Corps, en-route to Caen – "that is all the Americans need know" – and would affect his French identity immediately afterwards. Clearly, this was an operation of particular importance here in Blighty rather than within the collective allied cause.

"Who is coming with me?"

"Oh, the French military will be involved."

"Us, then, against the Americans?"

"Not really," came the languid response. "It's more a case of *they* having used *him,* one of their men so to speak."

"But he's not one of ours?"

"Definitely not. A potential embarrassment, so to speak."

Preparatory material was handed over at a Mayfair office. The target was Emile Bertrand, aged fifty, a lawyer, divorced and living alone an hour from Marseille in a small town whose claim to fame were Roman antiquities and a former cathedral. His bodyguard was an ex-legionnaire of legendary reputation, known as Spitz. The same age as Bertrand, he had been hired in Marseille recently. Danny assumed Bertrand must know he was a target.

The war in Europe ended and the day after Danny got the signal to go. A nauseous night crossing from Falmouth, in uniform, carrying a new *de Lisle,* the old one having been lost on operations (actually hidden in Wych Elm in a quarry shed) and a small suitcase of 'equipment,' he disembarked, followed normal procedure and drove by jeep to a rendezvous well down the Contin Peninsular. He was left standing outside a roadside café. Pierre Manon greeted him from within, looking a little heavier and pointing to two packed tents by the passage wall.

Danny changed and they set off down as direct a route as possible, assuming the guise of old friends on holiday, seeking the sun and *les femmes fatale,* both carrying fishing bags to conceal their weaponry. They reached Marseille on time, meeting their contact in the best hotel. Somehow, Danny was not surprised to see Baz Carew wearing a new light grey suit and club tie, well into a bottle of the finest red, giving them further instructions and updates. Carew was positively urbane in his attitude, speaking to Danny and Manon as though they were old family retainers.

Their cycles and tents were loaded into the back of an elderly van the following day and they were dropped within a mile of their target to make the necessary 'arrangements.' Already aware of the land from accurate maps and detailed observational work previously done, Danny selected woodland, containing a broad mature tree, just five hundred yards from the house with a clear view of the courtyard. Five days each week Emile Bertrand took lunch at a hillside restaurant a few miles from home. He was driven in a Citroën saloon, identical to the one Danny had blown apart in Picardy, a graceful machine he resolved to spare this time. On Friday, at 11am, Danny observed Spitz drive the car from the garage and get out. His shot-hit Spitz in the back of the head, leaving him sprawled on the cobbled yard. He immediately re-loaded the chamber. A full minute elapsed before Bertrand appeared at the side door. He could see the car from the door, but not Spitz's body. As he stepped out, saying something, Danny fired a shot which hit him in the centre of his forehead, spinning him around. He fell facing the open door of the house.

Pierre Manon appeared, calmly walking through the gate. Danny placed the carbine back in the fishing rod canvas, shimmied down the tree and walked toward the house. Pierre emerged as Danny reached the gate. He was carrying a leather bag. Nodding to each other they took their cycles from the roadside ditch and cycled south, reaching Marseille late that night. They were booked into a small hotel and used the telephone to contact Carew the next morning. He arrived and collected the bag. Quickly examining the contents and declaring his satisfaction he gave Manon a rail ticket and a significant sum of money. Pierre left immediately. Danny was relieved of his carbine and told he was sailing to Malta. Within the hour he was on board a small boat. The following evening, back in uniform, he was flown by transport plane, sitting among crates and wearing an old army greatcoat for warmth. He landed in a remote East Anglian airfield, totally exhausted and needing food and sleep.

His debrief occurred on the air base, his controller showing some delight as the bodies had only been found the following day: *first class job, well done* etc. He was told to report to Welwyn for a further week, followed by some leave. There would be further interviews, but until contacted at Welwyn his time was his own.

Summoned to a meeting in a woebegone office in Kensington (it might have been Wormwood Scrubs a month or two earlier), Danny was told demobilisation would start early in the following year. He could continue with the Intelligence Corps rather than return to the railways. Danny had long discounted the railways as an option, not least because he saw the lack of money for virtually anything looming on the horizon and the idea of servicing a nineteenth-century technology, just to get by, had no attraction for him – and he said so. But it soon transpired in the conversation that there was another option.

"His Majesty's Government could utilise your services in a more circumscribed way, part time, possibly freelance, so to speak."

"Go on," replied Danny.

"This would, of course, be beyond the normal terms of service and would require your working in a capacity which allowed for time away."

"Self-employed, you mean?"

"Ideally."

"I was already thinking on those lines."

"The family stone business?"

"That is now being transferred to my mother and me. We have a day-to-day manager in mind. My sister has taken her share in cash and wants no further part in it."

"Will it be enough?"

"Until we start building again – roads, houses, serious stuff – it will just tick over. So I'm looking at options in the entertainment line."

"This may help."

The rather seedy looking civil servant – club tie, worn blue suit, shabby waistcoat, but supporting a significant gold watch chain – pushed a white envelope toward him. Danny picked it up from the desk and saw his name, Captain D J Hird, written in immaculate copper plate in black ink across the front.

"No ceremony," said Tattersall – that's how he had introduced himself. "Do open it. It may assist your decision making."

Danny reached for the silver letter opener, handily placed in front of him, slit the envelope and withdrew a cheque, drawn on Coutts & Co London bankers, for £1,000. He gave no outward reaction, but looked at Tattersall, raising an eyebrow. Today such a sum presently might be useful for day-to-day living but in 1945 it was a small fortune.

"That isn't your standard gratuity, by the way – that will come at the end of your war service and amount to a little less than half of that. No, that is a personal gratuity from above."

"For what?"

"For service rendered."

"Which service in particular?"

"Oh, the small detail at *Vaison la Romai*n."

"Bertrand."

"Quite."

"And you want me to do similar services on a part-time basis?"

"In peacetime, still serving HMG, as a craftsman and receiving a monthly retainer for future services,"

Tattersall intoned, allowing himself a smile. "Rather like having your own plumber, on-call, day or night."

In this way, Danny found himself recruited into the Special Operations Branch (SOB) attached to MI6. Less than three hundred service personnel were recruited and those who were had key skills needed to extend the country's reach abroad. Many skills were linguistic or, increasingly, electronic but Danny had several and had been earmarked very early on.

This initial meeting led to two others outside the capital and by April 1946, he was duly signed up to this particular firm. He was subject to the infamous Official Secrets Act which had to be signed, *with due ceremony*, in the same office in Kensington, with Tattersall and a female managerial type present. She was obviously ex-military, introduced herself as his Director of Operations, Miss Wells.

"But do call me Madge, off duty. These military habits do tend to stick a bit and can so easily gum up the works. Don't you think?"

Danny agreed.

"So, back north then Danny, and await the call. Hope business progresses well. Music and light entertainment, I understand."

"Yes," Danny replied. "I have negotiated the purchase of Wych Elm's one-and-only cinema – closed due to the fact there are five in Bolton with comfortable seats, a proper roof and a decent range of films. When it rained the noise on the tin roof tended to drown out the dialogue. I remember watching Flash Gordon as though it were a mime."

"You made sure you bought the Queen's, the whole plot with the building for £90. Given time the land will double in value. Your district council contacts should ensure a viable little business. Keep them sweet."

How did she know all that?

That was clearly Madge's warning. *She and they knew.* But, Danny reasoned to himself, what he knew could equally be a warning to them. Neither party entirely trusted the other. At least in this scenario nothing was likely to become personal. It was more about acts and deliverance, based on self-interest rather than ephemeral notions of love, respect and loyalty.

Chapter Five

It is a truism that the older we become, the more detail we recall from distant past memories as opposed to those from the previous week. It does not, of course, necessarily make them true. Our memory can deceive us. At least that is what we tell ourselves, especially when things go awry.

In Danny's case, the previous day was becoming a struggle but his recollection of the beginnings of *Danny's Place* were as clear as a bell. In four years he begged, borrowed and stole materials to fit out a dance hall, cloakrooms and decent washroom facilities so that by the beginning of 1950 it was a going concern. Early on he paid the American military, at their base in Padgate, £20 for two record players and speakers which he used as a dual system, just like the way things were done in Marseille –he had observed it there and once in Paris – so that the venue became famous for continuous dance music. At the start it had been little more than an elaborate youth club, which paid its way. By 1950 it was making good money, much of it in cash, which could be husbanded carefully to avoid the voracious tax regime which dominated much of the UK in the immediate post-war years.

Local councillors were squared for music licenses, the victuallers for a drinks license – eventually secured for six days excluding Sunday – from 1951, with the proviso that the bar was separated from the dance hall and, as a calculated bonus, allowing younger teenagers to use the facilities at lunchtimes and for early evening sessions, without the influence of alcoholic refreshment permeating their minds and making potentially less than agreeable adults of them. A shilling entry provided up to two hours at lunchtime with a free bottle of lemonade and American records. There was no Rock n Roll at that stage but everything at the old Queen's, as some continued to call it, was thoroughly up-to-date, inexpensive and, above all, desirable. Factory hands and factory girls met, went out and often married after a few lunch sessions and the more extended themed evening events. Jazz was an initial success on Tuesdays and later the emerging taste for folk music, with live bands on Wednesdays in the 50s. By the end of the mid-60s the venue had become a permanent Friday night draw, attracting people from all over the northwest. Coach loads of fresh-faced teenagers decamped for an evening in Wych Elm.

Danny could equally recall the labyrinth of the French legal system that eventually secured his mother's right to the family home in Amiens. She spent a considerable sum updating the services and decoration. By 1952, having stayed just a few summer weeks there in the previous four years, she rented the property out to a young family. They made permanent roots and proceeded to grow older for the next thirty years. They paid the rent on time.

In 1948 Danny bought a new car, replacing his parents' pre-war Flying Standard. It was a Ford Pilot, a heavy and essentially old-fashioned saloon with an eight-cylinder side valve engine, which anyone with wartime experience would recognise at a glance and repair quite easily. The car had presence, was comfortable and, unusually at the time, had a good radio. Danny drove this green monster for more than 10 years and swore by its reliability.

Danny had described the car to Sandra before she had to attend tend to other people in her care. The next thing invading his consciousness saw Danny aroused from a reverie by the voice of Mary Hobson refusing to go down to the dining room for lunch. Her designated carer, Andrea, was clearly getting exasperated as a cut-glass tone had entered her voice. For Danny, that was far from a good combination. Andrea was younger and taller than Sandra. She had incredibly good legs and Danny had told her so on the first occasion they had spoken. But she was the type of woman who not only brushed off a compliment but gave a sense of entitlement in her reply *–she not only knew this already, but her current partner also rated her hair.*

Danny had heard enough. Attractive as she may be in view, her voice had the timbre of a chainsaw and grated on his ears. He had never liked loud women and this voice cut through him in a ragged sort of way, blanking out any positive notes from her body. She reminded him of a young, aspiring pop singer he had supported forty years earlier who had opted for a wealthy marriage rather than a career auditioning for London impresarios with Danny as her agent, taking over fifty percent of the fees between them.

Mary was in full flow.

"You people will kill us with all the food you keep throwing our way. It's not necessary. And, no, don't bring me sandwiches. I've barely digested breakfast and here you are again!"

Andrea smiled as sweetly as she could.

"Mary, is there anything you do want?"

"Yes, there is. I want to be out of here and living with my family. Most of the people in here are either disinterested or on their last legs. I spoke to one lady in the lounge yesterday and she fell asleep while I was speaking to her. No manners."

"That would be Mrs Hewlett. She died."

"That doesn't surprise me in this place," Mary replied and without a pause went on to demand an appointment with a doctor.

"You don't listen to me; my family don't want me and you are all trying to kill me."

"Well Mary, if you do want anything later, press your bell."

"A lot of good that will do! I rang it last night. Four and a half minutes before anyone came."

"Whatever, Mary."

"And I'll have less of your cheek. I pay your wages, remember."

At that point Sandra poked her head round the door and, smiling, pointed across the corridor toward Mary's room.

"Do you want lunch, Danny?"

"No thanks, petal," Danny replied. "Just bring me a ham sandwich and a cup of tea when you have time."

"You haven't forgotten Jan Dale is coming in to see you at three?"

"How could I forget such a charmer?"

Danny had first met Jan Dale in the dance hall as a 16 year old. She was at the grammar school and had persuaded him to do an article for the school magazine on the current pop scene. That would be May 1968. Danny calculated she would be near on sixty this year and didn't look it from a distance, nor in the half light. Close to was rather different. He had followed her career in journalism and latterly done some careful checking. The 16 year old who had pushed him into a free article had gone on to do a history degree in London and had a Sapphic affair with a café owner who happened to be the niece of one of the capital's gang leaders of the post-war era of rationing, shortages and general want. She had secured a permanent position with one of the national dailies on the strength of articles surrounding this connection and the London crime scene in general. A book had followed on the link between rationing and organised crime – *what year was that? It must have been 1975 or 76 – a time when long political memories were around to ask awkward questions in parliament.*

Since then, she had engaged in an affair with a government junior minister (married) and an American female CIA agent (unmarried then but more recently attached) and had seen her father, Jack Barnsdale, die of a stroke in police custody, here in Wych Elm, being questioned about an historic murder case that is still, to this day, unresolved.

As far as Danny was concerned Janet Barnsdale had moved from being one to watch to one who needed watching. Her journalistic instincts and sheer luck could prove awkward. She had interviewed him for thirty minutes some four weeks ago, ostensibly about *Danny's Place,* but the drift of her enquiry was less about pop music and more about his staffing arrangements and his work as an entertainment agent after the club had been sold in 1970. She had been deferential in the kind of way someone might be to a live chicken they intended to kill and eat.

He had wondered whether she had got hold of his wartime record or maybe, worse, his work up to 1955. But she seemed unconcerned with the bland titbits he threw at her. She seemed to be barking up an entirely different tree. There was something incredibly cold about her, in the way she appeared to show an interest in something you had said and then raise a totally unrelated question. There was an agenda and Danny had only agreed to see her again to discover what she knew, or what she thought she knew.

Anyhow, she was back again and this time Danny was more prepared, not least with questions of his own. The woman who had appeared on *Desert Island Discs* in 1982, had a weekly music radio show from 1988 to 1990 and still did the odd journalistic book was, among her fellow news people particularly the music critic of the *Northern Times,* "about as popular as the pox in a convent." One respected editor in Manchester had expressed the opinion in a phone conversation with Danny that she was the type to have slept with the Nazi hierarchy, one at a time, to gain an advantage and that her true sexuality was still a matter of speculation. She was seen as self-promoting and self-regarding.

Danny had volunteered to him that he had known her father, Jack Barnsdale. It was his company that had rewired the old cinema building and had the contract for the electrics until well after Danny had sold the place. He was, Danny maintained, typical of Wych Elm's business community: masonic and trustworthy within a contract, but personally a quiet mystery. No one *really* knew him. It was like seeing someone permanently behind glass. Her mother was considered an attractive catch in her day. As time went on she seemed to have disappeared into a sort of domestic bliss only to reappear occasionally on high days and holidays.

Jan arrived on time. Danny was in his wheelchair, for convenience, in the ground floor lounge. Sandra had taken him down in the lift and placed him by the window. The sill had a couple of plant pots on it but Danny saw her arrive, between the foliage, in a black Porsche and emerge wearing a red trouser suit, well cut and similar to the grey one she had worn last time. Then, Danny thought she looked funereal, but today she resembled a 1980s airport hotel receptionist. The white-blond hair had a stiff perm, something he had worn for a long time on similarly coloured hair, becoming a trademark on television programmes and during outside events. In the last few years he had let it revert to grey but he still kept the waves fairly long.

Jan signed in at the desk. Andrea happened to be in the hallway as she arrived. She gave a beaming smile and greeted her warmly as "Miss Dale."

"Oh, call me Jan, please. You make me sound like one of my old teachers at the grammar school down the lane."

"Fine," replied Andrea. "He's waiting for you in the lounge."

She pointed to the closed oak door, her eyes transfixed on Jan's walk as she brushed by. She was rewarded with a flash of a smile over the older woman's shoulder, a trick Jan had perfected early in her career and used effectively in photoshoots.

Jan entered, closed the door behind her and expressed her satisfaction that there was no one else in the room. Danny explained that everyone else had been directed to the bigger lounge on the second floor, at least for the next hour. A notice had been placed on the door handle. Jan sat opposite Danny, in an armless lounge chair, and placed a recorder between them, checking he had no objection to her recording the interview.

"As I said last time," Danny replied, "our memories are slipping a bit now but I'm sure I've nothing to hide."

Jan gave a watery smile, started her rather antique machine and went into warm chat mode. This was her preferred and well-practised approach. Danny was unimpressed but played along.

"Danny, today I want to speak about some people from your past – in particular, Linda Haslam, Jennie Johnson and Liz Layne."

"All three worked at my place for a year or two. Let me think, Linda was from Wych Elm and worked for Reg Smith, the solicitor, Smith & Co. She used to sing the introductions – *Have you heard, He's in the stars* – usually on Friday nights. She had a good voice. At one time Liz Layne sang with her. Jennie didn't, because she sang on Saturdays with Lindsey Morrell."

"Lindsey married and moved off to New Zealand," said Jan. "She died of cancer last year."

"Sorry to hear that," he replied. "I didn't know her well."

"But you knew the others?"

"I can remember them, but *knowing* them is rather a different matter. They weren't girlfriends or anything like that."

"Have you ever had a steady girlfriend, Danny?"

"Yes, a few – and so have you."

"Mine are a matter of record." Jan did not miss a beat. "Whereas you are an enigma in that area. Never married, never engaged and close to your mother."

Danny noted the innuendo but kept his face on hers.

"My mum, Princess, lost most of her family during the war and I supported her as well as I could. She was a priority. My sister lived away, with a family of her own. I was here."

"Then there was Cliff Hindle? He helped you out, didn't he?"

Clifford was the best friend Danny had made after the war. A few years older, he had served with the Eighth Army in North Africa and Sicily where a misplaced shell in support of his company's advance put shrapnel in his right leg, sufficient to place him on light duties. He had been a keen amateur boxer and played rugby league into his 20s. De-mobbed early in 1945 he had rejoined the family business in Aspen Hill, selling boot polish and insoles, plus doing simple shoe repairs from a small shop in the village. It doubled as the local barber's shop where his father cut hair with hand clippers. His mother had managed the shop with his father but cancer took her in late 1950, and while his father continued to cut hair, Cliff answered Danny's ad for a security supervisor at the dance club.

Cliff was solid, quietly spoken, enjoyed a pint but never to excess, and could handle himself and others well. He was always well dressed, wearing good suits or blazers. His black curled hair invariably had a smooth continental oil dressing. When necessary he could deliver a right upper cut to lift a bigger man off his feet. The interview – in Wigan pub *Legs of Man,* down the Old Arcade – had taken all of 20 minutes. In later years Cliff had been Danny's driver and was a custodian of a few secrets, but the very idea he was some kind of homosexual would have made him turn in his grave. Cancer took him, like his mother, a year after his father succumbed to a coronary thrombosis. Bill died in February 1967 and Cliff followed the following March. Cliff, Bill and Jane were buried in the same plot at St Elizabeth's in Aspen Hill. If anything, Cliff was asexual, with more interest in sport, horse racing and cards. Danny had gleaned this aspect of his character very quickly. He was the type of bachelor totally unknown today and would be the type to arouse suspicion of some suppressed sexuality or dark longings, awaiting the forensic pen of someone like Jan Dale to expose his shadowy secrets to the world.

"The problem you have, Jan," said Danny firmly, after giving her a brief but succinct description of Clifford Hindle, "is your presupposition that everything about a person is defined by their attitude to sex. I left

France at the war's end and watched that nation spend thirty years trying to reconcile Freud with Karl Marx. What a waste of time. Here, we spent thirty years trying to make sex open and accessible and wasted our time. Now it's a commodity that everyone your age is trying to control, like smoking and our diet."

Jan was discomfited but tried not to show it and asked him about smoking.

"You were a smoker, were you not?"

"Most people were. In the army, the cigarettes compensated for the awful food. Everyone smoked Woodbines or Capstan, Players or Senior Service."

"You didn't smoke a common brand."

"I smoked *Alfred Dunhill* and only gave up before coming in here."

"Did you ever give cigarettes to younger people? Girls?"

"Yes," he replied with a smile. He had done his homework on her.

"The only blot on your copybook at Wych Elm Grammar School was smoking - Embassy Regal, I expect, on two occasions."

"But I wasn't being given them by an older man."

"I can see the drift of this conversation and I cannot say I'm too keen on it. This is a story so old it has a beard."

Jan ploughed on.

"And what of Alan Thompson? You and Cliff Hindle drove him to London – to see an agent. You say you left him there and he…"

Danny grimaced at the memory, brought on by the very mention of Alan's name. It had a deep resonance for him. Alan was not related to Arthur Thompson, the pub landlord in Eccles. It was a common surname. It was more the coincidence of the name being mentioned so soon after his recall of the murder and trial. Alan Thompson was altogether a different matter, one that had cost time and money.

Danny told her that Alan had some talent and a decent backing group from Manchester, but there were mental issues which curtailed his progress.

"I introduced him to the best agent for his type of music and, within a week, he…"

"Disappeared," said Jan.

"I still sometimes see his mother; well, I did," said Danny. "Nothing has been heard of him in thirty odd years except for journalistic rumour designed to get a penny or two. You know well enough, on the back of a cock-and-bull story, that they dug up half a suburban churchyard in Lewisham 10 years ago looking for his body and then switched to Bolton, of all places, until the police came to their senses."

Jan had been heavily involved in this particular story, convinced both Danny and Cliff Hindle were at least implicated in Alan's disappearance.

"Do you know where he is?"

"If I did, I would tell his mother, then the police and as I don't there's nothing to say. His old group did reasonably well up here – don't forget that. They were originally *the Motors* and later called themselves *the Carrs.* All of them are still alive. Ask them what they know."

She had and none of them could shed any light on the alleged mystery. All of them showed at least contempt for Alan Thompson or open hostility. All thought their careers had been blighted by his affectations and sense of entitlement. The pop music industry could be as acerbic as journalism.

"I think we've said enough."

Jan tried to continue but Danny waived her away and swung to his left, propelling his wheelchair to the door. He went to the lift and as he pressed the button to go up, he looked at the standing figure eying him in the distance.

"Don't come again."

Jan was angry with herself for losing control of the conversation. She should have stuck to the girls rather than introducing the Alan Thompson angle so early in the talk. The group, calling themselves *Junior Jumpstart & the Motors* had their first single reach number 22 in the charts in March 1967. Danny had guided Alan Thompson and provided the backing group, a successful black harmony sound from the Manchester club circuit. The problem was, Alan wasn't black but wanted to be. He loved black music and the soul sound. To emulate it he went to extraordinary extremes to tan his skin, dying his straight, light brown hair black and trying to use a mid-Atlantic accent in everyday speech. Danny's influence at that time was basically northern and he used the *Heim & Rhyme Agency* in London's Soho as his sole London contact for likely northern acts, taking, at first, up to 20 percent and expenses.

It was as though the capital swallowed Alan. In an agency owned flat for four days he simply disappeared without trace, but not without rumour. Levi Heim wished he'd never met him and said so to the police who even then seemed far more interested in his longstanding male friends than in tracing this daft kid from the north. The backing group returned with little regret and had 10 good years on the Manchester circuit, re-forming a few years later to take part in the *Northern Soul* revival, earning considerable fees and excellent reviews.

Danny wheeled himself down the corridor to his room, raised himself and sat in his easy chair. He was concerned rather than angry and made a few phone calls to contacts outside, making it clear that Jan Dale was no longer welcome in his company, explaining why and that anything out there on *her* would be gratefully received.

"Never you mind," smiled Sandra as he told her the tale. She was due to finish her shift at 3.30pm but had called in to see him. "She'll be barred from now on in."

"Barred? I'd have her behind bars," said Danny firmly.

"Father John, the priest, might pop in this evening. He performed the last rites on one old lady last night and said he might call in."

"He wants something," replied Danny. "He's a peculiar priest. He's English for a start, doesn't drink beer, just fine wine, no interest in horses or football. His hobby is archaeology, you know, digging old stuff out of the ground. Not bodies, at least, not recent ones - more stones, pots, necklaces, that kind of thing. He's not into socialism, which is a good thing and he hates what he calls parish buffets. Never eats the stuff. Waits till later and orders a Chinese. No, he's fairly sound. He wants something. Money, I expect."

"I don't know him that well," replied Sandra. "He seems nice."

"So do I," smiled Danny. "But I'm not."

"Get away with you," she pecked his forehead. "See you tomorrow."

"God willing," said Danny.

He was left wondering just how the divine would view his life. Not in the sense of *so far* as it had progressed as far as was likely to go. He would be judged on all that had gone before. Anything in the future would be a bonus. His time was limited. Would he be condemned more than most? Silly thoughts, really; how can anyone – priests, bishops, the Pope – actually know? This was not the type of thinking suited to the elderly. It is more a case of continuing to look forward and as little as possible, back.

Chapter Six

The mention of Cliff Hindle brought back a host of memories for Danny, not least his reliability in managing the day-to-day business when he was away from Wych Elm. Latterly it had been agency work for aspiring pop stars involving trips to London, negotiating after rehearsals with Levi Heim. Danny often said it was easier to do a deal with the Gestapo a wistful comment not lost in its irony on Levi himself. Both men were in this business for the money so the easier the better. Levi had established himself just before the war, acting as the British agent for one particular American concern, a mutually beneficial link which lasted for over fifty years. Levi had the contacts, Danny the time and patience, as well as the access to the northern scene.

In many ways, *Junior Jumpstart & the Motors* had been a distraction. Before them Carla Wayne (actually Carole Entwhistle) from Bradford had been the first real success. Danny had managed her career for 12 months before sending her south. She now lived in Sacramento with her longstanding husband and still sent birthday cards to Danny. Eddie Wise was another, still doing pantomime in his 70s but scoring two chart hits in the late 60s. He was an apprentice plasterer from Daisy Hill. Even in the late 80s Danny had discovered *the* group of that era. They may have only lasted three years and two American tours under his control but *Poke Me Quietly* had made Danny more than a million and secured a financial legacy which Danny was now actively enjoying in a world economy slowly going to the dogs. Had they been dogs, or cats, Danny would not be concerned. People were a different matter and some could be of major concern, needing attention.

But this is to jump ahead. Cliff and Danny secured the dance hall reputation by dealing firmly with trouble. He or Cliff had often taken teddy boys or an aspiring Marlon Brando round the back, where a dogleg extension hid most of the yard, bouncing them from wall to wall until they saw things the managements' way. Reefers were an occasional distraction. A warning was given once and if ignored the local constabulary were informed. The night-beat regularly visited *Danny's Place* — through the rear entrance gate and up the fire escape – for coffee, tea or stronger in the back office. It made life easier for them and for Danny when mutual concerns arose and allowed both to keep an eye on things.

Danny had a double garage built on his mother's bungalow plot, using quarry stone, with a single flat above, and there was some sleeping accommodation above the dance hall. Cliff tended to use the flat – he got on well with Danny's mother – but they did sometimes interchange, as circumstances determined, until Danny bought his own cottage near the reservoirs; *handy but quiet* as he used to say, which left Cliff permanently in the flat. In 1958 Danny had bought an Armstrong Siddeley saloon, leaving the Ford Pilot for Cliff to drive around, although he did act as Danny's chauffer a few times on longer drives, especially down to London.

The longest Cliff had to look after *the shop* was in 1953 when he, two other male retainers and the two permanent females were left on their own for a month. That was a real assignment, unlike a terminated job early in 1951 when Danny was sent, with a Welrod, to one of the Tyne ports, looking for Russia-bound public schoolboys who had dirtied on their own doorstep. At the time Danny doubted the intelligence and did not expect to meet them. He finished up with a chill and a severe hangover from indulging in one of the quayside pubs, locked in, past 3am. The idea that they might run for Mother Russia via the Norway ferry from North Shields was laughable and, in any event, he felt sure the service wanted them out, not dead on a Tyne quayside. He had called, unannounced, on his sister Helen and her husband in Whitley Bay for breakfast on the final day and been met by an atmosphere as cold as charity. He left Newcastle Central station on the late morning train to Liverpool, as far as Manchester Exchange. Helene and Nichol had treated him like a flu virus, neither believing his cover story nor showing any willingness to play long lost happy families.

But the 1953 expedition was different altogether and preceded by a letter, received at his mother's address, inviting him to renew his acquaintance with Bernard Carew at his Oxford college where he tutored in philosophy for a living and, as he expressed it in his note, made it his mission "in this male arcadia" to encourage young female students in the university to "make their way in the world." Hence Danny had to drive down for a pretentious day or two in Oxford and suffer all the delights and dignities on offer during his stay.

A further letter gave an address in north Oxford to call on before meeting Bernard in college. Danny stayed overnight in war-damaged Coventry, arranging to see some former army friends from the city and imbibing a glass or two in one of the older intact pubs that the Luftwaffe had missed in November 1940. It was quite close by the burnt-out shell of the cathedral, the medieval stonework still bearing the scorch marks of the incendiary bombs dropped on the city. Paris and Amiens had got off lightly by comparison but at least Britain had not been occupied, except for the Channel Islands. His old acquaintances were all working in car manufacturing or engineering and earning good money. Danny noted the lack of a *Danny's Place* and made a mental calculation as to the clear profit available in this prosperous wreck of a city. Wages in Wych Elm were lower. What could you expect from textiles and the railway?

The drive down to Oxford was uneventful and Danny found himself reflecting on how a German occupation may have developed here. The usual arseholes would have done well out of it, provided they weren't Jewish. That would have affected Manchester, less so Liverpool. 'Yet having won the damned war, here we were,' Danny whispered to himself, 'just out of bloody rationing.' Danny had used his Jewish tailor in Bolton to produce the suit he brought with him. It was the latest American style − dark brown with a grey pinstripe, worn with a trilby hat encircled by a two-inch ribbon. He drove in a pair of grey flannels and an open-neck shirt, with an older sports coat on the back seat. He had started to wear his hair longer, to the extent that one old army chum in Coventry asked him if the barbers were on strike in Lancashire. Short back and sides was still the male urban norm. He was less conspicuous in Oxford.

The Oxford house was a small brick terraced property on a tree-lined street. Each house had a stone step up to the front door. Most of the paintwork had seen better days, but number nine was in good condition with some evidence of recent maintenance. Danny knocked on the black paintwork and the door was immediately opened by a small, elderly and rather intense lady whose hair was incredibly white and worn in a tight bun. She spoke quickly.

"You must be Mr Hird, yes?"

"Yes." Danny nodded.

"Madam is expecting you. Follow me."

Danny was shown into a comfortable and well-furnished, pre-war style lounge. A dark haired lady who may have been forty, but appeared 10 years younger, rose from one of the easy chairs and, in a voice with the smooth consistency of warm butter, bade him sit down. He did, taking in her petite body and a most becoming maroon woollen dress which showed her figure to perfection.

"Forgive me, I am Suzanne Carew."

She swung her head as she spoke, eyeing Danny up and down, without being too obvious. He reached over and shook her porcelain hand fleetingly, feeling almost dumb. She was a real class act, from the clothes to the body language and the soft accent doing little to betray the clipped tone of the landed gentry.

"I hadn't realised I would be meeting Bernard's wife."

"Did he mention me much in your war service?"

"Only in passing," replied Danny honestly. "But this is a great pleasure."

She smiled and rose, walking to a small corner table and returning with a large manila envelope, unsealed. She sat and passed the documents to Danny. This was to be very much a business meeting.

"All of your instructions, tickets and funds are in there. The usual rules apply, read overnight and, apart from the tickets, destroy."

Danny gripped the envelope, Suzanne inwardly amused at his apparent discomfiture. She allowed herself to smile. She had not had an effect like this on a man for quite a while and it was all the more amusing to find he was no country bumpkin, still less old military, like guards' officers, in style and manner. There was something quite distinct about him, decisive, unobtrusive, confident; indeed, a set of qualities the service wanted to develop but in Danny Hird they were manifestly there. She broke the momentary silence.

"Like you, Bernard was essentially a field operative and he still does a little for the service. His skill set is rather different from yours, but he will advise on some aspects of this operation. However, I am office based and look after the structure," she said, "as well as the plan."

Danny recovered his composure, accepting this unforeseen development, and pointed out that he had been expecting a brief in London. Suzanne replied that London had effectively come to him, this house being her "pied a terre" in Oxford.; Bernard had rooms in his college and normally only slept in this house at the weekend. Their main home, Danny later discovered, was an inherited manor house in Gloucestershire, set in over a hundred acres of parkland. This was a lifestyle easily managed in an academic year amounting to little more than three five-week terms.

Suzanne was remarkably well informed on Danny's general progress, leaning forward to stress the need to get involved in specific charitable work. He mentioned his support for St Jude's, a school for double orphaned Catholic girls on the outskirts of Bolton. Through the local priest, Danny had provided a set of cycles for school use and a grant of several hundred pounds for the appointment of a part-time languages teacher. He had given free stonework for a chapel extension and was now installed with two priests, one lawyer, several nuns and a lay nominee of the bishop on the governing body. The equivalent larger boys' home, 10 miles further out, had been provided with cycles and a racing trainer who had been part of a team in the 1948 Olympic Games, but Danny had refrained from joining that governing body, citing time constraints while promising a grant toward a new gymnasium in the next financial year. Some of the girls and boys had been on special trips to *Danny's Place,* though, at the nuns' insistence, never together.

While Suzanne agreed it was a start, she did advise some national donations in the next year, "so as to assist your profile."

"And another thing," she added. "Your own beliefs are very much your own, but don't be *too Catholic*. It gives rather a working class, Irish, generally chippy impression."

"I treat it as I would in France," replied Danny, not the least offended. "I avoid all the Irish dancing and the rest of the Celtic fringe social events. I suspect Catholicism behaves better in Oxford."

Danny had seen this donation lark as some kind of cover and took the view he would do what he could in areas that interested him. He soon discovered that his natural generosity in certain areas had a more utilitarian point as far as the service was concerned, but Danny took Suzanne's message on board.

He checked his material and, declining an offer of tea, moved off to his hotel and prepared to meet Bernard at two. He avoided lunch and ran through the documents again, placing the tickets in his wallet and using his cigarette lighter to burn two of the papers in the wastebasket in his room. He then took a hot bath to ease out the discomfort of two days on poor roads, slow speeds and queuing traffic. An easy walk took him to Bernard's college, a small medieval place tucked between two larger institutions. At the gate office he was directed to the archway off the quad which formed the entrance to a staircase, off which Bernard had his set of rooms.

"If he is sporting his oak, sir, walk away and come back later."

The porter's phraseology left Danny looking askance.

"Ah, I'm so sorry, sir. What I mean is, if his main wooden door is shut he doesn't want to be disturbed. If that first door is open or ajar, walk in to the next door. Knock on that and walk in."

"Thank you," Danny replied firmly.

Danny walked up the stone stairway, found the heavy door open and the second lighter door ajar. He tapped the wood once and walked in. Bernard was sitting in the type of patterned sitting room normally associated with elderly spinsters. All that was missing were a couple of cats and a parrot. Bernard was rising from a deep armchair, wearing a plain blue jacket, yellow shirt, club tie and casual trousers in a distinctive peacock blue. His shoes were quite light in appearance, black but not at all heavy in upper or sole. This allowed Bernard to virtually dance around the room as he poured brandy and bade Danny to avoid the large sofa and sit in the other armchair.

"You've met my wife?"

"Yes, a surprise and a pleasure."

"Surprise?"

"Her role."

"Ah, I'd forgotten you were unaware of her being in the tent, so to speak."

"What is going on in Italy? It's not as though we saw them as real enemies in the war. They'll be communist, the rate things are going. Mussolini's lot won't be back for a while."

"The target is a Frenchman," said Bernard firmly. He refilled their brandy glasses and waved his arm in the air. He went on to say it was a pity the target wasn't in France as it would be easier to control him there and any elimination much more easily done.

"It is, of course, connected to your last operation down there, at Vaison. Our target was a good friend of Emile Bertrand and, I understand, an accomplished jazz pianist."

Danny sat right back in the chair, raised an eyebrow and said he had noticed Bernard's award of a French gong for that operation.

"It wasn't just for that and the event was not mentioned in the citation," Bernard drawled reflectively.

"And you will get yours, eventually. It's just that the French cannot award you just yet for killing their own. My German tally was higher. But yours will come – eventually."

"I can wait."

Bernard then took on a graver tone, lighting a cigarette which served to emphasise his diction.

"Our target is an ex-employee at number four, *route de Champ d'Etrainment* in..."

"Paris."

"Quite so," continued Bernard. "The semi royals still leave a trail of potential embarrassment and the connection with a voluble Sicilian Count, loose women, blackmail, narcotics and a quite imaginative criminal record under Mussolini leaves us and others with little option."

"When did he work for the pair of black sheep?" Danny asked.

"Just last year," replied Bernard. "But his former employer was Emile Bertrand, friend of the sheep and no longer with us, courtesy of you. This will be a similar job, this time near an Italian fishing village, handy for Rome."

"And my contact?"

"Just follow the plan. You don't know him; he'll be based in the Rome embassy. He is considered *very good.*"

Danny took in the information, delivered in similar style to the last job in France having no reason to doubt the arrangements, nor the gratitude which would inevitably follow. Thereafter, Bernard asked Danny about his impressions of Oxford. Danny was quite blunt.

"It's a small town full of churches, chapels and places like this." He pointed out of the latticed window. "It's like living in alms houses or cottage hospitals. Cambridge is much the same, only flatter and colder."

"You stayed in Cambridge briefly." Bernard was smiling.

"Yes. The natives were akin to aggrieved peasants. They seem more bucolic here. Like everyone else, they have an eye on the main chance."

"Most of the dons here think *this* is normal. Most did war service of one kind or another but saw it as a holiday. They enjoyed the company of the chaps in their regiment or unit, did all that was asked of them – and in some cases more – but saw it all as a passing phase, waiting to dine with the chaps here."

"You teach here," said Danny. "Mostly young men I expect. Don't you get bored?"

"Ah," Bernard responded, quick on the uptake. "There are a number of women's colleges here, populated by Sapphos, bluestockings and the earnest families of note who allow their girls here as a sort of finishing school. You know, to meet the right type. The influx of grammar school boys will put paid to that. But there are some dreamy girls from the grammar schools, clever and wanting to learn. Just *my* type, some of them anyway, even though there are some appalling accents. I actively seek to tutor those while most of my colleagues stick to the chaps."

"Hence the large sofa?"

"It can be useful but on some occasions a straight wooden chair is more appropriate. One young beauty insists on calling me *Caroo* as opposed to *Carey*. I've told her more than once and I'm sure it's deliberate. Her father, a naval gunner, went down on the *Barham;* mother never remarried. She lives on private means and the naval pension outside Plymouth."

"Sounds very Freudian," commented Danny airily. "Makes you a kind of substitute father figure."

"Freud," replied Bernard, almost choking. "That charlatan! Still, idiots can be useful, if a little long winded."

Danny listened to what Bernard had to say on the operation, querying little and admiring the economical way it was delivered. He was a natural teacher, oozing confidence and certainty. The importance and need for a clean result was heavily stressed.

He left Bernard to his assumed *loco parentis* duties and his weekday diet of college dinners consisting of brown soup, stringy meat, vegetables boiled tasteless and desserts amounting to hidden things under thick yellow custard. He was clear in warning Danny to avoid college food and, anyway, Suzanne would pick him up from the hotel at 7pm and take him to dinner. The culinary ills of college did provide a topic of conversation at table in a pleasant country hotel that evening. It served to pass some of the time.

They both chose fillet of cod with scallops and potatoes and drank a bottle of indifferent wine — described on the card as French but Danny dismissed the description as a printer's error, saying it had been found in a trench. The taxi had arrived with Suzanne sitting languidly in the back just before seven. The driver was sent in and Danny was already suited and booted in the lounge, nursing a whisky and dry ginger. Seeing the car pull up, he met he driver in the hallway. They reached the rural restaurant in 20 minutes, Suzanne promising on her part not to mention work, provided Danny refrained from questioning her about the project in hand.

This had led Danny to enquire about her family and she readily revealed that she had a 14-year-old daughter, away at boarding school. Danny remarked on Bernard never having mentioned her. A knowing smile came over Suzanne's face.

"He isn't her father. We married in 1940, almost a year after Evelyn's birth."

"Do you mind if I ask…"

"Not at all. I married her father in 1938. He was the tall dark army regular in the Tank Corps. He was killed in France in May…"

"1940," Danny joined in, thinking of the heavy, under-armed machines used by the British forces early in the conflict. Not that the later machines were much better. Some of them had been constructed in the railway workshops in Wych Elm, but never reached France. The experience of the tank engagement at Arras put paid to that. Wych Elm's machines were held in reserve for the invasion that never came. Had they been needed they may have made useful road blocks.

"How long had you known him?"

"We knew each other as children," replied Suzanne. "So I suppose I knew him in a family sort of way, but *really* know him? How far do we really know anyone?"

Danny was listening and thought he detected a lack of regret in her tone but wondered more when she said that Evelyn had never seen him except in photographs. She added that Bernard and Evelyn got on well most of the time.

"After all, he is, to all intents and purposes, her father."

She sipped some of the wine.

"You are close to your mother," said Suzanne. "Have you never considered marriage?"

"Not really," Danny replied, more quickly and honestly than he had intended. There was something so compellingly ladylike about his companion that he felt his emotional wall, carefully tended and maintained, was having a chisel knocked into it at a vulnerable spot.

"Don't worry," smiled Suzanne, sipping from her wine glass. "I know you aren't one for the boys."

"Bernard calls them…"

"Chaps," laughed Suzanne. "He also maintains chaps are never arrested, except in London and, only then, if they are terribly indiscreet. In Oxford, they are obsessed by other things like college politics, promotion and that sort of thing."

"Bernard is not interested in politics or promotion?"

"He sees himself above it." Suzanne smiled again.

She drew on a cigarette and looked at Danny through the plume of smoke.

"Are you a sincere Catholic?" she asked suddenly. "Do you believe in God, confession and the rest?"

This was not an uncommon angle of conversation at the time; usually the questioning was sincere, unlike the present, when it is used as a conduit as to how gullible or stupid a person you are likely to be. The experience of war left people wanting to know things and there was a keen interest in the future.

"I believe in the sense that a godless world would be even more dangerous and pretentious than it is," Danny responded. "Without God I would be far worse than I am, with far more to confess."

"You have us walking a knife edge," said Suzanne. "A knife edge between this, the world and…"

"An abyss."

"What do you confess?" Suzanne smiled, regaining the initiative.

"A liking for money," said Danny. He thought for a moment as Suzanne fixed him with a long stare. "A penchant for ladies and a liking for girls."

"To make you think less of the abyss?" Suzanne bounced back the tennis ball of conversation with the dexterity of a true champion.

"Spirits do just as well," replied Danny. "Whisky and decent brandy, that is, but maybe the Holy One lends a hand. I perhaps haven't noticed."

She swung the conversation around to music and mentioned Evelyn's likes and dislikes in that area. Danny spoke of the vogue in Hollywood for musical films, describing them as entertainments to help us to forget. She had seen *Oklahoma* and *South Pacific* on the London stage, preferring the latter. Danny had seen the first in Manchester and the latter not at all, although he did know the songs. He had used a recording of

Wonderful Guy in *Danny's Place* for a few weeks, encouraging the girls to sing and allowing the boys to feel wanted. It had served a purpose.

The taxi ride to the hotel found Danny entertaining her with some of his wittier jokes and he briefly adopted his stage persona to enhance the performance. All the time he wondered what approach to make outside the hotel, realising that a suggestion of tea in his room left no space for ambiguity and, while he would have done anything with Suzanne, on that night at least, he felt a sense of dread based on his own need for security rather than loyalty to anyone else.

Suzanne made it easy, stepping from the taxi and embracing Danny on the street. She gently kissed his ear while whispering she did not mind being the subject of his next confession. Bernard would be in the house on her return.

"He probably mentioned his weekly afternoon with the gauche female students allocated for his care and attention. He tells me everything and I listen."

Before Danny could reply she kissed him softly on the mouth, wishing him a safe journey home and to take care in his assignment. The taxi took her away into the night and Danny retired to his cool provincial bed, unsure whether to feel disappointment or relief.

An early breakfast of fatty bacon, toast and tea saw him away in the Ford Pilot, heading out through Banbury and on to Warwick to make a prearranged call to the widowed mother of another army colleague who survived the war but, as a regular, found himself in Korea the previous year. He had died in a military road accident, the sort of event that could have happened almost anywhere to anyone. He gave his best wishes to his friend's prematurely-aged mother, leaving her on a note of bemused anger at the sheer arbitrariness of it all – quoting John Donne about the bell tolling for thee.

Wych Elm was encased in a shroud of rain. Soft globules of water dripped from his hair as he walked up to his mother's door. She wanted to know all about Oxford as she prepared an omelette for him and, as he ate it, he told her. The colleges, the spires, the clean streets, the clean air – he related all of this and then described Bernard as his friend, portraying his college rooms, his lifestyle and his love of the ladies. He then described his wife and their dinner together. Catherine listened with a childlike intensity until the end.

"Your friend Bernard loves the ladies, you say," she paused before continuing, "Not the ladies, Daniel. He prefers the naughty girls."

Danny laughed, agreed, and thought to himself just how alike in that respect he and Bernard really were.

Chapter Seven

Danny had rarely queried the arrangements made by the service and indeed, on this operation, all seemed to be in order as far as Avignon. Travelling by rail through France, the channel crossing and the overnight stay in Paris went well. He was using the same identity as he had utilised in the war, though with better clothes and, at first, access to superior accommodation. Using a previous name or back-story was not normally recommended but he accepted the reassurances he had been given by the agent on the Calais ferry and now, in the south of France, he was enjoying some good food and, as far as he dared admit it, an element of relaxation. He could understand why the Popes had left Rome to live in Avignon. The red wine was the best he had tasted, the cuisine decidedly Mediterranean. The contrast with England was stark.

However, his contact was a day late and when he did finally arrive, his general brusqueness and air of agitation made Danny alert in a way he had rarely experienced since his time in occupied Paris. Gianfranco said little, standing red-haired with inflamed skin and light grey eyes that gave nothing away. He said next to nothing as they drove a circuitous route in a new Fiat saloon as far as Nice and insomuch Nice had any low rent property, they were in it and shared a room overnight – in sleeping bags – setting off early the next morning with nothing but a cup of coffee. Eventually they arrived in Genoa and at a hotel rendezvous with embassy staff from Rome.

"Don't mind Gianfranco," said the embassy man, Hoskins, airily. "He is very useful in slip-in and slip-out duties."

Danny and Hoskins stayed the night and over breakfast were joined by a wiry character called John Montroni, who was to be Danny's co-eliminator on this little enterprise. He was barely five foot three with jet black hair and, in the right clothes, he would have passed for a bookmaker at a northern racecourse. There was, however, a distinct Roman nose and a command of local Italian which Danny could never hope to match. He did confide in Danny that his mother and father had an ice-cream business in Sheffield and at the outbreak of the war, his father had been interned in the Isle of Man as a potential enemy and supporter of the Duce. He did, in fact, noted Montroni with heavy irony, support Sheffield Wednesday. There was another English city, like Coventry, whose centre was an open space due to the attentions of the Luftwaffe. Rebuilding had scarcely begun, with everything at drawing or planning stage. But the Montroni café had survived. Montroni's military speciality was surveillance and *sweeping up* after operations. He said they were still sweeping up in Sheffield.

They drove down to the coast by Rome, sleeping in a low-level khaki field tent on the wooded outskirts of two hunting and shooting estates nearby. It was basically scrubland and any beauty it possessed came directly from nature. Their interest was in the estate owned by an Italian Count who, despite his attempts to hide it, had a Sicilian background. There was a substantial criminal record against him during the war and he now made a living selling narcotic drugs through a network of street girls in Rome and controlling a chain of cafés in the suburbs. These outlets dealt in almost anything that carried a premium.

"The local police, the *Polazia di Stato* and the *Carabinieri* are in his pocket and local politicians attend his summer musical parties, held al fresco, where men hunt girls in the woods who are carried back like trophies for more party games."

"It won't be Monopoly or Snakes and Ladders," Danny replied.

"Any games played involve a price or a favour," continued Montroni and he elaborated on the varied schemes he had been involved in. "But he always keeps a barrier of vulnerable staff between himself and the action. Some of his people have been successfully prosecuted but no one has touched him since the time of the fascist government. He sponsors classical concerts in Rome and provides a few musical scholarships. Gratitude regularly comes his way."

Danny listened carefully to the background Montroni was providing and then began wondering how long they would have to "live in a hole and bury their shit" as he expressed it on the third day of this frustrating exercise. Surveillance with field binoculars had given little information of use and the target had been seen, very briefly, just once. Danny was no nearer to deciding whether a close call with the Welrod was preferable to a long shot with the carbine, and his uneasiness was getting more manifest by the hour. The following evening, 9th April, proved decisive. The Count had left in his car, driving alone, and Henri Berlot emerged onto the lounge balcony. There was a slope of land running down to the shoreline. Danny had used the bushes and dimming light to hide low alongside the marble balustrade. He fired the silenced weapon from a distance of less than a foot into Berlot's lumber region and as the man fell his body began twitching on the tiles. Danny then went through the awkward reloading process and fired again into his head.

A female voice filled the still air. A call of "Henri" came from behind where Danny was standing, from the direction of the shoreline. The voice carried as the slightest of breezes brushed by. An attractive girl was approaching with a paper parcel in hand. She had obviously seen a glancing view of Henri between the trees, walking some one hundred or so yards away. She walked on, oblivious to what had happened and continuing to call Berlot's name. Danny decided he must take her out and swung himself back over the balustrade in time to see Montroni leap from the bushes and grab her from behind. He covered her mouth and dragged her back toward the sea water. She was a slight thing, no match for Montroni's deft handling of her body. He held her head, nose down, under the surf and in moments she was drowned. There was barely a struggle and she lay lifeless in his arms.

Danny ran down and removed her shoes, skirt, suspender belt and stockings with an efficiency Montroni admired. He returned with them, launching them over the balcony through the glass doors into the confines of the house. Meanwhile, Montroni dragged the body into the slow current and left it in the water. The two of them used old branches to sweep the evidence of their footprints from the vicinity of the house and then eased their way back to their little hide, clearing all the elements of their presence, Montroni changing his wet trousers. He carried them over his arm as they walked down nonchalantly to the fishing village of Torvaicanica. They had parked the car there four days before and were able to drive uninterrupted as far as Pisa. There they made contact through the embassy, using a café callbox and were directed to a small hotel where they cleaned up, shaved and found a complete set of clothes waiting. Their old clothing was placed in a waiting suitcase and collected by a man in a three-wheeled van just thirty minutes later.

Only then, driving overnight to Milan, did Danny express some misgivings about the whole operation and its organisation. Montroni said that a moving target was more difficult than a static one and the location was the one place Henri Berlot could be pinpointed for any length of time. After all, he maintained they had succeeded and the girl's presence was just bad luck. His worry had been any necessity to eliminate the Count. A young girl was, at a pinch, disposable while Counts, by their nature and standing, were not.

Her body was actually found at Torvaicanica on the morning of 11th, but no mention was made of anything or anyone else. The police concentrated on the girl Wilma who, on examination, died a virgin and whose family simply wanted to avoid the taint of suicide. She had been engaged to a local boy in her Roman suburb and had, on the face of it, everything to live for. She was eventually buried with the full services of the church and her reason for being in Torvaicanica was given as her need to bathe her new shoes in sea water, so as to ease them. She had travelled there by bus. No shoes were ever found, nor were her missing clothes.

Danny travelled by train from Milan, arriving in Berne to be met by the ubiquitous Hoskins from the Rome embassy. Over dinner he congratulated Danny on his work and explained that the onward rail journey was cancelled. He was flown the following morning from Berne directly to London in an unmarked private aeroplane. The debriefing was handled efficiently by a character called Bright whom Danny had never met before – a fair-haired ex-army type, efficient to the point of rudeness. He seemed anxious to get Danny away from the capital as soon as possible and thus he found himself on a regular army transport flight into Manchester – bumpy, uncomfortable, chilly and back in Wych Elm before 11pm. Duty done, his mother made him a light supper and lemon tea, asking nothing other than the state of the weather in Europe this year.

Danny lay on his bed, recalling the blank week that followed nearly sixty years ago. The detail was vivid in his mind. Huge numbers in the club and a consignment of records from America brought in through Liverpool. Over nine days elapsed before a letter arrived arranging a meeting in the *Legs of Man* pub in Wigan. It took less than half an hour over two large brandies and Bright, clearly uncomfortable at the bottom end of the bar surrounded by market traders, eventually handed Danny an envelope.

"For your loyal services rendered."

"Are we looking after the girl's family?"

"That's the Italians' business, not ours. What happens next is entirely their concern."

It was made clear to Danny that a job of this kind was unlikely to arise again in the near future and, in any event, the department was undergoing a reorganisation. If he was affected by the new arrangements he would be told in good time. Bright seemed glad to leave and Danny watched him fairly bounce down Wallgate toward the station. Not for the first time Danny smiled at the contrast at what he had done and its farcical completion in a Wigan pub.

Danny opened the envelope in the car. A cheque for £1,200 was folded inside. Someone had wanted Berlot very dead indeed. He was being told to keep quiet, something that in the past would have gone without saying. This was obviously special. The following year saw Danny's type of work abandoned by the service, although a retainer was paid monthly for the next 20 years. *Was this insurance or hush money?* Danny did not care. Everything now went into his own business. His private, personal war continued, but in other fields. The methods and moods remained pretty much the same.

Andrea woke Danny from his late afternoon slumber, aggressively poking him in the midriff and sounding impatient as she spoke.

"The priest is here to see you."

Danny roused himself, pushing his hand through his hair. He slipped from the bed and settled into his armchair.

"Send him in," he replied, "and close the door."

The priest strode in, ignoring the form of Andrea as she brushed past him and closed the door.

"Ah, *c'est le cure n'est ce pas.*"

"Hello Dan," replied the priest, the Reverend John Stannard – he never called him Danny, it was either Daniel or Dan. He had a smiley countenance which showed humour and also an element of intensity. Danny liked him for the distance he kept both from men and women. This was a priest who did not wish to be everyone's friend and did not engage in a faux jollity. Life was far too serious for that kind of thing.

"I must have a word, Dan," he went on. "The curia office, up at the diocese, have been approached by the press about your time helping out at the two St Jude's, you know, the girls' and boys' homes."

"I see," replied Danny gravely.

"And you'll be aware that all this went on in Father Mallon's time," the priest continued, "and most of the records have been misplaced or destroyed, except for the registers and…"

Danny gave him the gist of his conversation with Jan Dale and Stannard immediately became reflective, saying that the two of them were very much in a similar situation. At one time, everyone seemed to be obsessed by sex on their own behalf. Now everyone wanted to stand in judgement on everyone else, often from the most ridiculous moral point of view, based on nothing in particular – usually what was fashionable or unfashionable, one week to the next.

"The modern world is suspicious of anyone conspicuously single and when you're a celibate, like me, the suspicion doubles. A married parishioner, with a husband working in Saudi Arabia, invited me to dinner in her home last month. Oysters, I ask you? She was as unambiguous as a pillar box."

"Did you make your excuses and leave?" Danny smiled.

"Not immediately, the oysters were fine and the bottle of Pinot Grigio, from a vineyard near Trentino, was the real thing. None of the supermarket rubbish."

"So you left after the dessert?"

"Swiftly," Stannard replied, with a knowing grin.

"I must ask you, Dan," his tone changing. "Is there anything to find? Anything I need to know?"

Danny quickly explained how much money he had given to both institutions and how the girls' team had won the northern cycling championship of 1956. The boys won their competition in 1958 and 1959, the girls coming second in 1957 and 1958, before winning again in 1959. Stannard donned his steel-rimmed spectacles and began writing in a small notebook. Danny continued, describing how he and one of the younger nuns, Sister Monica, had devised a reward system for the girls which involved a trip to *Danny's Place* in his car, six at a time, squashed into the two bench seats. A similar system was developed for the boys a year or so later. The girls had Friday evening, once each month and the boys had Wednesday.

"Many of the girls had lost both mother and father, all of them came from poor backgrounds and a trip like that was a light in their lives," Danny said firmly. "Some of them begged a cigarette or two off me and I danced around with some of them, sometimes the odd kiss of gratitude came my way. There was nothing beyond that."

"Do you recall a young lady called Myra Kearns?"

"Yes," Danny replied. "She was rewarded one week, with five others, and absconded the next. That would be in 1958 or 59. She met a bit of a bounder called Mervyn Griggs at the club, an apprentice boilermaker. Between them they devised a plan for her to escape and meet at the club one Thursday night. The local police gave me the nod on the lunchtime and when young Mervyn arrived with his gang of poxy little boys Cliff Hindle persuaded him to get lost. The silly bugger seriously believed he could move her in at home, with his mother and five siblings in a two-bed terrace."

"Persuaded?"

"Mervyn fancied himself as a latter-day teddy boy, all mouth and bravado. He swung a punch at Cliff and became the proud owner of a busted nose, mainly because Cliff rather assisted his fall onto the pavement. The local constabulary told him not to be so soft when he and his ghastly mother went to the police station to complain the next day. She frog marched him out of the building when the desk sergeant started to ask about missing girls from St Jude's. She was bawling and yelling at him to keep away from those dirty little cows."

"And what of Myra?"

"I had the whole staff on the lookout and she was picked up, paying her shilling to come in the door."

"Then what? How was she handled?"

"I let the police know and offered to drive her back once my introduction song was over. They happily agreed and Sister Monica was waiting for us on our arrival."

Danny went on to say that while corporal punishment was not a normal feature of life at the girls' St Jude's, at the boys' place it was a daily routine; Sister Monica agreed to forestall the severe caning which would have happened to any girl absconding from the site. She said that the incident was down to her not having a father figure in her life and no father would have allowed his 14-year-old daughter to date a boy like Mervyn, let alone run off with him. She told Myra that my avoiding any further police involvement and preventing any scandal had been a case of me doing a paternal duty for her – and she should be grateful. Myra had been a picture of misery all the way back in the car but Danny did detect a small element of relief in her face. However, Sister Monica continued with a ''back me' look at Danny and told her Mr Hird would now finish his duty and give her the good spanking she really deserved.

"And did you?" asked Stannard.

"How could I refuse?" Danny smiled. "She did deserve it, although these days it would be seen as a form of sexual assault."

"Sister Monica was there all the time?"

"Yes, telling her she would still have to confess the sin."

Danny was not embarrassed by the recollection and added that six strokes from the Mother Superior would have been far worse than five minutes over his knee with Sister Monica in the parlour.

"Did you see her again after that?"

"Yes, a year or so after. She appeared in the club on a couple of Saturdays. I seem to recall someone telling me she married young and moved away."

Stannard put his pen and notebook down on his lap. He then recounted the information he had been given, adding that Danny's description of events matched with Sister Monica's recollection. She was living in a home in York, aged eighty-two and as bright as a pin. Her religious order had been absorbed into a similar nursing order some 20 years ago and she was effectively in the care of her own. She had studied Jungian theory and closely followed the work of a Dominican friar, Victor White, corresponding on such matters for years. She was regarded as a pioneer within the field of religion and psychology.

"God, where are we now? Lord help us, Myra would be, let me see, 14 in 1958," said Danny, thinking aloud. "God, she'll be sixty-six this year."

"Yes, and she is part of a group action of seven females trying to sue the religious order for various types of abuse they allege was inflicted on them at the home."

Danny wondered if the case had any chance of success after this length of time and, as he pointed out, he might be alive for now and so was Sister Monica, but for how much longer? Father Mallon had been a regular visitor to both the boys' and girls' homes, hearing confessions and saying Mass on a rota; he knew far more of the intimate details of both places than anyone, then or now. Stannard was unaware of how well Danny knew him. He had died the day he fell asleep in an armchair, nursing a large whisky and his fortieth cigarette of the day. The presumption was that the lit end of the cigarette fell onto the armchair and set it alight. The ground floor of the presbytery suffered severe damage. Mallon was identified from dental records and the gold rings he wore on a relatively unscathed hand.

His two successors, appointed in 1965 and 1969, had stayed for just four years each, organising folk groups and other banjo banging arrangements at the services. Danny had often made a point of saying the Second Vatican Council had a lot to answer for. The next lasted less than two years, leaving the priesthood to marry a widow of means from his previous parish. Finally, Stannard's immediate predecessor lasted until 2000 before retiring to the family farm near Limerick.

Danny told Stannard he would inform his lawyers of developments and the diocesan legal team could then contact his people and work together. It wasn't the first time this sort of thing had arisen but the name of Jan Dale circulating around such issues was sufficient to make everyone a little wary. Stannard seemed satisfied with the proceedings and, before leaving, gave Danny a blessing.

Andrea came in almost immediately and took his order for dinner. She kept looking at him in an inquisitive way and eventually asked what the priest had said when he had his hand on his forehead. Danny surmised she had been listening at the door for at least some of the time, a trait he had noticed in her before.

"He looked like he was christening you or something," she said.

Danny explained the nature of a blessing and Andrea said she had seen him do the same to Mary Hobson, but thought it was just for women. She then added that it didn't seem to do much for Mary.

"You shouldn't be spying," said Danny. "You'll get a poke in the eye."

"I think you're past poking anything now, Danny."

He accused her of brazen cheek but had to reflect that, cheek or not, she was right after all. He could equally do without this nonsense at his time of life. In the past, he had refrained from paying off trouble and was not going to start now. Once Andrea had left him alone he used his landline to speak to the office manager at his solicitor's in Manchester. He gave her the basic details. He was told to expect a call first thing and, duly, it came at breakfast the following day.

Danny sat in his room telling Chris Babbage what had happened to put a private detective agency onto Jan

Dale's past and to speak to the diocesan solicitors, *Brannighan & Morwick*, at the Preston office. Allen Morwick himself was supervising progress there. Sandra left Danny alone during the call, but he called her in part-way to massage his right foot which had gone to sleep on him.

"Are you upset?" she asked, as he replaced the receiver. "Not that I'm prying. It's just that Andrea was on the phone last night…"

"Was she indeed? Saying what?"

Sandra blushed a little, enhanced by the colour of her light blue overall, and she continued to massage his foot while kneeling by him on the pile carpet. Danny asked if she had mentioned the blessing Father Stannard had given him and Sandra said she had.

"And what else did she mention?" Danny was now smiling at her discomfort and reassured her, stroking her hair and making a hand gesture to say his foot was fine. She remained kneeling with her head away from him. He stroked her again.

"She thinks you are some kind of pervert, saying you were doing things to young girls in the past - something about a school or a home?"

Danny sighed and quickly gave her the bare bones of the real story. Sandra sat on the bed, as he finished his story in the chair and she reached for his hand. She said she would put her straight but Danny said not to bother – he would tackle her this evening.

"If she eavesdrops again, I'll be informing management," he said firmly. "She's a real Keyhole Kate."

"She's a hard worker," replied Sandra. "But everything is for herself. She doesn't really care about anyone. If she loses her looks, she'll be very lonely indeed."

"She could hide behind a glass partition," replied Danny drily. "Or, as I recall reading somewhere once, a fellow who could hide behind a spiral staircase."

"Well, I don't think you did anything wrong," Sandra went on. "My Dad walloped me once for giving my mother some lip. He was right to do it."

Danny simply said times were different then and people reacted very differently to lots of things. It wasn't better then, just different.

"My mum said she remembers you as a bottom patter at the club," Sandra was now laughing softly.

"That's true," said Danny. "After all, it's woman's finest feature."

"Till it slides down your legs," she smiled.

"Not a problem for you," Danny reassured her and gripped her hand. "You are class, something Andrea neither knows nor appreciates. You have class and depth."

Sandra appreciated the compliment.

"You've lived a lot, Danny. Is there anything you really regret?"

"Having done, or not done?"

"Yes – is there anything at all? I know it's a funny thing to say, but how much of what we do really matters?"

"Not a lot," said Danny. "Regret can lead you astray so easily and you have to keep in mind at all times that the past is past – it has happened and while we can sometimes make amends, it doesn't fundamentally alter a thing. I should regret smoking, but I enjoyed it for years. I should regret having missed a couple of good groups in the 60s, but catching them, would I have missed others I did see? I miss my mother, but no one can live for ever, even if Mary Hobson thinks you can. No, and I don't regret spanking runaway Myra's bottom. Same time, same place, I'd do it again."

"I do agree," replied Sandra. "Yet everyone I meet, except you, seems to be dwelling on something and can't move on. Andrea had a boyfriend who works as an actor, mostly adverts – he's doing the cinema ad for Northern Bank just now – and even though she's lived with her boyfriend for three years she told me last week she'd ditch him tomorrow if Clive, the actor, would have her back. And I wouldn't mind, but she ditched him!"

Sandra went off to finish her morning duties. Danny lay back in his chair, facing the window, watching birds darting around the trees. Regrets? Wilma, possibly, but perhaps it was more a case of regretting the necessity in a job less than well done. Perhaps there were two candidates, but certainly one. Danny drifted off and scenes played themselves in his mind as he floated back to 1961 and a disaster that crowned a series of entanglements which were to fall, in timely fashion, like dominoes in a line.

Chapter Eight

Regret rarely faces you, tweaking your nose or clipping your ear. It lurks in the undergrowth or hides in the weed bed for months or even years at a time and emerges to create gaps beneath your feet and voids lacking any meaning in what had been a previously familiar environment. Danny experienced a cacophony of daydreams which seemed to last for hours, but the nature of light sleep in the void of reality meant all of it lasted less than three minutes at a time. He saw Therese walking by the cathedral in Amiens, Wilma smiling as she walked toward the Italian lodge and the scorched remains of an old textile mill, bricks the colour of a well-used teapot with black streaks soaring upward, glassless window gaps, discarded furniture and stacks of blackened burnt timber lying on the ground. This was the remains of the rival club, opened in Bolton, to thwart Danny doing the same; it formed the penultimate act in a three-year rivalry that played like a card game where the stakes grew in proportion to the egos involved.

Quite early on, the police acting as go-betweens, Danny had met James L Connah who had started with two snooker halls in Wigan before the war and during it, secured the tenancy of two pubs for each of his sons, later moving into the social club business in and around Wigan. He had his eyes on the coast, Southport possibly, to expand and develop his line in illegal gambling – cards, football and horses. In short, he was into anything that brought in a lot of cash and gave ongoing enjoyment to the customer. The police turned the proverbial blind eye to the Connah activities. The Connahs informed on others when it suited them; they kept order and did not overstep the mark, a flexible line of parameters that had moved back and forth over the years but never very far in either direction.

Old man Connah had watched Danny's progress in Wych Elm with a dispassionate interest and made it clear to the family that there was nothing to be gained by moving in. However, he did recognise a good business and had no wish for Danny to extend his style of enterprise into Wigan. A meeting was arranged, in the *Legs of Man*, neutral ground, to have "a little chat."

The Connahs often arrived at meetings en-masse, each driving a black Triumph Renown, with John, the elder son, driving his father up front and Albert driving behind, accompanied by two employees, Eli and Elijah Ainscough, twins who had been reputable amateur boxers when young and now acted as professional enforcers. When not enforcing, they operated as travelling bookmakers in the Connah business. James was rotund and balding with a restrained dignified presence. John was dark-haired, like his father, but taller and feline in appearance. Albert was his father's double, big in every way with black brylcreemed hair. The Ainscough's were red haired and sprightly with pale blue emotionless eyes. All of them wore black herringbone suits, ordered from the same tailor, with the latest style of tie, white shirts and mother-of-pearl cufflinks. Danny came to know all of them as acquaintances and Clifford Hindle knew both Albert and the Ainscough's to speak to from mutual yelling and encouragement on the terraces at Wigan Rugby League Club.

The 'little chat' with the old man was a strange sort of success. Danny respected James' approach to the issue of competition and assured him Wigan was not on his expansion list. Both of them had an eye on Bolton and maybe Manchester but there was no intention on either part "to tread on one another's toes." Connah already knew of Danny's police contacts and there seemed to be a mutual view of the world, how it should be and how it should be organised. Both of them believed in keeping the police onside.

"Watch out for the Holcombe's, young Danny," said Connah. "A dirty little group living in Bolton now - used to be in Salford, into women and pubs. They give the protection business, any business, a bad name."

Danny knew of the Holcombe family, two cousins and an elderly uncle who had served time for burglary and assault. The cousins, both called Edward and distinguished as Ed and Ted, were rumoured to have murdered a business rival a couple of years before and were ruthless with any opposition, within and without their operation. The Holcombe's did not cooperate with the police and for some years had been involved in a running war with them in and around Bolton. Uncle Holcombe, Fred, was the very image of a kindly, grey old man. His appearance was completely at odds with his nature. Old man Connah was disparaging in his summary of "those nasty buggers."

"All this time wasted, having to put them in order, when they're trying to run knocking shops in my town."

"Are they doing drugs, reefers and worse?" asked Danny.

"They'd be into baby killing if there were money in it," replied Connah.

Danny made clear his agreement on this point. The two of them began to extend their meeting and drank some pints of bitter accompanied by a meat pie. They found themselves discussing people in the area who seemed to have done very well out of the war, without actually fighting. A respect grew between them and over the next few years, they met very occasionally to discuss mutual concerns. By 1958 James was slowly passing control of the business to John and Albert, near contemporaries of Danny. That summer, James was on holiday touring Ireland with Maureen, his wife of forty years, when Ted Holcombe rolled into the original Connah social club in Wigan strongly suggesting a sale of the business at a reasonable price. The police later suspected that the Holcombe's wanted to move out of the prostitution business and take over some more legitimate concerns. Girls no longer made serious money. Ted Holcombe kept mentioning the fire risks in a club like this one. Albert and his doorman threw Holcombe out.

In the same week, Ed Holcombe arrived with two women at *Danny's Place* and pulled Cliff Hindle to one side, saying he provided a good fire insurance service for a place like this. Cliff quietly advised him to leave, which Ted did, but not before warning him to buy an asbestos suit. The older Holcombe was clearly encouraging his nephews to clear up the opposition as quickly and, if necessary, as ruthlessly as they could. Police intelligence sources confirmed that Fred Holcombe had judged the elder Connah as "past it," saying "his sprogs were soft" while Danny Hird was seen as a "soft Nancy-boy" who'd been lucky but was "right out of his depth."

The following Saturday night saw a van drive by the Wigan club, back doors opening and a Molotov cocktail launched into the entrance. There was little damage and the van appeared to drive away. But half an hour later it was in the car park with Ted Holcombe directing operations. Six men dressed in boiler suits burst through the rear entrance, kicking over tables and smashing up the bar. Albert Connah had one of them in a half-nelson and was about to launch him into the wall when two others hauled him off, dragging him outside and into the van.

His body was found in sacking by the roadside near Aspen Hill the following morning. The police enquiry met a wall of silence, though the Holcombe's openly boasted of their exploit for months afterwards. Later in the same week *Danny's Place* suffered some fire damage at the back. When Cliff Hindle went out to investigate the noise he was jumped on by three men who proceeded to knock seven bells out of him using a hammer. He protected his head and flattened one of them with a kick to the groin. Danny arrived from the front with his two doormen, sending one of Cliff's assailants flying over the back wall. He and others escaped and Cliff was left unconscious. Danny dealt with the fire with water buckets and an extinguisher.

Danny then went into full military mode, getting all the details of the Holcombe family locations from his police contacts. The carbine and *Welrod* were brought from their hiding places, tested and oiled. Cliff Hindle was in hospital for 10 days, recovering from concussion and five broken ribs. Danny identified where the uncle, Fred, now in his 70s, was living – a detached house outside Bolton in its own somewhat limited grounds. He lived there with his third wife who managed the 'women' side of the business for him. He had no regular security and Danny found it easy, after a couple of nights' surveillance, to enter in the darkness of a late evening, over a wooden palling and through a glass sliding door, into the dark kitchen area.

Fred Holcombe did not react when Danny walked into his living room. Wearing black trousers and jumper, a black woollen hat and carrying the *Welrod* in gloved hands, he could not have mistaken him for a casual visitor. Danny got the distinct impression Fred was expecting him and momentarily wondered whether he had been drawn into a trap. Fred's face suddenly took on a blank expression. This was an old man who simply reacted. Initiation was now a stranger to him. Danny was automatic in his response.

"I'm Danny Hird. Your little boys have burnt my club, injured a friend and they've killed a friend of a friend of mine," he said quietly. "This is where you pay, sunshine."

Before Fred could reply a bullet entered his forehead. He was sitting on a sofa with an open box of gold jewellery on his lap. His body slipped to one side. The muffled shot brought some movement from upstairs and Mandy, the third Mrs Holcombe, came down the stairs asking Fred whether he was alright. She thought he'd fallen or knocked something over. Totally unsuspecting the real situation, she pushed at the lounge door and began to walk in. Danny's black gloved hand chopped across her throat, felling her instantly. He had not lost his touch. She was stone dead. He was quietly satisfied with his handiwork. It could have been a training exercise.

He walked around the house in a leisurely way, collecting more jewellery, cash (£2,000 in various drawers and tins) and even a heavy box of sovereigns which necessitated careful handling over the garden fence before placing in the boot of the car. When he did eventually count them, there were 850, all from the early years of King George V.

The subsequent police investigation was based, at least in public, on a burglary. Ed and Ted had every good reason to doubt that it was a simple burglary and, like the police, were struck by the sheer efficiency of the operation, thinking either Connah or Danny, or both, had hired professional help. Six months elapsed and the Holcombe's were busily organising a mass revenge attack on the Connah businesses in Wigan. James was tipped off and he contacted Danny. He was amazed to find Danny, Cliff Hindle and three 'specially selected' staff arrive at the car park outside the Holcombe's *Rialto Club* in Salford, the rendezvous for the Connahs' own pre-emptive attack. The Holcombe gang were meeting there prior to their car caravan heading for Wigan. Their reputation depended on something like this and, for them, reputation was everything. Danny had equipped his group with steel knuckle dusters for the occasion, each one having a bauble on one edge and a spike on the other.

A running fight of medieval proportions over two streets and gardens ensued, Cliff Hindle laying out Ted Holcombe personally while John Connah accounted for three on his own. The police arrived conveniently late to pick up the Holcombe dazed and wounded, charging all of them with affray and carrying offensive weapons. Ted Holcombe served six months and emerged from prison to find he was suffering from liver cancer. He was dead within the year.

James Connah followed shortly afterwards, a coronary thrombosis taking him while he was tending his greenhouse plants; John, his remaining son, took over seamlessly, consolidating the whole operation and, when the gambling laws were shortly afterwards amended, creating a first-class betting shop chain which covered the whole of the north and down into Birmingham. Danny expanded his club, started the agency work and planned new ventures locally. The Holcombe's were struggling financially, had lost their air of menace and only the sale of Fred's house kept the operation afloat.

Ed Holcombe had to sell some of his own premises – rented flats and a small drinking club. His organisation was still on its knees but he was utterly determined to bounce back. He took a lease on the second and third floor of an old mill warehouse in Bolton. The first floor was occupied by a kitchen furniture workshop and entry at second floor level was gained on the street side into a foyer which, in reality, was a small landing where a single flight of stairs went up to Holcombe's new *Top Floor* club and down to the kitchen workshop. A door off the foyer served as a cloaks and toilet area. On the other side, the building stood at a full three floors against the cobbled lane close by a small flowing river. The tall lower windows faced the river – the floor level panes of the workshop dusty and blackened – while those above were regularly cleaned and had silk curtains – acquired from a defunct cinema – which were pulled at night and gave a ruby illumination effect into the invariably damp air.

Money had been spent inside the club on modern décor, an attractive bar and an expensive tape machine to play the latest pop music. A sprung dance floor had been added and comfortable tables with Scandinavian style round chairs. At first sight, it appeared the height of sophistication. But the single access up a wooden stair and the lack of any fire escape eventually proved to be a disaster.

Ed Holcombe recruited a manager and sent young people out to other clubs with leaflets advertising his new premises. He made a point of making *Danny's Place* a target and let it be known he was out to break Danny Hird. Tiring of the innuendos Ed was throwing in his direction, Danny went to the *Top Floor* to warn him off. On arrival, he noticed the plush interior, the one-armed bandit installed in the foyer and the availability of wines as well as spirits. Had it belonged to anyone else Danny would have expressed how impressed he was, but Ed was not there on this particular night and the manager had him thrown out by the staff as an act of humiliation. Use of phrases like "we don't want your sort in here" rather added to Danny's discomfort and he decided there and then that Holcombe needed to be taught another lesson.

The following Monday, May 1st, Cliff Hindle drove Danny into Bolton. They parked the Ford Pilot some streets away and walked toward King Street, down the stone steps to the riverside. They then forced an entry into the premises below the *Top Floor*. Inside, Danny found a tin of paint thinners among the chaos of cheap wood cuttings, plastic and drums of paint. Opening the tin he jammed a discarded cloth inside, lit it with his cigarette lighter and threw it on the floor. He and Cliff walked out.

Staff upstairs could smell smoke and the manager made a slow descent of the stairs to investigate. The doorman was already looking further down the stairs and was certain he could see smoke. Bob Bartelli, the manager, went on down and could see puffs of smoke coming from beneath the workshop door. It would not open. It had no lock so he kicked the door in and found a wall of flame which effectively chased him back up the stairwell. He yelled at the doorman to open up and ran upstairs to the club area to warn everyone.

The tape was playing *Hoots Mon* and everyone was moving to the sound of this old hit. The next was the popular and smoochy Elvis' *Wooden Heart*. The strains of the song provided a backdrop to the developing chaos, lasting until the tape melted in the heat.

The fire moved up the stairs from below the wooden steps and cut the upper floor off, enveloping the club in oily smoke. People crowded behind the bar, others smashed windows and jumped toward the river, many crashing down onto the cobbles and dying where they fell. Fire appliances came from all the surrounding area but their ladders were too short to reach the *Top Floor*. Some did get out, a few were eventually rescued but 19 died in a tragedy that made national headlines. It was a secret Cliff and Danny held hereafter, not least because Ed Holcombe would guess who was responsible and the police could not ignore an event like this. The irony of it all lay in the fact that there was an escape route through a loading bay door which opened onto the King Street side of the building. The barman had tried to open it but the new dance floor was an inch higher and the door would only open when lifted off its hinges. It was close to the bar itself and a furniture delivery van had parked directly outside. It would have been an easy jump, just a few feet, and no one need have died.

Danny and Cliff drove back to the site at 1am. The whole area was soaking from fire hoses which had created a flow of water in the streets. A pall of black acrid smoke was at eye level. It took a good half hour to spot Ed Holcombe in the crowd, trying to identify which of his staff were safe and who was missing. Police and firemen were trying to cope in an environment not seen since bombing raids in the war. Police cordons were generally less organised in those days and the need for ambulance access made the scene quite chaotic. Cliff grabbed Holcombe and dragged him, as though rescuing him, toward a shop, one that was genuinely being used by the ambulance service. Danny came from the car and tried to bundle him inside. He struggled and fell with the back of his head on the kerb. He lay there.

"With him gone, humanity will be none the worse off."

Danny said this as the two of them drove off. Cliff said nothing at first. Only the following day, in a tone of regret rather than admonition, he remarked, "You would have been better shooting the bugger, like his uncle. It would have saved a lot o' bother."

Holcombe's death was connected with the enquiry. It was assumed he was trying to avoid responsibility for the death trap of the *Top Floor*. No one had seen the struggle but many remarked on his agitated state; he was concerned more for his business and his staff than for his paying customers. His death was, eventually, listed as accidental. His wife proved to be a waif of a thing and subsequently left the area with her child to live near her mother in Blackpool. Fire regulations changed, inquests were held and no specific cause for the fire was established, even though the open tin of thinners was found. Danny did not regret Ed Holcombe's end, just the messy way it happened. He did feel for the 19 innocents in the club. *That* should not have happened. He consoled himself with the thought that under the new fire rules, *Danny's Place* passed with flying colours. Anyhow, far worse had happened in the war.

Danny had breakfast with his mother on the Tuesday morning – eggs and fresh bread with lemon tea. She asked if he was ill. *Was he working too hard? Did he need a break?* His reassurances were weaker than usual and she insisted on him seeing the doctor. The diagnosis was a form of depressive fatigue and tablets were prescribed. He was told to take care on the dosage. Amphetamine became a companion, on prescription, for quite some time. His mother talked about the fire for weeks afterwards, as did most of the local population exercised by the equipment failure of the fire service. Tall blocks of flats were being built everywhere – what would happen in a fire 10 floors up when three Victorian floors had caused such a problem?

Within three months everyone was discussing the Berlin Wall and the events surrounding the fire and the ensuing *Top Floor* disaster passed into history. Danny was able to buy the *Rialto* club in Salford through agents in 1964 (using some of Fred Holcombe's own money) at a knock-down price. It was demolished and replaced as *La Dolce Vita*, opening in January 1965 as a top–of-the-range nightclub, which thrived for 15 years under various managers but always under Danny's direction. It was sold in 1980 to a national chain of entertainment clubs at a huge profit and as a going concern. It was demolished three years back in 2007 to make way for a new link road.

The office and flat at *Danny's Place* were totally refurbished and Danny took on more permanent staff, installing a sprung floor in the main dance area and Mediterranean-style furnishings. Prices went up but so had local wages. The quarry plodded along until the proposed new motorway, linking Manchester and the M6 north, was confirmed. The road opened in 1969 but Danny had received an offer he could not refuse three years earlier from the national company which eventually built the road. He and his mother were now, technically, in the millionaire category. The quarry was totally exhausted, landscaped in turf and small trees. Its existence today is only confirmed by old photographs.

He sold *Danny's Place* in the same year. Cliff was gone, managing hordes of restless youth had lost its appeal and Danny had his own television show, *Hird's Hits*, broadcast on Friday evenings at 7pm = 30 minutes of live performances and dance recordings of the popular music of the time. He grew his hair long, dyed it steel grey or sometimes white. He affected a cool persona who knew what *should* be a hit and what was just popular. Magazines listed him as the most influential disc jockey of the era. He gave interviews, hosted parties and judged talent shows. His television programme ceased its Manchester production in 1977 and from then on, it was broadcast from London.

For many, the mid-60s and 70s were a blur. For Danny, it was rather a bore, too easy, no real challenge and he felt the need to constantly perform. He rented a house in Chelsea and was lounging around one weekday afternoon when the doorbell rang. He was living entirely alone and was a little wary, especially of female fans 'just passing' and invading his privacy. In true Wych Elm style he flicked the front curtain and was amazed to see, 20 odd years on, Suzanne Carew at the doorstep. Well into her 60s, she was still the essence of elegance which had so entranced him in Oxford. He answered the door to a long remembered and becoming smile.

"Hello, Danny. Do you remember me?"

Every ridiculous cliché went through his head. *How could I forget,* and many others, the types of phrase people mimic from novels or films.

"Come in, Suzanne. What can I get for you?"

That was at least a nice variation on the theme. As he ushered her into his lounge, far less tasteful or homely than he had remembered hers being in Oxford, he had sudden and irreversible thoughts. *What does she want? Am I back in demand? Or, am I in trouble?* He dismissed the last one in short order, the second was pretty unlikely at his age. *So, what does she want?* Danny remembered the encounter as though it were yesterday and rather wished it had been. Today was a regular trial.

Suzanne had an uncanny ability to get Danny talking. He would have much preferred to listen to her. She still had a most viewable body, petite, symmetric and utterly feminine. Her voice was much the same, possibly a tone lower and her hand gestures, as she asked questions, remained as he remembered them. For two hours they sat drinking Earl Grey tea with lemon, Danny recounting a version of the last 20 years while she made encouraging comments framed around his mother and his status as a celebrity within what she called "the bubblegum world of popular culture." This was not a slur, just a simple observation and, from Danny's standpoint, fairly accurate.

"It wouldn't be so bad if it were just bubblegum," stated Danny with more than a hint of disapproval. "I am well aware we're in the business of hope and fantasy but it's the illusions we create that bother me. There's a lack of experience out there, people are more cosseted than they used to be and it's not a matter of enjoyment now. They need to actually believe this stuff."

"You mean girls obsessed by unattainable men? A lot of the pin-ups are into other men – or boys."

"Boys? Girls? Both at once, plus wacky ciggies. And," Danny wasn't laughing, "I've been to some parties where there was more heroin than in an average hospital dispensary. Then there are our so called elected representatives. If anything, they're worse. An MP, not 20 miles from Wych Elm, has been farming disturbed boys for years. Some of those bastards couldn't pass an asylum without popping in for a quickie."

He calmed himself.

"Sorry, Suzanne," he said, this time with half a smile. "I'm ranting."

"How do you keep yourself sane?"

"I spend as much time as I can at home, listen to good music and read a lot. I even spend time in the garden."

This was true. He had missed the convenience of Manchester for film and television appointments. He needed a London base but resented the ever-increasing cost. He did keep an eye on one or two people but did not mention it to Suzanne.

"So, your great partying image here in London is just that." Suzanne smiled. "Just an image, I imagine."

"Ok," said Danny, "why are you here? And before you answer, tell me, how is Madge Wells these days? And for that matter, how are the others? Bad luck Bright copping it in Africa – awful luck."

Suzanne acknowledged his commiseration with a nod and a shake of her head.

"Madge takes charge of one of the all-female colleges in Oxford in September. She'll be good at it and it'll be good for her. She never got over the Philby thing."

"Neither did I," replied Danny. "I nearly got pneumonia hanging round the Shields ferry. Who did come up with the ridiculous notion that the two fugitives would head north rather than south. The Soviets left the north to their trade union officers. They would never have trusted them with an escape plan."

"Madge had marked a few of them down years before as odd, something not right. You know the feeling? It certainly wasn't wisdom after the event, it was actually on record. Then all the other stuff began to tumble out."

"Will the public *ever* know?"

"Depends on who's in Number 10," replied Suzanne.

"And, presumably, what they want to keep hidden."

"That's how it works – and if they have nothing to hide, the cat will inevitably emerge from the bag. That isn't our concern. You have made a name for yourself with the Royal British Legion. Over half a million pounds in donations? Not bad at all."

"No publicity," said Danny, "I feel strongly about that. Our generation has seen some reward, but nowhere near enough. Every problem we face in this country can be traced back to the sacrifice made then. Those following us have a shock coming. The Americans and most of Europe did not give a toss. Suez, the nuclear trigger, TSR2... we are treated like a daft maiden aunt who needs to be humoured from time to time."

"It is about to bring you a gong," said Suzanne. "For services to charity, I understand and, may I say, not before time. The French aren't ready to make you a member of the *Légion d'honneur* just yet, but it will come."

"Is that why you are here?"

"Danny, I'm retired now."

"No one ever retires from the service. You are either pushed or die."

"You can be hauled back in."

"I see," answered Danny. "And where might it be this time?"

"Not far. We, or should I say, *they*, might require your services within the UK."

"After all this time? Where... oh I see, the United Kingdom of Great Britain and Northern Ireland you mean. They want me in among the steeples of Ulster, do they? Can't they cope on their own?"

"We have to operate with one arm tied behind our back. You know that well enough. The SAS could solve the problems in a week, but eliminating a third of the Ulster population would be counter-productive and for what? It seems to be a three-hundred-year-old view of the world?"

"The Americans live by it."

"Do not go there, Danny. No president can afford to alienate the Irish lobby."

"Until they have bombs going off over there," said Danny, with a shake of the head. "I'll happily arrange that."

"Are you able to make yourself available, if asked?"

"Why now?"

"You are booked into a Belfast concert next May. It's surveillance. Not a wet job."

"Ok," he replied. "Let me have the details when you can."

"Not me, Danny." She smiled. "I am retired. I just happen to live around the corner. Really, I do. Mr Bright junior will be pleased. He's in charge of operations there. He said to mention his brother's visit to the *Legs of Man.*"

"Both are blasts from the past," said Danny. "One of the better disc jockeys referred to old records as "Revive 45s." Even the younger brother must be nearly into his pension."

Suzanne did not react to this attempt at a fishing expedition.

"What happened to you and Baz?" said Danny, changing the subject.

"We parted, amicably, in 1961. He took up a professorial chair here in London and enjoyed the swinging 60s for four years. He married the divorced daughter of a city broker, with two daughters in tow, and aimed to live happily ever after."

"She died in a car accident, didn't she?"

"Yes, it happened three years into the marriage, leaving him with Julia and Naomi, a 14 year old and a 12 year old. Their real father used to take them over the Christmas holiday but Bernard brought them up. She *was* stone drunk, by the way. She drove straight into a bridge wall."

"Are you still in touch?"

"I get a telephone call, maybe twice a year. He lives in what was our old house in Oxford, retired but still an Honorary Fellow of his college."

"And you?"

"What of me, Danny?"

"Are you re-attached?"

She gave a knowing smile.

"I live just a street away and have my family home in the Gloucester countryside."

"So it's still very much the same as before."

"We could perhaps discuss it over dinner? It's getting late and, unfortunately, I do have somewhere to be."

Suzanne recommended a pleasant little restaurant within walking distance, which Danny had used before and they fixed a date for the coming Friday evening. Danny felt as though he had been effectively manipulated over the preceding two hours but, and this was the strange thing, after 20 plus years, he did not really mind. He imagined his old security file being dusted down and Suzanne's report being filed on top. No, he thought, re-jigging his thoughts. It is probably all computer tape now.

Still, the old file will be pretty thick. *Surveillance in Belfast? Who or what, I wonder.* He was pleased no attempt had been made to warn him off activity in London. He and Nathan Heim had the odd enemy or two.

Chapter Nine

Suzanne was more forthcoming over dinner. It was the type of restaurant in which to be seen eating and a photographer managed to take a shot of them in deep discussion between the soup and the green lasagne. She looked classically attractive in black, no mean feat given the sartorial standards of the 70s. In retrospect, he looked passable for the time, a good jacket in lime green, a white shirt and restrained kipper tie and black tailored flares; the effect was offset by the bouffant hair, lots of it, with side boards resembling stuck on Weetabix down the sides of his face.

She mentioned a few acquaintances they had in common, mostly MPs of every party, none of whom seemed to have sought high office. One in particular was highlighted as having stayed at Peers Park, her Gloucestershire family seat. Danny took the hint. It had been an on-and-off arrangement for a couple of years and was now firmly off. After all, he was a good 10 years her junior and had eventually married one of his researchers, 10 years *his* junior, and his wife and young family adorned the election leaflets of his London constituency.

The photo appeared in a tabloid newspaper in the middle pages two days later under the line *Danny's Girl?* The image probably flattered both of them. The same shot appeared in a popular music magazine under the title *Has Danny found Love at Last?* which was rather wide of the mark and less flattering for the inaccurate gibberish that tumbled for paragraph after paragraph down the page. He was only questioned on it a year later, at an open-air concert in Margate, by a local journalist who had at least done her homework and knew who Lady Suzanne Peers actually was.

Suzanne mentioned her daughter who was living in Norfolk and married into a farming family. She was building an organic vegetable business, successfully, and breeding ponies rather less so. She was, as Suzanne put it, married but not breeding, unlike her school contemporaries, most of whom were unmarried and breeding copiously. Little of this conversation would be considered in any way novel or newsworthy. At the time, it gave an air of modern semi-sophistication.

Bernard had taken the death of his second wife rather badly. He had withdrawn from the London social scene for a year or so before re-emerging to receive an honorary degree or two and making a well-publicised speech about the weakness of the British Army in terms of equipment and training. It had earned a rebuke from the then Labour government, which he actually supported, serving to make his case appear all the stronger and causing passages from it to be quoted in the House of Commons to this very day. His tag line of everyone wanting necessities on the cheap has been regularly quoted since, often dragged out of context and concerning things that Bernard would have hardly cared for and, in some instances, would have been positively against.

Suzanne had then asked about his family. Danny mentioned the weddings of his two nieces, Helene's daughters, one back in 1967, which he, in the role of rich uncle, had arranged and paid for, ensuring several transient pop stars performed at the evening reception in the grounds of a stately venue in Northumberland. Esme continued to live in Whitley Bay with her teacher husband and their daughter, Diane. The younger niece, Catherine, had married six years later, quietly in London. She had studied history there and joined a left-wing pressure group intent on a Trotskyite future of everlasting protest against anything the rest of society happened to be for. She had split from her husband after two years and was back in Tyneside, teaching in a primary school and looking after her three year old son, John.

"I did meet Cathy's husband once. Thin and very hairy; he resembled a doormat on legs. He looked and smelled as though he had yet to discover a bathroom. I don't know what happened to him."

"He's a councillor in Lambeth," Suzanne replied. "He's responsible for housing."

Danny scrutinised her face. Suzanne gave nothing away. He had said enough to raise a file.

"Helene is devastated by the whole thing. Catherine and Esme don't speak, and Catherine only speaks to her mother when she wants something – childminding or money. Her Dad, Nichol who doted on her, is only contacted when Helene refuses her something and that causes rows between all of them."

Suzanne listened carefully.

"Maman is worried and furious at the same time. She has never seen John, and last saw Catherine, named after her, as a 14 year old. I'll never forget that weekend. She told Helene and Nichol she needed a firmer hand. Both were offended and we drove back early on the Sunday with hardly a *bon voyage* as we left."

"Relationship is often the worst ship there is," said Suzanne. "At least we can choose our friends."

"We still see Esme and her husband. Sometimes they come down and stay with Maman and I occasionally drive her up north. We stay in a hotel. Their daughter, Diane, is nearly 10 now and I've got to admit, a bit of a favourite. It makes up for the problems elsewhere."

There was none of the awkwardness of their Oxford dinner date on this occasion. Danny walked Suzanne to her home; he wasn't invited in and did not expect to be. The merest of pecks on the cheek heralded his return, but not before Suzanne assured him she would be in touch. That was true insomuch she called him after 10pm one night the following year, just before he was due to depart for Belfast and a pop programme. She simply said that his services would not be needed as other more permanent arrangements were in place. Danny was perfectly polite in reply, business like and to the point, assuring her that permanent arrangements were superior to temporary fixes and used less time and energy. He said he was pleased to see Madge Wells' Oxford appointment announced in *The Times* and to pass on his best wishes. He made no mention of Bright.

In 1979 Danny received an OBE at Buckingham Palace. When Sandra brought in his mid-morning coffee he gave her all the details he could remember of the day. In reality it was confined to waiting around, protocol and the sheer joy Maman took in the events and engaging with one of the family, speaking in French, which extended beyond the ceremony itself. That, with three nights in the *Dorchester* and much recollection of the pre-war years over bottles of decent wine, probably exorcised some of the ghosts of the past and drew a temporary veil over the rift with Helene. She and Nichol had been invited. They declined by return of post.

"What happened to your sister, Danny?" asked Sandra, still luxuriating in his tales of the palace. "Do you miss her?"

"She died 20 years ago, 7th November, two days after her seventieth birthday. Helene never seemed to have any luck in her life. Had her first husband, Bob Brown, survived the war she'd have stayed in Wych Elm and remained close to her mother. Not that Nichol was a problem. In many ways he was your typical Geordie – strong, liked a drink and looked after his family. He perhaps relied too much on Helene in family matters, even looked up to her. She probably needed a bit more input, more direction."

"What took her?"

"It was a combination of losing Nichol two years before to a heart attack and her contracting pneumonia. According to her doctor, she was lacking the will to fight it. She died, he said, with a cynical smile on her face. I believed him. She had cultivated that smile since the war's end. I'd seen it often enough. It was as though she had placed a limit, a very low limit, on her capacity for enjoyment and disliked seeing it in others."

"A bit like Mary?"

"Similar," Danny replied. "People like that are not good to have around. No matter how many virtues they have and use to good effect, their presence deflates the world around them."

"You humour Mary when you speak to her."

"It makes for a quiet life," replied Danny. "It leaves me as the last door she'll knock on for an extended whinge."

Danny took lunch in the dining room. He enjoyed a large halibut with oven-baked vegetables from the menu. He chatted at the table with Ernest McGregor, a widower in his 90s who could clearly remember every pub in Wych Elm and their landlords and landladies. Danny would try to catch him out with one of the more obscure tenancies but had failed on each occasion. Ernest was an ex-railwayman, driving tank engines out of Bolton Great Moor Street station. He later transferred to one of the Manchester depots and had spent his last working years driving multiple diesel units on passenger duties between Manchester and north Wales. He reckoned the ultimate vision of hell on earth was the journey to Holyhead in winter. The experience allowed him to conclude that death was nothing to fear.

"Tha' knows hell is at least warm. Ah cannot stand cowd weather. Cowd sheets is worse. Ah keep askin' that Andrea girl to warm em up for me. Yuh know, ah might as well talk to mi bloody walking stick. She's as cowd a woman I've ever seen. She talks like one of them speak yer weight machines. They used to have 'um in public toilets."

"I remember them," replied Danny, with a laugh. "She's been spying on me. I'll be having a few words with her later."

Danny eventually retired to the small reading room on the second floor. There was no television in there and it was usually quiet. The view from the window was a combination of trees around the lawn and garden, and a majestic sweep of moorland grass, rising in defined stages up to the summit of Angle Pike. The days he could walk up the footpaths to the top were a distant memory and the times he could cycle to the top were now approaching pre-history, but fondly remembered, just the same. The exuberant pumping of the legs cranking through the gears, and the shimmering sweat and giddiness on reaching the top remained a fixture in his mind of good, competitive and happy times. *The individual who strikes out against the world* – a motto worth having and one he had tried to live by.

He did read a lot when he was younger and hadn't entirely given up now. Like most serious readers in the 1950s he had read Durrell and had first editions of the last three of the Alexandria Quartet. The descriptions of warm lands, blue seas and the exotic guise of foreign cities and people was essentially an immediate post-war fashion. The author had been living in France, another plus. His five books based on a vision and highly descriptive version of Avignon had entertained Danny in the 80s and these, with lighter reading from Wodehouse and Wheatley, provided quiet sustenance outside the noise and chatter of popular music. He remembered referring to Liz Layne as *Justine* one evening in the club; well, actually, in the office. Danny could not recall why he had called her up there. Jan Dale had Liz on her list, Jennie Jones too. Hadn't he given her the name *Sappho*, or was that someone else?

Drifting into a hazy sleep, Danny found himself afflicted by dream sequences, real enough in theatrical performance but within the dream Danny was aware he was dreaming. It was hardly a Shakespearean eve of Bosworth scene. The emergence of faces and forms, in front of his face, saying nothing but staring at him was haunting. It was an exercise where they appeared to scrutinise *his* face. Helene loomed toward him, retreated and then the Holcombe's, uncle and nephews, immediately followed by Maman and Therese. They appeared to be askew of a true time sequence as both were physically as Danny had last seen them. He was thinking throughout the process, *I am dreaming,* but nevertheless woke with a start and began to feel a trickle of pain down his left side. His mouth was dry. The pain ceased. This is what had brought him in here. A general infirmity and two serious falls at home, both preceded by a brief pain akin to warm water being poured within his bones, had finally persuaded him that independent living was no longer a viable option; to the relief of his doctor he followed the medical advice first promulgated three years before.

He slowly made his way down the broad stairway back to his room, sat in the familiar armchair and promptly fell asleep. When he eventually awoke (Andrea had entered the room to give him his afternoon medication), no dreams were remembered to pass judgement on the rest of the day. He felt genuinely refreshed.

"I hear you have been eavesdropping on my private conversation."

"Who's told you that?"

"You aren't denying it then?"

"I can't help hearing when I'm doing my work outside. Anyhow, Sandra is a sneak. She likes to think of you as *her* client. She only looks after you for half a day. She's after something. I cannot think *what* that might be," snapped Andrea, with a knowing look.

"Stop trying to turn this around," Danny replied firmly. "I don't want to get anyone into bother and I cannot believe you are jealous, it's not in your nature; you simply want to be in control, without responsibility, on your own terms. Don't listen in again. If there's anything you want to know, ask."

"Alright," she conceded. "But I wasn't deliberately listening."

"And I'm not a pervert," said Danny. "If I were, I'd be pawing you left, right and centre. Now give me those tablets and have done."

"Sorry," she replied, handing him the small white pills from a small plastic container. He swallowed them with a glass of water. She departed through the doorway, closing the door softly behind her. Danny watched her near perfect form move away from him. Being married, or in partnership as they say today, would be hard work with that one. Any motor engineer will tell you, a good body is no guarantee of top-class performance. Where had he first heard that *bon mot*?

It was probably in the garage in Wych Elm, a business long gone which serviced the Ford Pilot. The foreman had used it in connection with a new continental model which was in for a blown gasket. The second time was clearly etched in his brain. The Percy House pub, in High Percy, a few miles and two social classes down from Helene's home in Whitley Bay. Catherine was living there, having raised a mortgage for half its value to pay Esme her half of the inheritance. Catherine remained the type who only called when she wanted something and Danny had acted as a referee between the sisters over the price, terms and conditions affecting the former family home when Helene had passed away. The family solicitor was a decided oddball, the ultimate hypochondriac who operated a long established firm, *Wood & Co,* in Newcastle, Armstrong Street, a steep roadway which went straight down to the city quay on the river.

Essentially Peter Wood saw his business as a land agency dealing with county property – a few large transactions per year with a high fee. It had worked well until the end of the 60s but high inflation and cheaper competition had taken its toll, so he had succumbed to dealing in small house conveyancing for people he knew. As he lived at the coast, most of his house sale and purchase business came from Whitley Bay, Tynemouth and North Shields.

The office was Art Deco, including the wall lights which were largely untouched since the war. The wiring was almost certainly of historical interest. His elderly female secretary typed on a black Remington machine and his two-part-time filing and ledger clerks pottered around a general office illuminated by weak bulbs in green shades. Wood's office was off the reception area, behind a solid wooden door. It appeared small due to the huge quantity of files piled around. However, few people actually saw the inside because of his terror of the common cold. Once infected he suffered unimaginable agony, spluttering and sneezing for weeks on end but working on, alone in his office, communicating with the outside world with his black Bakelite telephone. An appointment to see him was rare and required a lengthy telephone interview as to when you had last had a cold and, in addition, anyone you had recently met or indeed were related to.

Danny had spoken to him through the crack in a barely opened door, with documents passed underneath the door for signatures and returned to the secretary the following day. It was a combination of Dickens and an unlikely Whitehall farce, but Danny had been amused by the whole carry on, taking the trouble of enquiring about Peter Wood among the local businesses in Whitley Bay. He lived in an ordinary 1930s semi, once owned by his parents. His father had died young and he had lived with his elderly and doting mother until her demise some 10 years before. The house was painted, once every two years, in cream and green; it was well maintained but remained in its original condition inside. When sold, an estate agent could have advertised it as *containing all original features* without fear of contradiction. It would have been equally true to describe it as *needing extensive updating.*

Eventually, the business concluded and Danny heard nothing more, apart from a Christmas card, until three years later when he took a telephone call from Catherine very late one evening at his home in Wych Elm. Her son,

John, had been badly beaten up outside a pub and the local police had been less than perfunctory in their investigation. Danny was persuaded to travel up the following weekend to visit John in hospital. The 18 year old had been well and truly worked over. He had a broken jaw, a broken eye socket and several broken ribs. It appeared that he had been meeting another young friend at a riverside pub called *The Bell* and had been attacked as part of a group entering with the intention of selling drugs. The owner of the pub, and two others along the river, was a local hard man, into protection. He was also the owner of a door security business, keeping undesirables out of pubs and clubs. It was a cash rich operation. He was a police informant and, surprisingly, against drug use or, as he put it, "the scum who sell the stuff." He was also an ex-boxing professional who was more than handy with his fists when he wasn't getting his own way.

A problem like this, in and around Wych Elm, was easily dealt with. When the territory is unknown, the police contacts unknown and the turf unknown, it becomes more of a conundrum. During the same weekend, staying in a local hotel, Danny established that Nigel Beveridge Mitchell, known as Bev Mitchell, lived in High Percy and owned three pubs: *The Percy Bar, The Bell and The Hadrian House.* He provided door staff for at least seven pubs and 10 clubs in Newcastle. His professional boxing activities were now confined to the streets and back lanes. He had a partner of 10 years, the usual orange-skinned blonde with two daughters, one of which was his own. His gang included the type of followers in awe of him and lacking much by way of brain power. Danny saw the whole operation as an extension of the school yard.

Assuring Catherine he would deal with the problem, he used his own law firm to put an investigation agency onto the job and while the information, when it came, was useful it was little more than a local presence could have discovered in a few nights. Initially Danny wondered whether a word in the right ear might result in a less tardy police response, but Bev Mitchell knew the score and enough of the right people. He considered paying an outside gang to wreck one of his pubs but traceability was a likely issue. For that reason, he took a week off and spent a quiet few nights in a Newcastle hotel, booking in as Jacky Brown – he had dyed his hair black en-route and had it trimmed. Although he was past 70 he looked more like a well-preserved 60. The black hair did enhance the lines on his face in a Michelin-tyre sort of way and he knew to avoid similar colouring in the future. He normally dressed down outside the studio or concerts and there had been fewer television appearances over the previous five years. His first evening, at a table in the Hadrian House, he found himself cheek-by-jowl with two men approaching middle age at the next table, engaged in banter surrounding the dark-haired barmaid.

Jack, slightly older, was obviously homosexual in a non-camp way, his hand gestures and lucid phraseology were strong indicators. He had longish greying hair and large spectacles with a metal frame which gave him an owl-like appearance. His thin-faced companion was almost certainly not gay, showing reservations concerning those who were, which became clear in their discourse.

"Ye? Marry Christine? You've not even asked her out yet!" Jack smirked at Keith, his companion.

They were sharing a bottle of brown ale and Jack was replenishing their glasses from the half-full bottle on the table. Keith's eyes were fixed on Christine, the barmaid, as she pulled pints and smiled at the people milling around for drinks.

"Shaddup Jack," Keith replied. "She would give you a good night's sleep, I can tell you!"

"Good night's sleep? You marry Christine, every day will be a rainy day. You won't be sailing the sea of life together – it'll be a stormy passage."

"Listen to yourself, Jack. What would you know! You can be a sarcastic bugger!"

"No, not even a stormy passage – more likely sunk in port."

"Just look at those thighs." Keith's eyes narrowed further.

"Thighs? You'll soon tire of those! Marry Christine, every time she goes to the corner shop for a loaf of bread, you'll be pacing the floor till she gets back." Jack was smiling. "It won't be a three course meal and your slippers when you get home from a hard day at work. No, it'll be a Dinkman's meat pie."

"You kill all my attempts at marriage and a family."

"No, Keith, it's just that you pick the worst. Her boyfriend's on his holidays in Durham. He has another year to serve yet. You, or anyone else sniffing round her, will be found with a brown ale bottle stuck up your rear end in a back lane somewhere. I have your best interests at heart. Anyway, all the women you wanted were either unattainable, married or on television. Did you ever hear from Flick Colby? How many letters did you send, care of the BBC? Seven, was it?"

"Eight."

"And never a reply," continued Jack. "See, I'm only thinking of you."

"I'll be 50 next May," sighed Keith. "Not much of a life, is it? Friday nights here with you, the rest of the week in front of the television or humping boxes for the Co-op. Welcome to modern Britain!"

"Never mind, pet. For your fiftieth I'll take you up to Shankhouse Club – they do a good pie and pea supper."

"Christ almighty, I can't wait."

At that point both Jack and Keith had begun to look at Danny. He made his way to the bar and, after being served by Christine, returned with a half of lager.

"You aren't a local here," said Jack.

"No, I'm not," replied Danny. "I'm up from Yorkshire doing some business."

"Oh," replied Jack. "What business are you in?"

"Canal boats," replied Danny, thinking quickly. "One of the repairers is preparing an estimate for me."

"Which one?" asked Keith.

Danny had passed one in his hire car and simply replied, "Elliotts."

"Must be a big order then," said Keith.

"20 plus."

"What do you do with them?" Keith asked.

"He sails them," said Jack, with a smile.

Keith glared at him.

"Holiday accommodation, house boats," said Danny.

"Some choice, a week in Benidorm or a week on a canal," Keith shrugged.

"A houseboat will be more amenable than a sterile hotel on the Costa Brava," Jack added.

"The rain in Spain falls mainly on the plain," Keith stated, with an air of finality. "In Yorkshire it rains everywhere."

Danny was concentrating on the figure who had just entered the bar – a bear of a man, typically Geordie; he had a shaven head, tight t-shirt top and tailored jeans with expensive white trainers. In any other town, apart possibly from Sunderland, he would have been passed off as gay. The men in the northeast had their own style, gay or not.

"Who's that?" he asked, as everyone seemed to part like the Red Sea to let him stand at the bar. He scanned the room before taking a swig from the pint of lager Christine handed to him. Drinkers were anxious to be seen saying 'Hi Bev' at every opportunity.

Danny could lip-read as Bev asked Christine if there'd been any trouble and who that black-haired man was sat next to Jack and Keith. She said she hadn't seen him before. He responded with a curt, "find out." Danny spotted an opportunity. Bev went into the back room to see how many were using the pool table, then doubled back and, in a whisper that carried quite a bit, said he was heading for *The Bell* to see what was going on. He stalked out of the door with half the drinkers almost bowing as he left.

"Would you two like a drink?"

Jack and Keith looked at each other.

"Kind of you," said Keith. "A bottle of brown please."

Danny walked to the bar. Christine eyed him up and down with the sort of look that would buy and sell you in under a minute. She was well made up in a black short skirt and low white blouse. She had gold rings on each hand. To say she was hard would have been simplistic. Under the makeup and chatter she had the consistency of a match strike. She may have interested him 30 years ago but the hard work and high maintenance of what was, in this instance, a commodity rather attenuated his approach. He was about to speak when half a dozen heavily made up girls burst into the bar warbling a pop song and making to smile to something unseen in the middle distance.

"Out of here, you lot," snapped Christine. "Into the lounge if you want to drink here."

"Oooh!" they responded in unison and waddled through an internal door into the lounge area.

"Little cows," said Christine, to no one in particular. "What can I get you?"

"A bottle of brown and a half of lager," he replied, pointing to the lager pump.

"You're not from round here, are you?"

"No. The name's Jacky and I'm up from Leeds on business."

"You're not the law, are you?"

"Is that what your shaven-headed friend wanted to know?"

"He's the boss. Be careful what you say."

"He could have asked himself. Does he do everything through other people? Or is he shy?"

"He sorts out trouble."

"So do I."

She was intrigued by Danny's manner and looked at him carefully as she gave him the drinks. She was about to make a further comment when Danny pointed toward the lounge.

"Do you let children in here regularly?"

"Only when they pay."

Danny returned to Jack and Keith. Jack asked, whether Danny had got anywhere.

"With the barmaid, you mean?"

"Why aye, Keith thinks she's canny."

"She's more like an old tin can," replied Danny. "Enter there and you come out with a few cuts, at the very least."

Danny finished his drink and walked outside. The street was full of boarded-up shops, down at heel hairdressers and one burnt-out betting shop. Boarded premises across from the pub entrance attracted Danny's attention. Walking down a side alley he found a door without hinges jammed into a rotted frame. He eased his way in. The smell of urine and defecation was overwhelming, but an iron staircase led up to the second floor where a missing cover gave access to the roof. The roof surface was rickety and uneven. The second floor would suffice. He lifted the remains of a pane from the front window and created a clear view of the street.

He returned the following evening, carrying the old canvas fishing bag and the *De Lisle*, freshly oiled and tested on the moor around Angle Pike. He had maintained the weapon regularly. The *Welrod* was now deposited in the lower reservoir in Wych Elm. A combination of deteriorating rubber seals and a less than satisfactory fit of the hand grip magazine had rendered the gun as a risk in terms of noise and firing capability. He still had the venerable *Bulldog* but more as a keepsake than as a tool of the trade. His physical ability was affected by his age but he was fitter than most. Nevertheless, even he doubted whether he could now kill with one strike. The *De Lisle* would have to suffice.

From the empty pane of the second floor he watched the comings and goings around the *Hadrian House* for over two hours. Just before 10pm a new Ford Probe eased by and parked nose first on waste ground immediately opposite Danny's lair. He watched Bev Mitchell get out and stride the 20 yards into the pub. Then, to his amazement, a dark coloured VW Polo drew up and an unkempt character in jogging bottoms, trainers and an oversized jacket got out of the passenger side and paced around Mitchell's car. He waved his own driver away. The VW reversed up the street and parked a few yards from the pub doorway. Danny could see the driver's lit cigarette moving within the black interior. The guy in jogging bottoms appeared agitated, even when still, as he was deciding where to stand. He produced a handgun from his jacket and in a momentary decision used the butt to break the driver's side window of Mitchell's car.

"Holy Moses," Danny whispered to himself. "He's going to do him."

The gunman waited within a boarded shop doorway on the street. He saw Bev leave the pub 10 minutes later. As he walked to his car he saw the jagged hole in the window and, as intended, he stopped briefly. The gunman emerged and, holding the pistol loosely, fired two shots, one of which brought Mitchell to his knees by his own car and the second that seemed to enter his lumber region. The gunman was shaking as though he had injected himself with steroids; he had difficulty getting into the VW as it pulled up behind him. It then screeched off into the night.

Danny watched Mitchell drag himself toward the street. As he squeezed his body along the floor Danny could see a profusion of blood flowing along the cobbles. He took a careful aim, but whether his grip was less certain or, more likely, Mitchell heaved himself with a lurch onto the street, the bullet missed his head and entered his back near the existing wound. In the seconds that followed Danny made his way down, along the back lane and along a dark pathway by some flats. He took care to place his canvas bag on the back seat of his hire car and drive off slowly, attracting no attention at all.

Back at the hotel he stripped, showered and placed all the clothes he had worn that night, including underwear and rubber-soled shoes, into a black, heavy-duty bin liner. He left the following day, changing cars, and that evening he burned the bag and its contents in an old dustbin in his own garden. The *De Lisle* was returned to store. The deceased Maman, or at least her garage, kept its secret.

A telephone call to Catherine elicited the remark – "You weren't meant to kill him."

"Someone else got there first. I feel a bit cheated really!"

The murder of Bev Mitchell produced no media interest outside of Newcastle. Most people assumed a gang rivalry. The police rightly assumed two assassins. The body had been hit by two .22 bullets, probably from a Magnum handgun. But there was also an unusual .45ACP round, a subsonic bullet, rare on the streets and not seen on Tyneside before. No publicity was given to the latter feature. There had been several arrests of various low-life criminals, but no one was charged. It became a story of hero worship and conspiracy theories which, when he spotted one, Danny read with some amusement. Here was Danny in 2010 and the case remained unsolved.

He was feeling a bit twitchy, perhaps a case of cabin fever and he shuffled himself out of his room. Lucinda, Mary Hobson's daughter, was passing in the corridor. She wore the strained visitor look of someone who dreads every visit but still cares enough to ensure all is well, carrying the weight of guilt piled on by the resident during each and every call. Mothers were notorious for this, though some fathers auditioned well for the part. Mary Hobson used a boiler shovel for this very purpose.

"Hello, how are you?" she asked.

"I'm alright," said Danny, not really convincing himself. "How's your mother."

"Still frail, but nothing wrong with her tongue."

Danny nodded, smiled and shuffled on. He entered the lift and managed to get up to the second-floor lounge. Sitting in a chair by the window he thought he saw the view change – the colours went from green to mauve and the trickle-of-water feeling in his bones returned. He was unaware as he slumped toward the arm rest, but as his body doubled over he felt a sharp cramp in his chest. He made to shout but nothing emanated from his mouth except a drool of saliva. He felt neither it, nor anything else, neither did he see the view. Life had simply ebbed away. He went somewhat gently into that goodnight.

Chapter Ten

There was a local radio announcement within 10 minutes of the news release. National radio and television did long slots on the 6pm evening bulletins. The internet had the story almost immediately. The bulletins concentrated on his popular music and television career. Newspaper obituaries appeared in the next three days. The most perceptive one appeared in the *The Daily Standard*. It contrasted a photographic portrait from 1970 – long steel-grey hair, a sharp smile and dark eyes looking straight into the lens, with a text that hinted at his earlier career.

Danny Hird

The pop maestro of the sixties and seventies Danny Hird has died in a Greater Manchester care home, days short of his eighty-eighth birthday. Responsible for the careers of many successful northern singers, he *promoted less popular soul music and achieved notable success in his latter years with the mega group **Poke Me Quietly**.*

*He was one of the first northern agents to break into the closed world of London agencies. He employed a ruthless approach honed on the Hird family quarry business in his native Lancashire which led Paul Ephraim, lead singer of one of his promoted groups, **Hot Wind**, to describe him as "mechanical" as far as people and money were concerned.*

Daniel Jacques Hird was born on 14th October 1922 at Wych Elm, Lancashire, the son of William Hird and Catherine Madeleine Verrier. His father served with the Royal Artillery in France and married Catherine, a native of Amiens, in France. Danny grew up in a wealthy bi-lingual household, attended Wych Elm Grammar School, excelling in languages and on the sports field, leaving to do an engineering apprenticeship at the local railway works with the intention of joining the family stone and clay business. He joined his local regiment in 1942 and subsequently served in SOE in occupied France.

His SOE service is clouded in mystery but his name was associated with the assassination of Hans Dietrich Held, second in command of the Gestapo in Paris, and Louis Darnand, commander of a Vichy unit in Amiens in February 1944. He was in Paris at the liberation and remained on the SOE payroll post-war.

He claimed to have invented the dual turntable for clubroom dancing and was certainly using this approach, with American equipment, in Wych Elm in 1946. Others, including a Yorkshire contemporary, claimed the credit for this continuous play system but it is likely both saw it first in Paris or Marseille where similar usage had been noticed pre-war. He managed a successful and popular dance hall actually a converted cinema in Wych Elm until 1969, by which time he sold the business to concentrate on management, promotion and television work.

His father had been killed in a wartime air raid and until 20 years ago his mother, known to him as Maman or la Dauphine, was a regular companion, accompanying him to receive the OBE for services to British music and his charity work for the Royal British Legion in 1972. He received the Legion d'Honneur two years later for unspecified service during the war. Unmarried he leaves two nieces, daughters of his late sister Helene, and a grateful legacy of northern musical talent forever in his debt. He established three charitable foundations, one promoting cycling in schools, another providing music scholarships and, his final venture, two private care homes for the elderly and infirm.

He died on 12th October from complications following a stroke. For some years he had been increasingly frail, living the last year of his life in one of his care homes. He will be buried in a prepared plot in the cemetery at Wych Elm and a memorial service is

planned in the Metropolitan Cathedral of Christ the
King, Liverpool, at a date to be arranged.

Jan Dale read this copy and heard the televised interviews with an increasing sense of frustration. Determined that the real story, her story, had to be told she now had no fear of a libel action. Her problem was the initial lack of interest in her angle. She could only move when the fawning stopped. One of her few close friends advised her not to be seen as "someone pouring manure in the coffin and spitting at the mourners." Suppressing her impatience, she bided her time.

There were three narratives already on tape, complete with photographs of the girls in their teens. Linda Haslam, now Mrs Smith, widowed and aged 72, was adamant in her story of how Danny Hird regularly groped the young girls in *Danny's Place.* The introductory singers were most at risk, both as they performed in public as a group and sometimes when alone in his office. She claimed he regularly gave her a cigarette and sat her on his knee while she smoked it. At the time, she was flattered by the attention but she came to realise he was a totally unsavoury man. This story was fed into the *Northern Times,* picked up by several tabloids and ultimately gained a life of its own on the net. She now lived at a seaside town on the south coast, alone apart from three cats, in a decoratively down-at-heel bungalow. Her retired solicitor husband had died 10 years earlier. She had one son serving in the army. Asked for more interviews, she demurred.

191

Janice Johnson still lived in Wych Elm with her third husband who was some five years younger than her 69 years. She confirmed Linda's story in some detail but also claimed that Danny Hird had the 'hots' for her friend Lindsey Morrell, now sadly deceased. She claimed he had full sexual relations with her, in his office, when she was only 15 and several times afterwards. As Lindsey had died of cancer in New Zealand the year before and her surviving husband knew nothing of these suggested events, the papers treated the story with a degree of scepticism, stating that without other testimonies there were huge questions as to its reliability. It was printed anyway, with suitable disclaimers.

Elizabeth (Liz) Layne was now Mrs Grant, aged 64 and living in Cheshire. Her husband had been a research scientist in Manchester and had recently retired. She had taught maths for many years at a private boys' school in Cheshire. She claimed Danny Hird was a well-known groper, bottom patter and spanker, with a taste for young teenagers. Her own claim in this regard was an incident in his office as a 15 year old when she was 'punished' for a late arrival.

The subsequent fall out produced various emails and letters of varying quality which either confirmed or denied aspects of the three accounts. Men who wrote in were at one in trying to keep their girlfriends or wives away from him. However, others hinted at the willingness of some of the females to indulge him, especially when he attained a national profile.

Meanwhile, electronic sentiment had begun to turn against "these old witches regretting their past" and at this point Jan unleashed her story about Danny's involvement with St Jude's in the early 50s. In doing so she successfully initiated an electronic *paedo* hunt where anyone remotely associated with the event – nuns and priests especially and churches generally – became targets for volumes of airwave venom.

Again, a fortnight later, she broke her story, implying that Danny and his friend and associate, Clifford Hindle, were implicated in the disappearance and probable murder of Alan Thompson, lead singer of *Junior Jumpstart and the Motors*. This was, however, an old story and one northern editor referred to it as "the bad penny much used by attention seekers and lazy reporters." She mentioned the two police investigations and hinted at the need for a thorough search of the Hird properties and land to uncover vital evidence. This was all very much old news as far as many newspapers were concerned, but it provided an opportunity to revive some old copy and allow some middle page spreads. Other news was lacking.

A police spokesman gave a statement saying that if Ms Dale, or anyone else, had new evidence concerning this or any other missing person case, to contact them. No one did. However, this flurry of press coverage caused three new people to contact Jan with information which was new and, as far as she was concerned, intriguing. In the meantime plans for a memorial service were shelved. The funeral service had proceeded quietly in Wych Elm's Catholic chapel and Danny's remains were interred near the family plot, his name as yet missing from the headstone. John Stannard maintained prayers for the repose of his soul. The solicitors began to deal with the estate. The church's lawyers began to issue statements questioning Jan's evidence and motives where St Jude's was involved and cited the lack of any hard evidence, in the form of files or any official documentation, from both institutions after this length of time.

Land rental income went to the nursing homes. His cottage was left to his two other charity accounts, as was the old family home. The contents of both were subject to specific orders prior to any sale. A London flat, purchased in 1981 and mortgage free, was, by way of a late codicil, left to Sandra. This development was to cause quite a bit of ribald comment among the office staff at the care home and there was talk of amending employee contracts to preclude pecuniary benefit from residents' wills and estates. The difficulties in drawing up such a contract multiplied as the lawyers examined it and a year later staff were employed by a newly created company which facilitated the managerially desired outcome. Sandra was surprised and rather shaken when given the news of the bequest, as was her immediate family, especially when her colleague Andrea began to imply it was payment for services rendered. In Wych Elm such a property may have commanded a price of £50,000. In Chelsea the figure was likely to exceed half a million. Sandra and her husband found it rather a basic abode of little distinction and spent the day regaling anyone who would listen about the cost of their return rail tickets. Once its potential as a rental property was established they took a different view.

His nieces were left a quarter of a million each from his cash holdings in the UK and the Isle of Man. The original will was dated in 1989. Given the structure of the will any challenge to the codicil benefitting Sandra was unlikely to succeed. There was no challenge.

Two months on Lisa Moores and Angela White, acting as agents for the estate, arrived at Pike Cottage to do an inventory and organise the sale or removal of items prior to marketing the property itself. They arrived together in a red Fiesta anticipating a couple of half days to get the job done. The dank weather did nothing for their spirits and neither did the tree-lined aspect in front of the house. The branches needed trimming. As it was they waved in the light wind, the bows crackling like alerted sentinels declaring their presence and heralding a grim determination to do their guarding duty. Another car pulled in behind them, a new white Alfa Romeo. Jan emerged from the driver's seat, immaculate in blue jeans, black boots and a Burberry top and jacket, waving a printed email in her hand. Discussions and phone calls followed, establishing that Jan was working for the *Daily Planet* on this particular case and, having given a series of undertakings, had finally got the agreement of the estate's lawyers to allow the newspaper, and Jan, access to Danny Hird's cottage. Chris Babbage, the estate solicitor, took a pragmatic view – friends close and enemies closer.

The three women gained entry by the front door. The garden was still tended on a monthly basis but it was apparent that a minimum amount of work was being done. The hallway was rather dark, with half-panelled walls and elderly coat hooks festooned with varied tatty jackets covering the wall behind the door. A door on the left led into a basic dining room. There was a fireplace, at least 50 years old, the grate covered by a brass fireguard. There were no ornaments and just one framed photograph of the late Mrs Hird, white haired, seated and holding flowers. This was another sentinel object, guarding the interior of this unsettling space.

The dining table and chairs were 1930s-styled, the table centre covered by an embroidered cloth. A matching sideboard completed the furnishings of the room, its coolness enhanced by the pale blue painted walls. The drawers in the sideboard contained nothing, but the two cupboards revealed Derby porcelain tableware and a set of leather placemats. Lisa and Angela both shuddered in the cool air while Jan scanned the room.

"Not a lot in here," she said. "Does it have the look of a millionaire's pad?"

Angela felt it was more like an undertaker's parlour. Lisa simply said it gave her the creeps. She kept looking up at the ceiling, watching the cherub faces in the cornices which appeared to smirk down on them.

The living room opposite was no better. The two settees did not match and had seen far better days. A low coffee table had two glass ashtrays and an open bottle of malt whisky. There were two stained teacups and a plate bearing several blackened crumbs. A pile of junk mail lay on the patterned carpet, slippers sat perched on the hearth and the fire itself was a two-bar electric contraption of uncertain vintage and, mercifully, unplugged. The flex lay like a damp stain trailing along the skirting board. The curtains were heavy and dark brown, matching the pair in the dining room. A bright day would enter this home like a thief in the night. Jan noticed the dusty yellowy-brown light shades and cob webs in the corners of the ceilings. Had no one thought to remove the whisky bottle or the cups?

"Has anyone been cleaning this place?"

"Once a month, under contract," replied Angela. "Evidence is hard to see."

The kitchen was on the small side and had an array of cheap looking units of a type fashionable 30 years before. The doors were a shade of tangerine, the surfaces white and showing distinct signs of what might be described as wear and tear. The stairway up to the two bedrooms still had brass stair rods securing an ancient striped carpet. Danny's bedroom had a dressing table of Victorian weight and curves, every surface scattered with varied bits of shaving tackle, perfumes and deodorant sprays, all reflected back by a huge adjustable triple mirror. The matching wardrobe contained just one grey suit, a purple jacket and two pairs of black trousers; a chest of drawers revealed the usual socks, a few ties and even some underwear. The overall effect was one of neglect and parsimony. The bedroom carpet was threadbare in places. An open, empty whisky bottle lay by the side of the bed, the bed clothes pulled up, cold to the touch and crumpled.

"This is just an old man's house," said Lisa. "It's cold, charmless and sad."

"The money he had…" replied Angela. "He could have lived like a king. Instead he seems to have lived like an old scrote."

"What was taken from here at the outset when he first went into care?" asked Jan.

"Money, valuables like jewellery and his papers," replied Angela. "There was a huge archive of letters, photos, press cuttings and the like. All of that stuff is in storage. The collection of vinyl records is due for auction next month. My boss reckons it'll bring in a packet."

The second bedroom contained a single bed and a small utility dressing table. One wall was dominated by a large bookcase, packed with various novels, bicycle manuals, car repair booklets and Penguin paperbacks, plus some novels in French, including several *Maigret, Camus' L'Etranger* and *L' Histoire d'O*. Jan took one or two down, flicking through the cool dense pages, checking for any stray bits of paper. There was nothing immediately obvious.

"What are the arrangements again?" she asked.

"For the contents, you mean?" said Lisa.

"Yes. I may be interested in the books," replied Jan.

"The furniture and crockery has to go to auction," said Angela. "Everything else simply has to be cleared."

"Offer 20 quid or so for the books, collect them yourself," Lisa said, with a nod to Angela. "I'm sure we could get that ticked off for you."

Jan had experience of old book collections and how they were used to store personal items, from bills to theatre tickets, even personal letters which, for whatever reason, were kept rather than thrown away. Danny would be no different in this regard. Everyone does it to some degree, provided they have books.

The three of them perfunctorily examined the bathroom and the separate brick garage outside. The garage was full of tools and two old racing bicycles with flat tyres. In all, Jan began to consider the impression Danny had given in the care home, his latter-day television interviews for various pop music documentaries and *this* his home and retreat. Even allowing for his electronic equipment and record collection being in storage, it amounted to very little. Was his public bravado a mask? If so, what was being hidden? For the first time she began to wonder about her own acknowledged obsession with this man, including her conviction that he knew more about the Alan Thompson mystery than he had ever been prepared to say.

Hannah Arendt had spoken of the banality of evil. This seemed even less than banal. She had some tantalising bits of recent hue, but in the whole scheme of things what did it all amount to? After all, he was dead. Was it time to move on? Katie Ross certainly thought so. She had been a friend since their university days in London and in the 80s they had worked as a team on an old Soviet spy story. Katie had been a young mother, pregnant at 16, but with wealthy parents in Chelsea willing to act as parents again, in their 40s, to Anthony, now a banker based in Singapore, about to celebrate his forty-third birthday. Katie had completed her studies and spent eight years teaching French to posh girls at a small private school in north London. She had eventually married one of Jan's old school friends from Wych Elm, made a widower by an Irish terrorist nail bomb in London which took his wife, his young child and four other passers-by. The marriage lasted five years. He had been living in Florida, fighting extradition for embezzling four million pounds from a housing corporation he managed in the 90s and was now God knows where, while Katie eventually lived with a boy half her age in Madrid where they owned a hotel together. She had worked hard at the business while he wrote silly ephemeral books of a type popular in the 80s. Love died. Katie had been alone and back in the UK for a few years; while she and Jan had kept in touch electronically on a daily basis, until now they had actually met just once, in Jan's now rented Camden flat, a few years before.

Having sold her rural, remote Essex house on the east of Mersea Island, Jan was back north in a large city centre apartment in Manchester. Katie was lounging in it, on her third glass of wine, speaking like an old mother to an exasperating daughter. Katie retained her looks, at distance. Jan was aware of it. She had used her linguistic expertise in the past and a desire to catch up coincided with a potential need in this matter. Katie had her measure but willingly participated in this "whirly little adventure with the dead." Katie played the dizzy girl quite well. It was an old and well-practised role which often provided a means of slipping by the best prepared of defences, be they emotional, rational or real.

"Where is all this coming from, Jan?" she was saying. "You once told me you had interviewed him for the school mag? Did he grope you? Attempt to kidnap, murder or sexually abuse you?"

"No, he didn't. He did have his hand on my pal's rear end throughout our talk."

"What did she do? Giggle?"

"More or less."

"And that was in 1968, 42 years ago. What are you trying to achieve?"

"He was a predator with young girls. For years he took them on car rides, cycling and had little talks in his office. He should be exposed."

Katie almost snorted. She reminded Jan that the pair of them entered the world in 1951, had seen the rise of the pop culture, groupies and to an extent in the capital – less so outside – drugs, pills and, everywhere outside the Celtic fringe, legal abortions. Katie reminded Jan of the

201

times she herself had used her charms to get a story, highlighting one occasion she had worn what could have been reasonably described as a gym slip when interviewing a government defence procurement minister.

Jan had the grace to wince at the thought but not to deny it. Katie ploughed on.

"Why didn't you say something when he was famous? You had the means, the contacts."

"No one would have been interested then."

"And did he attack all girls? Why not you?"

"He liked them girly and giggly."

"Or, to at least pretend they were?" said Katie. "That was never you. It could have been me. It was a role I've played often enough."

"I'm after some justice, for them and for Alan Thompson."

"Are you?" Katie went on. "People disappear all the time. Your obsession with *Junior Jumpstart* seems less about him and more about Danny. You cannot re-run the past. My God, I'd be pressing delete for most of mine."

Jan could scarcely admit to herself the truth of one aspect of Danny Hird. At the time, she felt he might be useful in her career and she had a crush on his screen persona. She had been decidedly disappointed in his Wych Elm attitudes and jokes. Her own sexuality had been complex – and still was – with her attraction to women and men, but leaving that aside, Katie's words were more *cutting* the chords than striking them.

She passes Alban Brooks' letter to Katie, a neat copperplate handwritten note on good paper. Katie searched her handbag for her spectacles and then read attentively.

"As you said, the chaplain at Strangeways Prison in the early 50s and he mentions the execution of a pub landlord who murdered his wife's lover, who came from Wych Elm. He whispers to him minutes prior to his death that the truth lies in Wych Elm and mentions Danny Hird. It's hardly a confession or an accusation. He says the police knew of the connection but did nothing and that he had met Danny Hird in France during the war, saying his training would have made him capable of anything."

"And then there's this," said Jan, passing a print out of an email received some weeks before.

Dear Miss Dale

I have read with some interest your newspaper comments and articles concerning the late Danny Hird. I have no wish to burden you further, nor to muddy the water, but I felt it wise to inform you of my late mother, Lydia Baines as she then was, a teacher at Wych Elm Grammar School. She taught Danny French and Italian during her time there and remembered him as a boisterous young boy, clever and linguistically gifted and, even at 11, old for his age.

She often told me of his rapid maturity and excellent performance in the examinations and how he ought to have gone on to university and achieved high academic honours. When he was famous, on television and writing magazine articles about pop music, she invariably told me of his time at the school. However, as she grew older and especially after my father, Robert James, died in 1988 she grew increasingly agitated by his television appearances. I was older and less interested in the pop scene and she had no direct interest at all. When she attained her eightieth birthday in 1992 she told me she had written to him and was awaiting a reply. She wouldn't tell me what her letter was about and seven years later, gravely ill and obviously dying, she confided in me.

My elder sister, Ruth, born shortly after my parents' marriage in 1937, had died in tragic circumstances in 1961. She was two years my senior and I had looked up to her. She had gone to university in Manchester and done a degree in French but, after graduating, could not settle. She ditched her long-term boyfriend and worked in a Manchester club behind the bar. In May 1961 she had gone to a club in Bolton with a casual boyfriend and both had been killed in the fire which enveloped the club. I was well aware of these events. Mum was devastated and Dad could barely speak of it afterwards. But Mum told me something I shall never forget. Ruth's father was not my father, but was the child of Danny Hird. Dad never knew the truth of the matter but Mum did. She told me she had put this in a letter to Danny in 1988, but had received no reply. She wondered whether he had seen or

at least read her letter and she died days later, leaving
me with this knowledge.

In the event I did nothing at all, until now. If you
discover he did know, perhaps you might let me know.

Yours Sincerely

Rachel Holden nee James.

Katie was quite taken by the message, its precision and obvious sincerity. She noticed Jan's encouraging reply. This woman, Rachel, was 70 or 71, haunted by a secret so recently revealed and one which amended her view of the past, her mother and her family. Nothing could change what had happened but both Katie and Jan appreciated that, like her mother, there was a desire for a closure of some sort, if nothing else just to tidy up the ragged edges of that murky memory we call the past.

"Have you found anything?"

"There's nothing apparent in the papers his solicitors are holding," Jan replied. "They did admit they had not looked too hard. They would not allow me any access, but who knows? They may relent."

Katie waved the paper in the air.

"Did you pass this to them?"

"No," she replied. "But I did give them her email address. I contacted her first of course, just to get her permission."

"You realise," said Katie, "there is more in *this* than all the rubbish about illicit cigarettes, who had who and when, spankings in the naughty girls' home and disappearing pop acts. At least this is human, grounded and, frankly, a tragedy. I hope he didn't know."

"Well," replied Jan, leading her into the dining area where four large plastic crates had been delivered and stood in a stack by the wall. "There is his remaining library from the cottage. We will search every book for markers, inserts, whatever may cast a light on the old goat."

Katie thought back to the number of occasions she had been the unpaid sidekick to Jan's sheriff, ploughing through old ledgers, report books, archives of letters and commercial documents, usually culminating in a well-paid story of at least national importance and, over time, in one celebrated story linking a field behind an Aspen Hill public house with the Hess flight from Nazi Germany. To be sure, Jan had rescued Katie from the north London desert of a private girls' school where she had taught French for eight years. They had both taken first class degrees at UCL, Katie in French and German, Jan in history; on graduating in 1973 they had lost touch, mainly due to Jan's affair with a female waitress in a Bloomsbury café who turned out to be the sister of one the capital's more celebrated villains and provided an inside track to the criminal underworld of post-war London. Her subsequent articles made her one of the youngest reporters on the staff of a national daily, and a later study of the post-war rationing era provided the material for a PhD in 1988. By that time the waitress was long gone, living in Tenerife with an African princess of a type, showing no desire to reside anywhere in her inherited estate.

Katie had made do with a short-lived marriage to a backbench MP who had denied office in the Thatcher years and thus turned to property dealing and alcohol in equal measure. Her subsequent tie with Jan's former school friend from Wych Elm was an indirect result of the Hess story. He was a widower, victim of a strange Irish obsession with a myth they held onto like a secular romanticism in ritual phrases and tendentious readings of history. It amounted to a romanticism of nail bombs in London, which romantically killed quite a few. It was this romanticism, which killed his wife and child. As he saw it they were sacrifices to the myth of Irish unity. His vulnerability at the time masked an emerging core so impervious his interests were measured in monetary gain, deaf and blind to anything else in the world. It was, as Katie was later to describe it, a form of asset autism.

Alone again, assisting Jan in varied journalistic jaunts across the country, the two friends lost touch again when Jan pursued Leonie, an American knight errant of odd style and attitude who had come fully formed from her pursuit of the Rudolf Hess story. She had stolen Jan's heart for a brief period of time, leaving Katie with the leisure to find a young physicist from Newcastle in an Ibiza hotel, spending four zany years with him until the assumption they were a case of mother and son grew to a clamour. It became so insistent that even *they* noticed and called it a day before dark night could begin its timely fall.

Katie had the genetic inheritance to maintain her looks, even at fairly close scrutiny and without much by way of chemical assistance. She was now pursued by men she would have readily encouraged in the past but her appetite for the great game, while not extinguished, was subservient to her desire for contentment, coffee and cream. Furthermore, she had developed an air of neutrality to almost anything and no longer went headlong into the emotive depths of her being, but saw much of the world from the outside, so to speak, with no desire to force a door and walk inside.

As she examined the initial pile of old paperbacks from the first box, with Jan flicking through others, Katie glanced across the dining table and twisted her face, simply to avoid the grin that was attempting to burrow its way through. Here they were again, history repeating itself. They had experienced it undiluted. Was this to be tragedy or farce?

The table was modern yet old in style; it was called 'rustic farmhouse' and to have such a furnishing framed in a huge triple glazed window which exhibited a seventh-floor view of east Manchester. It was a by-product of the industrial revolution if ever there was one, terraced housing, modern sports stadia, grey urban regeneration, half done, then re-done with rolling grey-green hills beyond. The vista was almost a parody. Two of Britain's more famous serial killer haunts lay within the eyeline. Katie found it almost amusing to think of herself and Jan, sitting either side of this wooden table, sifting through elderly paperbacks, fanning the pages to reveal any inserted material and only occasionally glancing at the titles. She found some admission tickets for *Danny's Place* being used as bookmarks, probably placed 50 or so years before. *What had interrupted his reading? Sleep? A meal?* Several more substantial documents were found, using a similar utilitarian fashion, including an electric bill from 1967 and two open-air concert tickets from 1970 featuring rock groups of the time, one of which was still performing their old hits in a smoke-ravaged vocal style which afflicts most singers in their late 60s. The backing tape had been used originally to back up the performance. Now it tended to hide the weakness of the main act. Katie mentioned that the tickets may have value in the collectables market, but her friend showed little interest. A photograph, a sort of publicity still, was folded into a copy of Hugh Thomas' *The Spanish Civil War.* Katie judged the date to be the late 60s from the attire Danny was wearing – a floral shirt with a large rounded collar and a hair style which for him could have passed as bouffant. Jan commented on his fixed smile which emanated no *joi de vivre* – merely a pose regularly performed, a smile for the camera and no one else.

Then from a hardback copy of an early *Biggles* adventure fell a steel disc, a DVD, in a thin paper wrapper. Jan seized it in triumph with a resounding "Yes" and examined the scrawled writing, written in blue maker pen, on the disc. There was a date, 2nd March 1985. Katie was shaking another copy of the boys' adventure books and two more discs fell onto the table, one marked 10th January 1988 and the other 14th February 1990. Jan made a hint of "our evening's viewing" while ploughing on for another hour where little of any consequence emerged. Finally an ancient atlas, stamped inside with Wych Elm Grammar School, revealed a purple typeface copy of a letter Danny had sent to the BBC, dated in April 1958, where he requested the corporation consider a programme specifically for "teenagers" based on "popular rock music" and shown on a Friday or, failing that, a Sunday evening, for half an hour, "utilising live artistes and a moving camera" and showing "the positive nature of teenage culture today."

As she shook the atlas again, Katie made the sardonic observation that he may have been ahead of his time but the battle over pop music on television was still being fought in their time, years later.

"He was spitting in the wind with that one – can you imagine? Televised pop on a Sunday?" Katie was saying. "Competing with Evensong?"

She did not see, at first, the faded white typescript that fell from the centre of the atlas but, as it landed on her foot she reacted, retrieved the sheet and read the faded letter. It was clearly the original, typed by Danny himself. He was still using correction fluid. Across the top he had written in pencil the word 'DISCARD' in block capitals. He had typed a reply to Miss Baines after all, referring to her letter and expressing profound grief that he had fathered a child so long ago and that she had died in such tragic circumstances. He commented on her name, Ruth, and referred to the biblical story of Ruth and Naomi, modifying the oft quoted line, "Whither thou goest, I shall go," amending to:

Where she has gone

I shall go

And where she is

She shall know me

And I shall weep tears of affection

For I knew her mother as mine.

He had ended with a brief line in French, calling the old lady Mademoiselle Baines, "my first mistress of mine." Katie translated carefully and said he was good. Jan commented that to use the word "discard" reeked of a well-paid, overcautious lawyer. The letter was dated 7th November 1988 and referred to hers written on 5th.

"And it never got there – do we give it to her sister?"

"Yes," replied Jan. "I think so."

A meal of pasta and tomatoes, liberally sprinkled with herbs, a glass of Frascati or two and a conversation where Katie recalled Jan's pre-menstrual agonies, now long gone, contrasting with her own easy passage through the menopause, and both of them stocking copious quantities of moisturiser to combat the residual dry skin, the last vestige of the battle with their bodily cycle. Then they tackled the earliest disc, which turned out to be a copy from a VHS tape with the concomitant ripples and occasional picture jumps that did not, however, diminish the content. Danny had obviously done this programme for French television, part of a series, marking 40 years since the liberation. Danny was filmed on location, in Amiens and Paris, the highlight being his description of his successful attack on the car – the two adjoining garages were still there – and his demonstration of the two shots from an updated Boys rifle. He gave his version of the aftermath and showed some emotion when he related the fate of his aunt and grandfather.

Jan was spellbound as Katie translated. Katie continually remarked on Danny's accent and pronunciation, saying it was close to perfect and that speaking French, a different character emerged in both his words and his body language, not so much softer but certainly deeper, Jan saw the resonance he had with the female interviewer.

"It is important to him that she believes him," said Jan.

Katie agreed.

"He seems so expansive," Jan went on. "What he says, rather than his personality, is the centre of attention."

"I can see the point the prison chaplain was making," Katie added. "He couldn't remember how many he shot in Paris, although he could point out locations. The Amiens incident comes over with a sense of pride."

The programme interviewed some of the local citizens, nearly all of them still living in the city, who commented on the same incident and the air attack on the prison. They agreed that the prison attack was a poisoned chalice for the city and its inmates. As for Danny's ambush there was less direct criticism but a strain of ambivalence was evident surrounding the reprisals generally and the awful outcome for the Verrier family.

Katie wrote up a verbatim translation of the 40-minute programme and Jan read through twice before retiring that night. She had been lucky in her earlier career, stories falling into her lap from acquaintances and lovers. The sense of professional jealousy still followed her around. Katie was well aware of her unpopularity among her media contemporaries. Jan wondered whether her luck was in again. This was book material rather than newsprint and any discovery of his special operations service, A James Bond to disc-jockey news headline, would have diminished the tale.

Chapter Eleven

The second disc was again a transfer from a VHS tape, readily identifiable from a running clock and fixed timer on the bottom left of the screen, plus a date, in the American style, which translated as 10th January 1988. There was no need for any linguistic translation this time. It was a series of interviews taken in Danny's home, given straight to the camera, with a female interviewer seen mostly from the rear, both of them sitting in the lounge. The room so recently dismissed as that of an old man. But now it evoked a rather warm domestic scene not dissimilar to a secular Christmas card. Danny was as Jan and Katie remembered him from his latter days on television, shorter hair, soft collars and a red three-buttoned cardigan which, contrasted with the steel grey locks, produced something of a Santa effect. It was disarming and welcoming at first but designed to frame what was then a controversial view of the history of British pop music, a view that, to their contemporary eyes, was essentially mainstream. However, its probable impact at the time it was recorded was not lost on either of them.

It was raw meat for an American audience; the interviewer, Charlene Roscoff, deviated from a prepared script and allowed Danny time to develop his theme at will with a stare straight up the lens in a tone brooking no contradiction. He made it clear that his own musical tastes were American, extolling the work of Ray Charles and of Nina Simone "long before she was used on a television commercial."

"I nearly changed the introductory chorus at *Danny's Place* from a variation of *Have you evah* to *Georgia on my Mind,* though getting a group of Wych Elm songbirds to do soul, let alone sound black at that time, would have been harder than the space race."

Charlene moved from "Danny" to "Dann – ee" in short order and asked him about his own music. "You know, what do you listen to when you're working?" Danny's pause was almost dramatic and he was clearly trying to be honest.

"Jack Hylton numbers from the 30s... Perry Como... Sinatra... Eddie Fisher... I used to dance a lot."

He drew on a cigarette and then held it at an angle upward from his head.

"And then there was Kathy Kirby, a fragile talent but pitch perfect in the manner of Doris Day. The Beatles I met a couple of times on the way up and their song writing was good in its time but, as a group, they performed better with American material. The best writer, at her best, was Jackie De Shannon."

Jan was transfixed and said to Katie that this was as she remembered him, quicker speaking, the occasional wink to the camera and the appearance, at least, of genuine thought when he spoke. Katie wondered how much of the interview was actually broadcast and then, laughing aloud, what Charlene might have made of Wych Elm. She had walked the streets in the electric golden hair, claret dress and "mauve heels to die for" and Jan wondered where she and her team had stayed.

"Manchester may have been a possibility or some five-star country converted pile in Cheshire, but I wouldn't be surprised if they'd flown up from London on a daily basis."

Both of them commented on the stack of vinyl shelved against the wall of the cottage and a pair of dustbin-sized speakers on the floor. The camera panned onto them briefly and later fixed on some ancient bone china around the room, swivelling to take a shot of silverware in a cabinet. At the time Danny was contrasting the Tamala Motown sound to that of Phil Spector, giving a crisp analysis of Motown's commercial "nous" being superior to Spector's "sense of superiority."

"The girl chorus was ditched in my establishment in 1967 and replaced with *The Happening*. Those were very good times."

"Dan-ee, are you saying Ray Charles was your favourite?"

"Sam Cooke ran him close and his rendition of *Nothing Will Change This Love* would accompany me if I were stranded in space for all eternity."

The mention of eternity spurred the interview along and Charlene referred to his Catholic faith and asked whether it gave him comfort. This was clearly outside the original parameters of the agreement and Danny seemed to wince a little before regaining his composure and fixing his eyes to the camera.

"We inhabit a random world which can show kindness and cruelty in the blink of an eye and comfort is largely a matter of perception. I believe we pay for our conduct in this life and I hope for little beyond it. We do kid ourselves, we Catholics, identifying our services and parishes with ancient times. Most of the stuff Catholics gabble about is nineteenth-century nonsense dressed up to be older than it really is. There's little difference in American Protestantism, except raptures, and cities on hills are even younger. There's a lot of spiritual adolescence about and it can be dangerous if taken too seriously, especially by politicians and broadcasters."

"So then, are you saying you despair of the world?"

"No," replied Danny. "I am saying we shouldn't listen too much to professional religious types. It only encourages them. Fear God and sit light to his representatives on earth. After all, they were born like the rest of us and didn't fall ready-made from heaven with wings and a halo, though they might encourage that thought to their own or their friends' benefit."

Charlene changed the subject and mentioned Danny's status of eligible bachelor. Was there no love in his life? Or are you so private as to keep your life in a secluded place?

"She is good," said Jan, staring hard at the screen.

"He's drawing on the cigarette again," replied Katie, watching with an intensity and curiosity to match Jan's own.

"When I was young, I had *une amie* and repeated the experience, with all its frailties and necessary compromises, in wartime. Since then such things have been like a gossamer sheen, experienced briefly and always at inopportune times. I've never had to pretend. I know what love is. It can't be bought at the corner shop." He gave a smile before continuing. "It resembles a gem found by a country pathway, immediately noticeable, not to be ignored and far from common. The gem is often small and can slip through your fingers and never be seen again, even though you know it lies near in the grass somewhere. I doubt whether it is ever a possession, for anyone, but it may be found again, a glimpse beyond the ordinary lusts of temporary enjoyment."

It was Charlene's turn to ponder briefly. Jan commented on her obvious awareness that Danny had been revelatory in a coded way, as though he were talking to himself but allowing an audience to listen.

Charlene suddenly seemed to feel a time constraint and asked some questions on his family, including his mother "to whom, people tell me, you are devoted." Danny let the comment pass, other than mentioning his mother's age and long widowhood.

Katie observed that it should be an easy task to contact Charlene and the American organisation to establish when and how much of the material had seen the light of day. Jan indicated she was ahead of her.

"Can you imagine the phone calls, letters and time needed to do this back in the 80s?"

"I was helping you. I don't have to remember. Just think of the three days in that convent in York, going through a school archive, returning home with sore knees and a cold closer to pleurisy."

The final disc contained what appeared to be a black and white home movie, transferred to videotape and copied to DVD format by someone either inebriated or suffering a chronic nervous condition. It was essentially a tour of *Danny's Place* early in 1969 where the maestro himself described the growth and development of this, his first business. The film jerked merrily along, Danny's voice varying in tone and pitch and had a huge reliance on him pointing things out for the camera, rather like a holiday film which had lost its original meaning and subsequently acquired an importance for what the camera inadvertently picked up in the background.

Jan identified an old school friend cleaning glasses in the bar, the mother of another sweeping the dance floor and, in a street scene outside, she saw her late uncle, her father's younger brother, walking along the pavement and carrying a shopping bag which he swung along like a clock pendulum as he strode away from the camera.

"The glass cleaner is Gary Lamb," said Jan. "Haven't seen him in years. Later that year his girlfriend disappeared in strange circumstances and hasn't been seen since."

"What happened?" asked Katie, aware that Jan rarely used the word *strange* in any way lightly.

Jan described the received story. He and his long-term girlfriend Jill Watton had attended a house party in Rovington village and walked back toward Wych Elm just after 11pm. They took a short cut down Hawes Path, an old footpath which, after about half a mile, developed into Hawes Drive, a small cul-de-sac of seven houses. Jill lived with her parents in the second semi on the right. Her grandma, on her mother's side, lived in the adjoining semi. There was nothing unusual in taking that route, even in the dark. There was a bright moonlight and they knew the path well. Jill used to ride her pony up and down the path and among the trees for its evening exercise. It was stabled in Hawes Farm, just beyond the tree line and no more than 200 yards from her home. It was a comfortable middle-class existence for her, while Gary's background was more prosaic. He lived two miles beyond the town with his mother and father, a housewife and engineer fitter at the railway works. It was a normal walk home, except the new motorway was under construction that year and the road bed cut straight across Hawes Path in a flat v-shaped channel. A footbridge was under construction, but at that time, unfinished. The two of them crossed the soft clay core at the bottom of the slope, their feet sinking and restricting their progress. Gary veered to the left to find firmer ground, looked back and Jill was gone.

"Vanished into thin air was the only way to describe it," said Jan. "You know, even by torchlight, as the local police, Gary and her Dad searched the area it was clear her footsteps had suddenly stopped in the clay, with no sign of forward or backward progress."

"What happened to Gary?" asked Katie, intrigued by the story.

"He was an ordinand for the Church of England and clever – three A-levels in Latin, history and religious knowledge achieved the following summer. He did his degree, became a vicar somewhere and slipped off everyone's radar. The police interviews were intense. They felt he knew more than he was saying. Her parents never recovered – the loss of their only child – but neither of them blamed Gary. It was and remains a mystery."

"And he sat three A-levels six months after that?" said Katie.

"His own family stood by him. But inevitably he changed a bit. From being an odd sort of ordinand who was into pop music and parties, he rather drew into himself."

"Did he ever marry?" Katie asked, with a quizzical expression on her face.

Jan surmised he had, but could not recall any detail and added that he rarely returned to Wych Elm afterwards and was certain both his parents were dead. She could not recall seeing him anywhere since his departure for university – in print, online or on the flesh.

"Well," commented Katie. "If he worked for Danny his views may be worth listening to, assuming we can find him."

Jan concurred.

A month passed while Jan corresponded with Charlene Roscoff by email and then had a series of meetings with Chris Babbage, Danny's solicitor, at his offices in central Manchester. It was conveniently four hundred yards from her apartment and, while initially unproductive, the meeting began to engender some trust on both sides, albeit rather an imbalanced trust due to Chris's father's dictum that no journalist was ever to be taken at face value and to "make the buggers pay up front." Eric, the father, had been the Hird family's legal man for nearly 50 years. He had started off with a one-man practice in Wych Elm, expanding to a three-partner office in Bolton and, 20 years on, a seven partner business in Manchester which employed 40 staff and retained the offices in Wych Elm and Bolton. He had also added a Spanish office in Malaga in the early 80s to deal with the sale and rental of retirement properties in Spain, the white pensioner business, plus child custody and desertion. Chris had worked there for three years before taking over the whole firm when Eric retired, aged 70, living in a Scottish castle in the rolling fields near Auchinleck. He was still listed as a consultant, even in his 90s and kept regular contact with the Chief Accountant.

Katie had returned to London for a couple of weeks to cover some domestic matters and, on receipt of a significant retainer from Jan's own bank account, undertook two appointments with two elderly ladies in Wych Elm, who were formerly on the domestic staff at *Danny's Place. She also spent* one full day in Durham where Gary Lamb was found to be living, recently retired from a university lectureship but retained as an associate research fellow in the school of medieval history. He was still listed as a priest of the Church of England but there was no record of him having any parochial responsibility beyond a three-year tenure of a parish near Basildon in suburban Essex which had ended in 1986.

The train glided into Durham station, atop a stone viaduct with a view of the old city to the east. Katie had come up from London on a drizzle of a dark morning, which had developed on the journey north to something resembling an Arctic expedition. She had never been to Durham before, but had passed by often enough on visits to Edinburgh and was aware of the dominant vista of the Norman Cathedral and castle. The view on this day – through sleet and forked lightning, clouds of dark grey, white and black rolling like the North Sea from whose

223

direction they came – gave an eerie ambience to what was still recognisably a former large mining town.

The chatty taxi driver drove through the slushy streets from the lower town into the old city proper, dominated by the shadows of the cathedral, depositing her by the north door and allowing a brief run into the still interior and across to the cathedral café where their initial assignation was to take place. Gary Lamb was waiting, sipping strong breakfast tea. He rose from the modernist table to show her to a curved modernist chair, proceeding to order coffee for her at the same time. As arranged, he was wearing a green Barbour jacket, opened to reveal an open-necked check shirt. She wore a red coat with a plain white scarf and was carrying a polka dot umbrella.

"Lovely to meet you," said Gary, lightly shaking her hand. Katie noticed the trace of Lancashire accent in the way he pronounced the word 'lovely' and remembered a similar trait, with vowels, accorded to Sir Robert Peel in the nineteenth century by those who met him. She had noticed this pronunciation with Jan in their earlier days but its appearance was far more a rarity now. They sat opposite each other and spoke sparingly as Kate's coffee arrived.

"Jan sends her best wishes," said Katie. "She would have come herself but the book she is planning, on Danny Hird, is proving a legal nightmare. She is in yet another meeting today, trying to access his papers."

"I'd be surprised if there were many of those," Gary replied. "I cannot help but feel this tome is coming 10 years late. Our generation may have a passing interest in him but the younger ones would need an additional primer explaining who he was. He rode the teenage market twice and earned a lot of cash. It couldn't be done today in any way resembling his methods."

"Did you know him well?"

Gary launched into a stream of conscious narrative where he was visibly striving for accuracy and the use of the correct words. He painted a picture of a man driven by money, watching every penny in the business and moving suitcases of cash around to avoid "Her Majesty's inspectors." Danny was free with his enigmatic advice to his younger employees and was intrigued by Gary's ambition to "take the cloth." He took his own Catholic faith seriously and remembered him saying that "any real power should be taken seriously, no matter how strange, sentimental or silly. But, once the power is gone, that's it, leave it." Gary also mentioned his turn of phrase, at least at that time. These words were never used on television but were a regular feature of his everyday speech.

"It was very like my own father, words such as *cheerio* and *courting, one over the eight, bloke* and a word like *book* was rhymed with *hook*."

Katie asked him about Danny's attitude to women. Gary stifled a smile, crossed his brown cords and revealed a pair of well-worn walking boots as he leaned back in the chair. He refocused and, looking directly at Katie for the first time, declaimed, slowly:

"Jan fancied him. She did a school magazine interview with him hanging on his every word like a limpet. Trouble was, she wasn't his type. He liked them to be young and dizzy, for temporary entertainment, either in his office or in his car. He drove them up into the wilds of Rovington in his Ford Pilot and showed them the ways of field and forest, his words. Or, as he made clear, especially in his later days, his eye fell on older, sophisticated and essentially feminine women, better if they are safely married, for more interesting, long term liaisons in good hotels or accommodating premises where the ways of field and forest can be developed accordingly. He had a reputation, but in his own way was highly selective and he made one point very clear. His big car, the Armstrong Siddeley Sapphire, was never used other than for transport and publicity."

Katie told him she concurred with his view on Jan and asked about Danny's family. Gary could say very little beyond what was already known. He referred to Madam Hird as having been a local character, well respected and known *about* rather than well known. He said that his time in *Danny's Place* was very much in its latter days and felt he had not seen it at its best. Indeed, his trouble, as he put it, started there. He had worked around the bar area in 1969 and 1970 before leaving for Oxford and had taken Jill Watton there a few times in 1969 before her disappearance in November that year.

"Jan gave me some of this background," said Katie, reassuringly.

"Danny was superb at this time. He spoke to my Dad and paid the fees for the solicitors, *Babbage & Co*, to help me."

For the first time, Katie realised that although Gary Lamb appeared insouciant, in his eyes were clear signs of someone still in the throws of an emotional kicking. He sensed her sympathy and visibly dropped his guard, ploughing on with the story. His language slipped into an increasing cascade of mild swear words, a sure sign of frustration and stress in what was essentially a flowery character much amused by his own episodic shrewdness. He lacked hair on top but wore what remained fairly long, to the extent it curled at the side. Designer spectacles framed tired eyes which only fully illuminated when he told a story against himself. He had been pleased when Jan had suggested Katie for this interview, not wanting to cover old ground involving schooldays and the disappearance of Jill. Yet with this stranger, similar in age but presenting herself much younger, he allowed himself to release feelings long secreted in the recesses of his mind.

While it was true he had scored a phenomenal first in his Oxford degree, showing a felicity for Latin translation rarely seen in his generation, he had gone off to theological college in Cambridge assured of a starred ecclesiastical career. Ordained into the Ely diocese, he had spent five years as a curate of the university church, staying on to embed a new incumbent while his original mentor had gone to be a bishop. Taking the best advice, he had read part three of the Cambridge Tripos, thus acquiring an additional first-class degree, and begun a doctoral thesis on the writings of William of Ockham. His tutor remarked to all and sundry that in 30 years he had not known anyone as adept with "medieval dog Latin," adding, "had we had a war on, Lamb would be breaking enemy codes left, right and centre."

Then, according to Gary's narrative, things began to change. A senior curacy in Manchester seemed to be leading nowhere. No offers came for college chaplaincies and anything he applied for seemed to run into sand.

"I'm as sure as I can be that something on Jill's disappearance was on a file somewhere, on the lines of either *take care* or *potential trouble*."

He described how he had met his first wife, Marianne Carson, while at Cambridge. She was a research student in English literature. They married in 1974. He was curate of the university church while she studied for her doctorate. She stayed on while he went north in 1980 to Manchester. They had a daughter named Molly in 1979 and Marianne stayed with him in Manchester for a year, before returning to Cambridge with Molly and completing her own thesis.

By this time, Katie and Gary were walking in the cloister as the Durham rainstorm battered itself against the ancient stonework. They skipped out of the gate, across the narrow street and into Gary's college where he was working on a new translation of the works of Duns Scotus for the university and an American academic publishing house. As they walked, opened the front doors, ascended and descended stairs in narrow corridors – the Durham colleges, at least the older ones, tended to be linked Georgian houses with odd extensions at the back – Gary continued his narrative unabated.

"Molly? Shades of Molly bloody Bloom! Marianne got a university lectureship and eventually a fellowship, leaving me to find a church living down there." He went on, "Bugger all. I finished up in a 50s vicarage on a council estate in Essex, the nearest I could get to Cambridge, seeing her half a dozen times in five years while she converted to Catholicism and had Molly learning Irish dancing from the age of five. You know the sort of thing, dancing and kicking your feet with your arms fixed to your side, as though you have a stair rod stuck up your arse."

Gary went on to describe the eventual divorce, she taking a professorial appointment in London in 1988 and living with a hotel chef. They had eventually married and Gary meanwhile resigned his living and worked briefly at a research institute in Rome. He returned to the UK in 1990 and lectured in classics for 20 years at Leeds before retiring and taking a part-time position in Durham.

"Do you see your daughter?"

"Twice in 35 years. She apparently operates a nursery in south London. You know the type of thing, a converted shop called *Little Demons* or *Little Gitz*. You know well enough, the sort of thing where allegedly hardworking families leave their offspring for the day. It's probably the biggest growth industry at the moment. Baby dumps."

By this time Katie was seated in his office, an L-shaped storage area with one window – an ill-fitting plastic frame enveloped by an old Venetian blind.

Gary produced a manila file from a desk drawer and handed it to Katie, saying it was a chronological list of all he could remember about Danny Hird during his time in Wych Elm. The original plan had been for another meeting in the evening to record his recollections but he now demurred, saying it would be a waste of time.

"You are staying at the County Hotel overnight? It's just down the lane over the bridge. Don't bother with dinner, come to us and meet my new wife. Shall we say 7.30?"

Katie felt their whole conversation had been one of gradation, three steps, and having surmounted two she was being allowed further into his court of confidence. She took the slip of paper he handed to her.

"Get the hotel to provide a taxi. We live on the Western Hill. It is a hill, by the way. At our age it's an iron lung sort of thing, or in my case a bus."

They parted at the oak front door and Katie walked, under her umbrella and holding her overnight bag, through the damp streets of grey stone and brown brick, to a uniform hotel which boasted river views and, due to lack of competition, London prices to match. Her room was of that type which, while being functional, could be anywhere at all, Durham, Durban or Damascus. The rain had finally begun to ease so, having showered, changed into jeans and warmer top clothes she ventured out again. She sat on a public seat on Palace Green and looked at the file Gary had provided. Apart from the first item there was nothing on the three closely-typed A4 pages that was not already known, at least in one form or another.

She called Jan on her iPhone, describing the meeting and saying she would contact a friend and academic at UCL to get any non-internet background on Gary himself and on his former wife, Marianne Carson. Jan recognised the name, certain she had been on the staff at either King's or Royal Holloway in the 80s. She was more intrigued by a name mentioned, Curtis Mead, a black Jamaican member of the London underworld, a man who had blossomed in West London for a few years in the late 60s and 70s after the celebrated gangster firms like the Krays, Richardsons and others of their ilk had been corralled into prison. This was Jan's original stamping ground in her early years in journalism. She knew who Mead was and felt intrigued that Gary had provided a photograph.

"If it is him, I'll know, and if I'm not sure I can find someone who can tell me."

Katie retreated to a city-centre coffee bar and spent some time looking at the photograph and what Gary had to say:

The first time I saw Danny, knowing who he was, on the platform of Wigan North Western station in April 1967. I was 15, 16 the following December, a train spotter catching a train to Crewe. It was the morning Windermere to London train and it clattered into platform 5, hauled by a filthy Stanier Black Five steam loco, poorly maintained, leaking steam from every orifice and sounding like a bag of rusty spanners. Nothing unusual then, as the steam stock was hardly being serviced at all, pending full dieselisation at the north end of the system and electrification to the south.

I produced my camera to catch a shot of this wreck, pounding and wheezing along with its 12 coaches; I clicked the shutter as it passed me.

At the same time Danny Hird appeared from behind me, crossing over toward the train. He had been standing with this well-made black guy, who walked with him, both wearing expensive suits and their heads close together in a controlled but angry conversation.

Danny is wagging his index finger into the black guy's face and the black guy looks as though he is about to bite it off.

It was only about ten years ago that I dug out this out with my other old rail pictures to copy and send to a magazine and realised that the black guy was Curtis Mead. He was a convicted murderer, sentenced to life at the Old Bailey in 1979 and was himself murdered in

*prison in 1990 – drugs or something - and the memory of
the day simply clicked into place.*

*When I worked at Danny's club two years on I never
mentioned it to him.*

The print was clear black and white; it was definitely
Danny Hird. Katie would ask about this over dinner,
while meeting his *new* wife. Further calls and messages
found Katie on her third coffee talking to a friend in
London, recently retired from teaching French literature
at UCL. The hunch Jan had about Marianne Carson was
correct. She had served as a judge for two major literary
prizes and held senior positions in two of the London
colleges, but had married a chef from one of the premier
London hotels and retired early. She lived in Kent. Her
daughter Molly owned at least two children's nurseries.

A brief walk along the river path saw Katie back at
the hotel, taking a nap before preparing for dinner *chez*
the Lambs. She made a mental note of points needing
attention and had the hotel arrange a taxi for 7pm.

Suitably refreshed and pomaded the taxi picked her
up on time. It was the same driver who had driven her
from the station. He was even more chatty, asking where
she came from. Katie explained where she was going
and handed him the details.

"Eeh, my God," laughed the driver. "This is the prof
we know as Tommy Cooper."

"Tommy Cooper?"

"Aye. He wears a fez when he's out at night. Not a red one mind, it's black. His wife must be half his age, Indian or Arab type. She dresses in silk, long dark hair under a veil thing. She's a stunner."

On arrival at the Lamb household, Gary was waiting at the door with his wife. The driver's description was accurate, although subsequent conversation and closer scrutiny put Aabirah's age just beyond 40, but she could easily have passed for 10 years younger. Katie noticed the black tarboosh sitting on the hall table.

Over their meal of lamb (at the Lambs!) and rice, with an aroma of spices based on coriander, the conversation was relatively easy, although Aabirah was both deferential and watchful as far as her husband was concerned, obviously showing some hints of distrust regarding Katie herself, or her motives, in the very early stages, but quickly accepting there were no hidden agendas nor dark avenues afoot. Gary went through stages of voluble bonhomie followed by considered silences as Aabirah recounted her story of a peripatetic family life, initially in Istanbul, then Abu Dhabi, then Mumbai and, following a brief marriage ending in a talaq divorce, she had trained as a pharmacist in London and was now employed at the local hospital in a senior capacity. She had one deep regret and this was clearly the emotional hurt that brought them together. It was the absence of her son, Aadheen, brought up by her husband's family following their separation. He was now in his 20s and working within his father's business.

Gary was able to state his certainty regarding Curtis Mead, saying later photographs in newspapers and television had brought back the memory of the chance encounter on Wigan station. The train had stopped at Warrington, Hartford and Crewe, where Gary had left the train, but he had been on the station for 20 minutes before making his way to the two locomotive depots in the town. Both Danny and Curtis had gone on. The next stops were at Watford Junction and London Euston.

"They were two compartments along from me, in the same carriage. I saw both of them sitting opposite each other when I got off at Crewe. So they both went on to London, or were flying."

"Flying?"

"Yes," explained Gary. "At that time, Watford Junction was used as a connecting stop for Heathrow."

"I see," said Katie. "Were they carrying any luggage?"

"I didn't see any."

"Hmm."

The conversation moved on through a fresh fruit desert and while Aabirah drank orange juice and Katie nursed a glass of Italian white wine, Gary was progressing through a bottle of malt whisky and a bowl of nuts. He slid onto the topic of Jill Watton again, revealing that a Lancashire detective had visited him in Leeds early in 1979, going over the same ground as before.

"He was polite, in a disinfected sort of way, looking for variations in my story and trying to establish what Jill had been wearing. It turned out that a body had been found in central Manchester, under an old car park which was being cleared to allow an extension to an estate agency. A part of a nylon dress and a plastic handbag had been found with the skeletal remains. As far as I know it's still unsolved. I began to wonder if I'd be interviewed after the emergence of every buried corpse in the north. But that was the last."

"At the time," Gary snorted an ironic laugh, "Mr Sutcliffe was running round those parts wielding a hammer. He killed at least 13 women and attacked heaven knows how many more. I wondered whether they had me down for that."

Katie noticed the frequent stops in the conversation when Gary explained allusions, metaphors and irony that Aabirah struggled to fully comprehend. Her own contribution showed her mastery of concise, scientific English and exhibited a wide vocabulary, but she seemed to find certain types of humour and irony awkward as she inducted them as literal statements, making sense in themselves, but appearing disconnected from the flow of the conversation. When this happened she looked directly at her husband and he would hold her hand and explain in a low voice using examples with which she was familiar.

"I have never been happier than I am now," Gary declaimed, after imbibing a large draught of malt. Aabirah certainly understood that; she glanced at Katie with a hint of triumph in her demeanour and allowed her face to show a glowing smile.

"I notice you are still officially listed as a priest in the Church of England," said Katie.

"You could best describe my views as a sceptic – of most things – but an Anglican one. Evensong in the cathedral still inspires me but then a glass of malt can have a similar effect. I drive Aabirah to the local mosque on Fridays and wait in the car. I even tried Roman Catholicism for a month or two, back in the 80s. Ghastly talentless singing, trips to places of alleged apparitions, Celts with a chip on either shoulder coupled with an undue deference to emotionally-stunted men – no, not for me."

"Are you asked to do marriages for friends?"

"Not recently. I don't advertise my clerical status."

Katie left shortly before midnight, same taxi firm, different driver. As the car accelerated under the railway viaduct, making rapid progress to the hotel, the driver – from his accent probably Polish – smiled to himself and then began to chuckle.

"The professor who saw you off, we call him Tommy Cooper. He wears a fez. Ha! Ha!"

Chapter Twelve

Jan exhibited several aspects of a singular life. She had not always been entirely single, but her life was one of singular aims and attitudes even when she shared her life, however temporarily, with someone else. It was a life lived in compartments, each compartment having a group of helpers. There were few links between each set of helpers and as time had gone by she had lost touch with some of them and some, by accident or design, had lost touch with her. She would be the first to admit she used people, but was reluctant to admit a close affection for any of them, although she clearly had for some. Katie fell into that category. Jan was a successful journalist when she recruited her old university friend on a complex case of wartime and Soviet spying back in 1979. Katie was teaching French in a private school attached to an acting and visual arts academy in north London and they had spent two of Katie's holiday breaks collecting information, collating it, travelling and interviewing before it had developed into something far more detailed and compromising than was apparent in its initial profile. The book Jan eventually wrote had been nominated for various prizes and Katie had been acknowledged as a major contributor to the finished work.

Much of what had been done then could, today, have been done with electronic equipment from a desk, and more recent revelations had drawn Jan to consider a new updated edition of *the Hess and Hamilton Story*, with more pictures and larger print, for the 2011 Christmas market. That was still be a possibility but the Danny Hird story was acquiring a momentum of its own and delving back into the 60s, to any depth, was going to need some old-fashioned knowledge collection and extensive legwork. The internet could take some of the strain but the memories of real individuals, the experience of older hands and an eye for linkage was still essentially a person-to-person affair.

Jan's helpers in this regard were her old editor Ben Fokker, retired, in his mid-70s and living in Norfolk; and Wesley Rhodes, aged 95, the doyen of security correspondents and now living in a retirement complex in a south London suburb. These two were demi-gods in her time as a successful, monetarily at least, freelance journalist. Katie had used both of them for the Hess book and the results of Katie's foray among the Lambs in Durham had indicated a need for her to do some digging into the past, especially where Curtis Mead was concerned. It was at this point that Katie expressed her desire to be actively involved in the eventual write-up of this story and to receive rather more than expenses and a mention in the preface.

Taken aback at first, Jan wondered whether she was losing her sense of perception. Katie had thoroughly enjoyed ploughing an information furrow in the past and had not intimated any rancour or jealousy in not being credited in the final outcome. Maybe now it was her age and maturity. Passing elation was no longer enough and recognition was sought, not for publicity but for her own sense of esteem. Jan had, she hoped, managed to hide her discomfort at Katie's proposal of joint authorship and royalties. Jan had simply said she would contact her agent who would, naturally, speak to the publisher on these matters. It was when Katie said she would appreciate some confirmation in writing or, at the very least, by email, that Jan realised how serious this had become.

It caused Jan to reflect, not for the first time but in greater depth, how far she had allowed these friendships and contacts to whither; the long delays in speaking, writing or just greeting had rendered these relationships into a basic commercial arrangement. She arranged to see Ben Fokker and Wesley Rhodes herself, the first being a huge personal inconvenience involving a five-hour drive to Norfolk's alleged champagne coast and an expensive overnight stay in a rustic hotel. The journey down was marred by delays and constant heavy commercial traffic, leaving Jan's mind to ponder and wonder about the Katie she knew.

Both of them had gone to UCL in 1970, Jan graduating in 1973 and Katie the following year to allow for her year in France spent at the provincial university at Nantes. Katie had lived at home with her mother in Hampstead – the type of mother who was in constant competition with her daughter, in clothes, make-up and, very occasionally, men. Katie's father had left when she was five, remarried and lived out in the country, breeding dogs. Her mother had acquired a succession of boyfriends, few of whom stayed the course for more than a year and Katie herself had returned from France with an aspiring actor who, after starring in two dog food commercials, broke off their engagement and returned to France to an existing wife and family. Her son, Anthony, had survived this environment and even Katie had to admit, her mother had brought him up well. Katie had referred to her French lover for years afterwards as "Rene the Rat", a name Anthony gave him, referencing a television puppet of a similar name.

Her father had died in 1981, leaving her a small legacy and a tiny flat in Chelsea. Katie had lived in the flat ever since. Her mother resented Katie owning the flat, as she had been unaware of its existence and for some impenetrable reason felt it should have been left to her. Katie had taught for eight years and then joined a commercial arts business for a further five; she was elected to parliament in 1987, having married Daniel Wade two years earlier and losing him, one step ahead of the sheriff, in 1992. She had last heard of him in a new housing development in Florida. She fought the 1992 election and scraped home, but lost by a mile in 1997.

241

She lived on her wits and her MPs pension. She had almost remarried in 2001, having lived with a handsome but nerdy beau in Spain, slightly less than half her age but a successful science fiction writer, then fashionable and very much in demand. Now, 10 years on, her mother dead for two years and a large fortune from the sale of the family home, she was totally secure. Jan decided it was all about esteem, pride even, or just possibly regret; certainly not money. Ben Fokker lived in Walsingham in a small cottage. He had moved there some three years earlier from a large house nearer the coast. His wife had died suddenly and unexpectedly from some kind of blood disorder. It had been a huge shock to him and their four daughters as they were a close family, despite the girls now firmly away. Esme, the eldest, was a lawyer with a London firm, specialising in commercial law. She was married with two children of her own. Naomi lived with her longstanding boyfriend in Dublin where they owned a small shop and restaurant. Eve was unmarried and a freelance journalist in London, while Angela lectured in psychology at one of the London colleges and was married with a child.

The girls were the centre of his universe while editing the *South London Times* and his devotion to Mary, his seemingly indestructible wife, was legendary among those who knew him in the throws of long hours, irregular days, missed meals and a propensity to smoke quantities of cigarettes. He was known to have had up to four lit, in different ash trays, within 20 yards of his tobacco-hazed office. Whisky was the standard cure for colds and influenza, dispensed in teacups and consumed on the move. Yet here he was, aged 74, still with a stroke-grey complexion, living in a picturesque village and pottering around a paved rear garden, surrounded by plant pots and preparing roses and geraniums for another season.

Jan had drawn up in her new black Porsche, hardly engaging the brake before the passenger door opened with Ben leaning in sporting a peacock-blue jacket and brown trousers. He was attempting to bring a smile to his funereal features, his black hair gone, white stringy locks swirling round his head. Jan hadn't actually seen him for 12 years but she had kept in telephone or written communication – postcards and greetings cards – over the time between.

"You look well," he said. "How's the hotel?"

"You look different," she replied, trying to smile away her surprise at his aged appearance. "The hotel is fine but damned expensive."

"The pub restaurant you passed in the next hamlet to yours charges £50 for a bowl of soup. The whole village is a second home haven for London media types. They keep it exclusive by pricing ordinary folks out. They're a supercilious lot, most of them with second or third spouses, insecure, with ghastly children in tow."

Jan discerned the old spark in him. He may have been older but his mind functioned as she remembered it. There was never any deference in Ben Fokker. That may have been why none of the big national papers took him on. But it could just as easily been a sense of comfort on his part. He was happy where he was, supported by a strong workforce operating like a tribe; they may have bickered within but proved capable as a unit. Young journalists were driven hard but loved the atmosphere and lack of ossified hierarchy which suffocated other titles at the time.

They sat among Ben's potential flower show drinking tea, Jan expressing her surprise at his abandonment of tobacco and he holding forth on her easy life, based on his observation of few lines on her face. She had already apprised him of the nature of her visit and produced Gary Lamb's photo from her briefcase.

"Yes, that is Mead. He's younger there, in that picture, than most will remember him. Like some of the older London criminals, he was, as they say today, gay. Then he was known as a black poof. He was dangerous, nasty, used rape as a means of control and intimidation, but very clever. He managed male brothels giving homosexual policemen access, female brothels using girls brought in from the homeland, Jamaica, and invested in other people's drug operations. He was also a key drugs informer for Scotland Yard."

Jan had been aware of rumours surrounding Mead's sexuality and contacts within the police and judiciary but had never had the details spelled out before.

"Danny Hird was never mentioned in connection with Mead although he did have pop music links, but then most of the serious underworld did in the 60s. They fed off each other. Gangster *chic* was more common then, endemic among young pop singers. Each one was seen as giving the other a sort of respect. Laughable, but it still goes on."

Jan immediately saw a link with Alan Thompson, although Ben knew nothing of the case, simply observing that disappearances then and now were far from uncommon.

"Hird was really a lightweight on the London scene," he went on. "He was thought of as a northern type, grasping and a bit chippy. No one tried to mess with him. I never met the man but those I knew, who did, agreed there was an air of menace about him. He was nothing like the figure he presented on television. One guy said he was like a policeman on point duty, doing one job carefully but watching elsewhere all the time."

Ben's narrative continued as if to a drum beat, saying that Curtis Mead was rumoured to be a supplier of boys to the wealthy and the famous – not, as he made clear, necessarily the same thing. He had some connections in the pop scene, not so much for his own entertainment but for the ready money it provided. It was rumoured he had access to more cash than your average bank manager.

"A lot of the big stars then were like babies when it came to finance and management. Most were badly educated or as thick as two short planks. One girl wrote £2,500 in cheques in one afternoon and couldn't understand why Lloyds confiscated her cheque card. She presents retro shows on the second channel now and was a judge on a couple of talent shows last year."

Mead's organisation was mainly of West Indian extraction -- hard, smiling and vicious. But, Ben continued with a laugh in his voice, offering an example of old habits dying hard.

"He wouldn't employ or work with anyone from Barbados. He said they couldn't be trusted!"

Jan and Ben drove out to the coast where they walked with a salty wind in their faces, reminiscing about earlier times. They shared a portion of fish and chips in a car park, swapping anecdotes and Ben telling some old jokes. Then suddenly a serious air overtook him and he brought up the security interest in her work.

"The *Hess* book, you mean?"

"Yes, Jan," he answered. "I know you pulled a few punches and kept back the odd name and the odd fact or three. They let you publish. But…"

He leaned deliberately into her face and wagged his vinegar-tipped finger toward her face.

"Don't think they've forgotten. They will retain a file on you till long after you are gone."

"Why do you bring this up, Ben?" Jan expressed a little alarm. "Was Mead working for them?"

"Damned if I know," replied Ben, looking beyond the car park and out to sea. "It wouldn't surprise me. But your friend Danny had a few vague whispers about him in that area. He definitely did hush-hush stuff in the war and his name cropped up in the early 50s. That came from an old friend, mentor and irritant at the *Evening Star*. Wesley may know more. I'm just saying… no, I'm warning you, to take care. There's nothing these people wouldn't do to protect their secrets…"

Ben had a coughing fit and recovering, added, "From us."

They returned to Walsingham with Ben in a calmer frame of mind, insisting he show her the Catholic shrine outside the village. He described the coach loads of "so-called pilgrims," either children on a day out or middle-aged parish groups, each trying to like Celtic fringe music and attempting to be pious in the countryside, desperately trying to show it on their faces. Some didn't bother, sitting with cans of drink in the sun. The Church of England's version in the village, often described as more Roman than Rome, was more like the theatre – highly organised with a shared series of assumptions designed for "increasingly elderly queens and their temporary camp followers." The place is crammed with cars and coaches in the summer, but the pace of everything is tolerably slow."

Jan spent the night in her hotel and drove back early the following morning, unaware the Katie was calling on their security contact from the *Hess* book days. She had done her own groundwork and found Michael Davidson living in Windsor with his second wife, he in his late 70s and she in her 40s, he a beneficiary of his service pension with a huge legacy from his late father, a

London accountant. His wife Miranda managed a recruitment agency in the city; she looked the part. She treated Michael like a favoured client, taking the morning off to sit with him during Katie's arranged visit. He looked an older version of the man Katie remembered and distrusted from the past. His hair was grey and well cut; his eyes were framed by small designer spectacles, totally at odds with the large 1980s steel frames that had lodged in her memory. He wore casual, cream trousers, brown leather slip on shoes and a white open-necked shirt, offset by a maroon phone in the breast pocket. Miranda was closely made-up with well-groomed honey blonde hair, a white blouse and stylish Swiss watch clipped to her wrist.

Katie explained that she was researching the life of Danny Hird, which, as she put it, "has morphed from pop stars and girls" into something more interesting, both in his private and semi-public life" and her spartan references to Curtis Mead, the *Heim & Rhyme* agency, seemed to produce a hint of recognition in Michael's pale blue eyes.

"Anything to do with him would not have been in my remit. Hird did have a wartime file, but then so did thousands of others. He may have worked for the service post-war, but not in any division involving me. As for old pop stars, in my experience they were pretty much of a bunch. Most wanted fame, others money and a few, very much a minority, were trying to be artists. Some did do temporary work for us, but then so have hairdressers, van drivers and engineers."

Katie asked if he could help with any background material, saying she would willingly pay for his services. Or perhaps he could shoo her to people who could be of more direct assistance.

"Leave me a contact number, Katie, and if I can be of assistance in any way, I'll be in touch. You must understand, I would need to ask a few permissions first. It will take a week or so."

He then proceeded to ask after Jan, Ben Fokker and all the others who had come together in the past, particularly recalling a turgid case conference held at Manchester airport in a temporary shed. Katie remembered that morning well. A bargain was struck to protect some of the interested parties while opening the door on others, effectively determining the outline of the eventual book.

This conversation was very much a diversionary tactic, nothing Katie had not seen before and she took the view that to employ this standard ruse meant that there was something to find here, possibly in full view rather than lurking in the undergrowth awaiting a eureka moment. For Katie it was crucial she saw Davidson's face. She never expected anything as a direct result of this little chat. She was able to focus on Miranda, noticing how she also focused on her, watching her body language, making little interventions to keep Katie talking so that her husband needed to say less. The fact this was happening convinced Katie she was on the right track. Taking her leave, the only issue was whether she said anything of this to Jan.

Nothing had been said prior to Jan's visit to Wesley Rhodes a week later. His retirement home was a self-contained flat within a large suburban house, dating from around 1900, which was set in what resembled suburban parkland. The land immediately south of the River Thames had little aesthetical attributes to commend it, even in the best of times, but the flat was well maintained and much of the furnishings Jan recognised as Wesley's own. He sat in a low armchair, enveloped in an imposing red silk dressing gown, still sporting a shock of white hair and still wearing bone-framed half-moon spectacles which he either looked directly through, or, when pondering a response, peered over the top, arching an eyebrow and allowing an impish smile to adorn his face. Unlike Ben Fokker, Wesley had constant difficulties with the ladies. Married twice, he had had several short-term relationships well into his 70s, including with a Maltese air hostess and a Chinese girl skilled in the art of acupuncture. His stories were both tragic and incredibly funny, and his costs enormous, but he seemed always to land on his feet, whatever the amorous disaster.

He was quick to point out that his only vice, latterly, was sloe gin, "mainly because I've no damned choice." He added a wry comment about the nursing staff who cared for him – "Nearly all male, some a bit Nancy and the few women are buxom Africans, jolly enough, but more suited to the local rugby club."

Jan permitted herself a giggle, noting that he looked smaller and far more vulnerable, but what can be expected of a sprightly 95 year old? He was reassuringly accurate in his speech and modulation. Hopefully his memory was still good. He reminded her of staff meetings in the *Printers'* pub, saying it was four luxury flats now, a sad fate for one of the best newspaper pubs in London, probably occupied by eastern potentates and used for entertaining.

"There are limits, Jan, to sand and Sharia!"

For her part, Jan asked about his daughter by his first marriage, the service having been conducted four days after the Dunkirk evacuation, he wearing his shoddy uniform and she, of necessity, her mother's old wedding dress. The marriage had officially ended in 1946; he had been in Egypt, based in Cairo, and later Alexandria from the end of 1941. He was a stranger to his wife and daughter and although some letters had been exchanged in the 50s, by 1962 his former wife and daughter were living in Australia, his daughter graduating from Sydney University and subsequently working in an administrative capacity for the Australian Navy.

"Died last year, car accident near Adelaide," Wesley intoned, as though he were making a radio announcement. "Her mother expired just five years ago, widowed for 10 years before that. If only we knew what lay before us…"

Before Jan could commiserate, he gave a wistful look and added,

"All of my loves are gone, every one, all gone before me and here am I, last in the line awaiting the final departure. The funeral is planned, paid up in advance, with a free bar afterwards. It should induce a few to come. Mind you, alcohol is rapidly being moved into the dog house, like smoking. The powers that be are making Methodists of us all. No wonder pubs are closing and people taking to drink indoors. The predication of all this is a potentially *better* life, dictated by those who don't know what living is – Bogart was right to drink, for fear of getting up in the morning knowing it was the best he was going to feel all day."

There was a short pause before Wesley began to giggle, recalling a tour of the House of Commons in the 80s, where he was introduced to a senior Minister of State who was comatosed from drinking brandy and ginger, slumped in a chair and snoring from the left side of his closed mouth "sounding like a Labrador with flatulence."

It was at this point that Wesley's tone changed, referring to her contact with Ben Fokker and casually mentioning he had contacted him by telephone. Wesley explained how he had assured Ben that he would help, but gave him no advanced details other than what Ben already knew.

"My contacts with the service have, like my ladies, gone before me, but I still have some avenues for messages and information. It's a two-way thing."

He then proceeded to warn her, like last time, that there were matters of the greatest sensitivity surrounding Danny Hird and, in a different way, Curtis Mead. There was a file on Mead and two on Danny, each with blue tags. The significance was not lost on Jan. Like the Hess investigation, the Crown had a close interest in these people with, at the very least, reputations at stake.

"Are you telling me Danny Hird was somehow protected? It would explain a lot, but pop music and pop venues in Wych Elm are unlikely to be high on a palace priority list, unless of course, you know differently."

Wesley did not answer directly. He spoke of Danny's war service, special operations and of subsequent service post-war, saying he was highly regarded in his field, mainly due to at least two successful operations abroad and, possibly, one or two at home. His message was much the same as that from 30 years past. She was being told, not advised, to tread carefully.

"The dead keep their secrets, provided they haven't written them down and, God knows today, left electronic messages where they can be read." Wesley was intoning again. "Not that Danny was into computer technology, apparently. Except in music, of course, and that was left to others – no, he was clear in that area. In other respects, he was like me, a fondness for money and for the girls. Only, he didn't marry them. Is that the key to success with tendencies like mine?"

"His tendencies went beyond sleeping with them," Jan replied, registering her old disapproval.

"We all have them, Jan," replied Wesley. "Unless we've outgrown them, or age and health curtail them.

Moral crusades all end in hypocrisy and, let's face it, are such a bore."

"What of the children, Wesley?"

"What of them? We must protect our own, if we can. I often spoke, over a glass or three, to one of the best columnists of his time on this very issue. Mind you, he was a poor novelist. But he reckoned available boys in prep schools, boarding schools, children's homes and care homes had always been vulnerable to buggery. Girls rather less so and rarely buggery, making the risks even greater. But the number of MPs, actors and artists who were into this thing – usually with boys – across generations, each pretending the last was far worse than they were, was an unspoken truism until very recently. In fact, as you should know, *very recently indeed.* At one time some of the better-off thought it was a price worth paying for a good education for their offspring, and sending them off to school kept the house free from clutter and noise on a term-time basis with only the summer holidays to endure."

"That is disgusting, Wesley." Jan grew cool and distant.

"30 years ago you would have taken this in your stride – and you did. You seem to be suffering from a collective guilt syndrome, one that seems to be all-embracing, like a psychosis, a prism through which everything is viewed. First it was Freud, followed by or conjoined to a western Marxism and now we suffer a ghastly municipal morality based on making everyone else responsible for our own failings. Society is as much in denial now as it was then."

"Why does everyone make excuses?"

"Jan, how often have you excused yourself?"

Wesley changed tack and directed her to the army records office and the official histories of the Special Operations Executive and then began to intone on Curtis Mead. He referred back to his previous theme and was quite clear in his assessment of him – "nasty and dangerous" and one who was rumoured to provide boys for the wealthy and well-connected. His activities were almost certainly used against some of his diplomatic customers and he made a substantial sum from this sideline.

"Was Danny Hird involved?"

He was emphatic that this was Mead's work alone, operated from a number of houses around the capital and at least one in a provincial city, used by some MPs "visiting their constituencies," and some suspect, at first, funded by the government agencies. He received money from South Africa, the United States and Israel while the Arab nations paid privately. The ramifications of this series of arrangements began to fall into place, overcoming Jan's acquired scruples and revealing yet again, in her experience, how far a good story has squalor follow it around.

By the time she had shared the contents of a teapot filled with Earl Grey and Wesley had repeated an old story about Harold Wilson and his pipe, Jan was at least smiling again. Wesley directed her to a couple of younger freelance reporters who would know more on Curtis Mead and his later career, especially the odd circumstances of his demise in prison, something he knew little about, other than the usual rumours when a big guy goes down.

"Let's face it," he said, "everyone today is suspicious of everything, even natural causes. When I go I trust you'll create an air of mystery and intrigue around me. It would be comforting to know!"

Jan reflected on this little meeting for quite some time, creating several computer files and even resorting to an old-style mind map on A3 paper stuck on her kitchen wall. Her reading and emailing on the activities of the Special Operations Executive(SOE) proved interesting, but only as a back drop. It was like touring the stage after the play, knowing little of the script and only being given items deemed safe. She paid researchers to obtain army records and found far more on Danny's father and Clifford Hindle than on him. A little of this was shared with Katie who, for her part, did some research of her own. She eventually found a retired prison guard who served at the London prison which housed Curtis Mead. Over a pint in a Kentish pub, quite unsolicited, he told her that no one on duty that day believed the official story. Mead was murdered by other prisoners, three of them, all recent arrivals for various petty crimes. Mead was quietly and efficiently strangled in his cell.

"I can say with certainty," he emphasised the point by tapping the oak table, "that this was a professional job, done to order. The three were tried, sentenced and split into provincial prisons. All of them were out within three years. But I'm as sure as I can be that Mead was killed by one of them – killed to order. The other two were just chaff – distractions to confuse the issue."

A couple of sentences provided the momentum for Katie to dig further and pass nothing of this to Jan. Perhaps she should call on Davidson again. Then again, she may provide something, a morsel or two, to show good faith. It was simply a case of providing the right morsel. To govern, as they say, is to choose.

Chapter Thirteen

The black taxi pulled up smartly outside the modern building, the type of building that could be anything – a top-end hotel, a football stadium, an academy school or an art gallery. Frank Sinatra's foggy nights in London town had ended some 50 years before but the weather in the capital still had the capacity to surprise, annoy and maintain itself as a topic of general conversation; and the variations in a day, let alone a week, still discomfited visitors from the continent as well as those from further afield. The rain was pelting down and the sky's shades of grey approaching black. Highlights of sulphurous-yellow heralded beats-of-bass-drum thunder echoing in the streets, water spouting off the pavements, rattling against plate glass and plastic fittings.

The tall, languid figure emerged from the vehicle, passing a note to the driver with a deft flick of the hand; gathering a patterned raincoat around him, he burst into a sprint to the glass security doors and with the same deft movement, swiped a nondescript security card through a wall reader, thus opening the glass panels. He met a gaggle of much wetter individuals on the inside, all congregating by a Perspex unit, swiping more cards and watched over by a lithe young female wearing a charcoal uniform, a white blouse and a silver-metallic ear piece that was glinting in her left ear. She in turn was observed by two shaven-headed white males, a combined weight of some 500lb, sporting black security trousers and boots, short-sleeved blue shirts and security vests with slung SA 80 rifles, ostentatious side arms and radios.

Michael Davidson was in the damp group and noticed the arrival of Sir John Arnold Bright, recently retired chief of the service and now chairing one of the larger banks in his continuing allegiance to the nation. Bright noticed Davidson's look of recognition and before he could be accosted, spied another acquaintance, Eleanor Tate, who had done a good deal of fieldwork for him in the 60s.

"Hello, Eleanor." He smiled, walking through Davidson as if he were a shadow and leaving him spinning in his wake. "No longer disguising yourself as a hippy these days!"

"Johnny, if I had to dress as I did then, people would assume I was some kind of vagrant and pass loose change to me in the street. Speaking at my granddaughter's school last week I found myself having to explain what a hippy actually was. Just picture that, explaining hippiedom to 16 year olds. We were supposed to be talking about the Vietnam protest movement for their history project. They were polite, as you would be these days to an elderly specimen."

Bright allowed himself a smile and a brief nod around the company when they were perfunctorily ushered to a carpeted corridor followed by a cloakroom area and then, after a few minutes, into a windowless interior briefing room, air-conditioned and containing a light-wood oval table with comfortable chairs and ample room for the eight figures encouraged to sit around it. There was a word-processed agenda at every space and place names. As they organised themselves, two females arrived, sitting by the wooded door and quickly followed by a short, grey-haired man in an expensive but crumpled blue suit. He was pushing what resembled a 1950s tea trolley on castors, with paper files on the two levels. The two ladies held small electronic devices. By the wall, a computer unit produced a flickering blue screen. A young man in shirt sleeves and no tie stood discreetly by it, appearing to take no notice of the proceedings.

The group had already been briefed, personally, at home. Neither emails nor paper correspondence was envisaged in this exercise. The agenda was simply a list of names indicating the order in which they would speak. Of the eight figures around the table, five were elderly men, former employees and operatives, and one was an elderly female, Eleanor Tate, who resembled the leader of a country parish sewing committee. The men exuded a quasi-military manner, with Sir John appearing to hold an air of authority, while Davidson held himself in, determined Sir John would not have the opportunity to snub him again. Davidson sank into a deep, dark reflection. Why on earth should Sir bloody John be here, when his elder brother, Francis, had been Hird's controller in the 50s? Like others then and later, Sir John had made a pretence of being a shit while practising a sound service. Davidson now decided he was, and had been one all the time. It was a rare thing for siblings to serve in the service, though Francis' death, from food-poisoning during an operation in West Africa in the mid-60s, had rendered any security qualms redundant.

The two women, sitting at what had become effectively the head of the table, were both in their mid–30s, although to Eleanor's eye the calmer one, Anne Luscombe, would win the race to 40. She had an air of studied fluidity, listening and speaking only when necessary, usually with a smile, and giving every impression, she was doing this job willingly, having been interrupted while vacuuming the stairs. Tracey Brown, on the other hand, was driven, with a sharp eye and spoke with a hint of a West Country accent as though giving instructions to a recalcitrant horse. Anne dressed easily in a broad skirt and jacket, offset by a patterned silk scarf. Tracey wore a maroon pencil skirt, matching fitted coat, white shirt and black cravat. Her stiletto heels gave her a good five inches in height. Her stance, in her chair, was designed to cut familiarity and her clipped tone reinforced this impression to everyone, except her immediate boss. Anne addressed her formally but kindly, as one might to a favourite guard dog.

The man by the trolley gave the impression of a family retainer, from a Wodehouse novel, but when called upon – and he was never called upon directly – he provided references in the files at his disposal including dates and salient points at will. He gave the briefest of nods to Sir John and, at the outset, a more definite one to Davidson. Charles Clarkson had been archivist to the service for as long as anyone present could remember. He dealt with all the paper files with a team of four and, level with him in pay and status, Karl Dodgson, the young man by the screen, handled all electronic files with a team of two. It was rare for both Clarkson and Dodgson to be in the same room together on casework.

Without introducing herself, Tracey called the meeting to order and in a clipped monotone gave an introduction much in the fashion of a battle plan.

"Anne has a heavy schedule at present, with her time and mine focused on internal matters here in London, East Lancashire, Manchester and West Yorkshire. Karl's team are on a 24-hour mode, dealing with internet providers reluctant to reveal or curtail their access routes to murder. You will forgive me if I seem a little abrasive, it's having to spend time coping with retired journalists and matters well in the past. Nevertheless something has to be done with Miss Barnsdale and Miss Ross. The note is on the screen."

At the far end of the oval, behind where Sir John was seated, the white wall became a cinematic screen where a series of notes were printed, starting with the death of Danny Hird and the activities of Jan Dale in the past five years and, subsequently, those of Katie Ross. The print was bold and defined, enabling everyone to read the material fairly quickly. A silence fell on the gathering, broken by a further intervention from Tracey.

"It will be apparent that Miss Dale's method is to ferret around until she finds something, anything - and then, without fully understanding the facts, elicits the help and complicity of others to build a sensational story, then to publicise and benefit accordingly."

"The recent intervention of Katie Ross is rather more concerning," Anne's languid tones interposed. "Having been involved in the Hess case she has taken a much more proactive role in this one. She was aware of our presence last time and..."

"Played the game," said Sir John firmly.

"Except this time she seems to be involved in a game of her own," said Tracey, glancing at Anne who went on to show how Katie's investigation, particularly reopening the matter of Curtis Mead, was more than a little disturbing.

"You can still buy Dale with chickenfeed, her silence and elsewhere, perhaps support for her book," said Sir John. "But you think..."

"Katie Ross is a former MP. She had a tainted husband but is clear of him and still has connections of her own," Anne continued. "The number of issues arising could multiply out of control. Wesley Rhodes has been in touch with us, trying to clarify a few points and what he wanted clarifying indicated a worrying drift."

At this point, Charles Clarkson made the first of his interventions, producing three files, none of them especially thick but visibly stamped in red on the brown covers and tied with blue tags. His seemingly urbane introduction, passing the files to Anne Luscombe, developed into an unmistakeable message. Danny Hird's reputation was to be beyond reproach.

"...his war record was remarkable, successfully taking out a senior German Gestapo officer, French collaborators and, subsequently," he pointed toward the second file, "a blue operation in France. There was a later joint operation in Italy, also blue, which was a success in its aim but left a few loose ends. Danny's performance supported Madge Wells' view that he was one of the best wet job operatives on the books."

A murmur of approval cascaded around the table at the mention of Madge Wells and a few voices began to raise questions beginning in the manner of "I've always wondered..." but Clarkson gently waived them away and continued his briefing in the same even pace.

"Tattersall, our esteemed keeper of the purse, paid him his dues and he built his music business on the back of it, with some his own family money and a degree of practical resourcefulness. He was still considered for advice and backroom work in the 70s in Northern Ireland and although there was an element of a loose cannon about him, his efficiency and essential focus when on service duty was one Madge vouched for on more than occasion. She and Suzanne Carew had great faith in him, not least because he tended to listen to women rather than men, and while Frank Bright was his line control…"

"Lady Suzanne pulled his strings." Eleanor laughed, speaking far more loudly than she'd intended and cast a quick glance toward Davidson. He responded with a raised eyebrow.

"He did get into the odd scrape, but nothing overly serious, except for two latter-day instances which are now of concern to the service and beyond."

"And this is the point of the meeting." Tracey Brown tapped her screen and cast a glance around the table. Clarkson lapsed into silence.

"Danny did do some freelance work in his time, most of it irrelevant now, but he may have been involved, for personal family reasons, in a very wet job up on Tyneside in the late 80s. We know he was there at the time and was using some rather antique methods. It appeared to the service then, and now, that he was privy to the elimination of a local criminal, Mitchell, one with– then and now – a following. Please, do not respond to anything on this case, unless directed from here. The outcome was in fact positive for the local police force and, as far as we can establish, Danny's role was essentially tangential. So, be clear, respond to nothing on the Mitchell case."

There was a silence signifying a general agreement around the table, broken by Albert Henderson who had connections in the north. In a stage whisper to himself he exhaled to no one in particular,

"Christ, how old would Hird be then? Freelance, at his age? I have trouble tending my flower beds."

Tracey glanced at Anne Luscombe, and then continued in the same vein. As she spoke, Charles Clarkson assumed the role of a Savoy waiter and in one movement placed a paper file, inches thick, by her left hand.

"The second case is of a different order entirely. The details are of critical importance to us, the service as a whole, as well as the state. When I say the state, I mean all of it."

Karl Dodgson put up the monochrome, cleaned up photograph obtained by Katie Ross, clearly showing Danny Hird and Curtis Mead together. All eyes were drawn to Hird's finger and Mead's hostile expression. John Pugh sat by Davidson, threw him a glance and gripped his wooden walking stick under the table. Davidson saw his whitening knuckles. Until now Pugh had said nothing. He had been known for his dour efficiency as a controller. Davidson had held him in high regard.

"Where did that come from?" Pugh almost spat the words into the air in a clear mix of surprise and annoyance. "For years that link was kept quiet, despite the media interest both acquired. There was already a public aura around Hird which he did well to control. Yet here we are, 40 years on, right on the back foot. Where did this come from?"

Clarkson stepped in to explain. Davidson watched Pugh's grip on the wooden handle of his stick grow even more tight. His left hand was on the surface of the table and as Clarkson spoke, the index finger began to drum on the polished wood.

"None of those buildings exist today. There's no possibility of claiming an electronic montage. This is dangerous – and all down to a damned train spotter."

Sir John was nodding. Eleanor was looking at Davidson, as if for a cue, while to his left, the asthmatic voice of Robert 'Bob' Wise made a hissing contribution from his slouched position in his chair.

"The locomotive might still have been with us, but for that journey. It was allocated to Bolton depot and booked into Cowlairs Works up in Glasgow for a heavy service. It had worked through to Preston on a parcels train and was drafted up to Windermere at short notice to relieve a failed engine stuck in Carlisle. That's why this particular old wreck finished up hauling the Windermere to London as far as Crewe. It was leaking steam from both cylinders and Crewe men later said it wasn't worth repairing. It was hauled up to Carnforth a month later, sold to a scrap dealer in Rotherham and cut up the following year."

"And your point is?" said an exasperated Tracey Browne.

"If it had been overhauled, as planned, at Cowlairs," he replied, bitingly, hauling himself up with a grimace as he did so, "the locomotive would have been preserved when steam ended the following year and we could at least have argued for a doctored photo. As it is the *Heim & Rhyme Agency* is in the firing line, with every media journalist this side of the Urals potentially putting their oar in. Do we still have the coordinates for young Thompson's remains?"

"Don't worry, Bob," said Anne, trying to soothe him. "We still have a handle on this. The meeting is to establish how we keep it that way."

Clarkson cleared his throat and sipped from a water glass. He waved a hand toward Dodgson who, simultaneously, put a time diagram on the screen.

"As you can see, Alan Thompson was taken to Nathan Heim at the agency known as *Heim & Rhyme* where Danny Hird had already established a working relationship for his *protégées*. A backing group, renamed *The Motors,* followed a day later and performed several items over three days to make a claim on a recording contract. Nathan Heim was, of course, on our payroll. He had a good record in intelligence during the war as a translator. Heim was unaware of Hird being with us and vice versa. Mead worked for Heim as a rent collector for his properties in the capital and had a sideline procuring males for other males. It transpired that Mead arranged a meeting with Sir Harry Hylton Jones MP and took young Thompson to a party in Kensington. Chemical substances and alcohol were in copious supply and..."

"Alan Thompson was subject to a series of sexual attacks by Jones as well as a currently surviving High

Court Judge, a senior member of Buck House staff and someone else who was part of it, but not staff." Anne Luscombe continued the story, "I know there were rumours then, but the threat of criminal proceedings kept Mead on-side for the service. Nathan Heim was aware of the background but only some of the detail. He blamed Mead."

"It was decided to return young Thompson home, Mead driving a hired van. Thompson was semi-conscious, still affected by a varied cocktail of stimulants. As they drove north the following day a plausible story was being constructed."

"It turned into a bloody shambles," Bob Wise hissed and then started coughing. Eleanor leaned across the table with a water jug. She filled his glass.

"You are all aware I was Nathan Heim's controller. John, you had recruited Mead. Francis was away in Nigeria and you, Michael, had been given temporary oversight of Danny Hird."

"Things did get into a mess," Davidson responded. "Frank Bright should never have been sent on that Biafra thing. It was a ridiculous exercise in economy, moving people on an accountant's whim between the home and foreign service."

"Mead did prove useful," Pugh said, with an air of resentment.

"During the drive north," Clarkson continued.

"I was responsible for Nathan Heim," Bob Wise intervened. "You, Albert, were in temporary charge of Mead, while John Pugh was given a supervisory role for this operation."

"For my sins," Albert replied. Pugh kept his counsel.

"But Frank was still technically in charge of Danny," said Wise, almost in a whisper. "But he was up the bloody river, in Africa. That Biafra thing was beginning."

"And you, Sir John," Eleanor joined in, "you weren't officially Danny's control until December."

"That's true," replied Sir John, allowing himself the merest hint of satisfaction.

"But you were on the planning team," Albert replied, with an air of triumphant pleasure, without saying directly that he, Sir John, had been below the rank of John Pugh.

"I was not in any way responsible for what happened. No one was. Well, possibly Harry Hylton Jones' gang."

"Possibly?" said Davidson, relishing his moment, looking at Sir John directly.

"We can't change the past," snapped Tracey Browne. "Charles, please continue…"

"Can't we?" Albert Henderson asked, to no one in particular.

"We have before." Eleanor smiled, directing her gaze to Davidson, Pugh and Wise.

Clarkson stood to his full height and in a homiletic style delivered the proverbial brick into the calm pond.

"Thompson began to bleed, from the rear passage, slumped forward against the dashboard. Mead described a pool of blood on the front seat. He did not realise until he pulled off the M1 to check him that Thompson was dead. He removed the body from the seat and placed it in the back of the van. He used a public telephone box to contact you, Albert, and you told him to wait."

Albert nodded, but said nothing.

"You, Eleanor, were sent, fast, to Wych Elm on your orders, John, to warn Danny Hird of an imminent arrival and to make adequate preparations for the disposal of the boy's remains."

"Hird could think on his feet," said Pugh. "My only worry was that he would kill Mead too and then Harry Hylton Jones. His constituency was less than 12 miles from Wych Elm. Eleanor's job was to make sure he and Mead came here to be briefed properly."

"I was on hippy duty in Manchester, keeping an eye on weed-smoking Trotskyites," said Eleanor sadly. "Danny was utterly furious, saying he'd finish Heim, Jones and the rest. I calmed him down with the promise of compensation for Thompson's mother and said that he needed the full facts before doing anything rash. I warned him of Mead's reputation. Danny saw that as a challenge."

Her description of the meeting at the office in *Danny's Place* and the trouble she had encountered trying to get in, dressed in dirty jeans and t-shirt with hair like rats' tails. She had driven a banger of a Mini, the floor of which barely existed, to Wych Elm and had finally persuaded one of the doormen to say a code word to Danny in order to gain entrance. When they did speak she spoke of his cold fury and scathing opinion of the way the service was going.

"You mean to say they've got you, embedded in Manchester, spying on middle-class kids who think they know something about the Soviets? What a waste of time. Those kids couldn't organise a booze-up in a brewery. They'll be in parliament next, collecting their expenses and oozing salaried compassion. Clem Atlee would have told them to get off the backs of the poor."

Mead eventually telephoned Danny's private line at the club. He was in a café in Bolton. Danny had him drive to the back of *Danny's Place* at 1am. Mead was made to clatter glass bottles on the ground to give the impression of a delivery while Danny questioned him and, eventually, he peered into the back of the van to view Alan Thompson's body. Eleanor was watching the proceedings with Cliff Hindle standing by her.

"This is a total mess, Cliff," Danny was saying. "The body needs to be buried now, at the back of the pike. Cliff, get some shovels from the quarry store, take the Ford, and come back here. Mr Mead will then follow you in this van. Once he's finished digging, at least four foot, the van has to be burnt out."

A full petrol can was produced from the club garage.

Eventually a cortege led by Cliff Hindle in the Ford Pilot – Mead in the hire van and Eleanor driving the Mini behind with Danny in the passenger seat – progressed up narrow unmade roads to the rough moorland behind Angle Pike. Danny had Mead dig the grave at gunpoint, producing what Eleanor described as a small pistol when Mead complained of tiredness and expressing it with a threat to Danny and Cliff's wellbeing. Once the remains were in the earth Mead made to burn the van.

"Are you bloody stupid, or what?" said Danny. "Burn it here and the flames will be seen as far as the Irish Sea. Drive behind Cliff again. We'll follow."

They retraced their journey, back into Wych Elm and beyond into Aspen Hill. Cliff drove along Mill Street, which petered out into an unmade track into a dip by a footpath and woodland. There the van was set alight and noticed only by a farmer, almost a mile away, rising for breakfast, at 5am. By then it was well alight and allowed to burn out. The group was well away. Back in Wych Elm Danny had sent Eleanor on her way to Manchester.

"It might suit your cover but that bloody car is a death trap," he told her, as she was pulling away.

Mead was allowed to bath and clean up at Maman's home, passed off as a delivery man whose car had broken down. He and Danny ate a decent breakfast in silence. Cliff Hindle produced an off-the-peg blue suit for Mead, shoes and rail tickets well before 11am.

273

Danny wore a grey pinstripe. Cliff drove them to Wigan station for a tense, simmering and quietly toxic journey to the capital.

Cliff Hindle burnt Mead's clothes, with assorted rubbish, in a brazier in the quarry yard. Nothing was left to chance.

Eleanor's spare narrative was compelling for its brevity. Clarkson continued in detail. He outlined the ultimately fruitless police enquiry in London and the myriad of theories on Alan Thompson's disappearance since then, including brief details of Jan's seemingly abiding interest. The truth is often prosaic but on rare occasions descends into a complexity far greater than any conspiracy theory could devise. After all, conspiracy theories are, more often than not, developed for lazy minds. Most of the major players were dead but the link with the London criminal world, sexual battery and in this instance, use of a leather-covered whale bone, a predilection of the surviving judge, served to silence everyone around the table. Other MPs had been regular attendees at these parties. Mead had been well rewarded, in money and in kind, for his supplies of fresh meat.

"As you can see, this is far from covering an embarrassment in the past," Anne Luscombe declaimed. "I have discussed the issues within the service and with the palace. Hylton Jones' limited reputation is expendable; his criminal connections can be confirmed and, if necessary, embellished."

"We are confident Jan Dale will buy that package, for a book or a television documentary. The Mead link will be focused entirely on the lawless elements he consorted with or controlled," Tracey added, quietly.

"Katie Ross wouldn't buy it," said Davidson. "This is the issue, is it not?"

There was an audible sound of throats clearing. Anne almost began to smile.

"Whatever happens in the next few weeks, we all follow the..."

"Party line?" Davidson interjected.

"No need to be facetious, old man," Sir John said, trying to exude authority.

"He isn't," Eleanor said firmly.

"There is only one game in town as far as this is concerned," replied Tracey. "All contact with Jan Dale, Katie Ross or any of their friends, no matter how innocuous, accidental, or apparently accidental, whatever, must be reported. If someone else even appears to enquire on their behalf..."

"It must be reported," Anne emphasised.

"Somebody's pension seems to be at enormous risk." Albert Henderson grinned at the group. Only Pugh, Wise and Eleanor laughed.

The meeting broke up quickly, taxis being ordered to the door, ritual goodbyes filling the air. The rain had stopped. The streets were still awash. Wise and Pugh left individually; Davidson and Eleanor shared a black cab and were dropped off at a nondescript pub close to where the old service offices had been. Davidson ordered a brandy and ginger, Eleanor a gin and lime. They spoke in hushed tones at a small corner table. Albert Henderson appeared at the bar and called across to them.

"You know, I thought I'd find you here!"

Davidson made a motion with his hand. Henderson joined them. He placed his whisky glass down and only half in jest asked Davidson which of the two lovelies caught his eye.

"We were trying to remember the name of the chap who did the wet job on Mead. It's all of 20 years ago. He was your man, wasn't he?" Eleanor was looking at Albert directly in the face.

"He was," Albert replied. "He organised things inside. He was in under a false identity, sentenced for wounding with intent. While inside he convinced others, as only an ex-con can, that Mead was a grass. Two dealers inside had Mead disposed of, in his cell, asphyxiated with a dry cleaning cloth forced into his throat and, for good measure, a tube of toothpaste stuck up his rear end."

Albert took a swig of his drink.

"Organising subsequent events was less easy than in the old days. But my man, our man, went via the open prison system and was gone within the year."

"Where is he now?" asked Davidson.

"At first, he was in Majorca with his wife," Henderson replied. "His gratuity bought a bar and a little income. Daisy, his wife, went off with someone else and Kevin, our man, returned to the UK and bought a burger van and a small caravan. He had a pitch outside Haworth up in Yorkshire. He sold Bronte burgers – Anne was a plain burger with lettuce, Emily was a quarter-pounder with cheese and onions, while Charlotte was a half-pound affair with bacon, tomatoes and onion. He'd completed an Open University degree a few years before and this was his inspiration."

"Where is he now?" Eleanor asked, her scepticism clearly visible.

"The truth is always stranger than fiction," Henderson responded. "It is amazing the variations and tales that have to be put out these days! He found the trade was only good for six months and moved to a pitch outside York – Minster burgers and Roman burgers, plus Viking fried fish. He made a living. Unfortunately, six pints of beer and an electrical fault in the caravan did for him a couple of years ago. The fire didn't kill him, the smoke did. What was left of him was cremated at the local crematorium. I was there."

"Will there be a wet job on Katie Ross?" asked Davidson. "That's the clear impression I had, and all for a few old skeletons."

"It depends on whose closet you are emptying," said Eleanor. "This is less a closet than a walk-in cupboard. Or a palace, perhaps?"

277

"I'd have said both of them were at risk," Henderson replied. "There'll be little by way of give and take where those two lovely ladies are concerned."

"What was it DH Lawrence said about women and harlots?" asked Davidson, very much in the air, then suddenly recalling himself, he apologised to Eleanor.

"Don't apologise for Lawrence," she laughed. "I daresay he said a lot, though I don't think people read him much these days."

"The one you're thinking of is – *If a woman hasn't got a tiny streak of the harlot in her, she's a dry stick as a rule.* That's the one, or should I say two?" said Henderson. "My round?"

He drained his glass and trod to the bar, ordered a double for himself and fresh drinks for his erstwhile colleagues. Placing the drinks on the table he interrupted their discussion of Sir John, briskly telling them to finish their first drinks and not to fall behind. He let his eye rove and with an arched brow entered into a strongly held tirade, something which may have once been rehearsed but was now part of his nature.

"Frank, the elder brother was first class, a sound operative and good judge of ability as well as character. John, the youngster was a bit of a Uriah, the one in David Copperfield, ambitious for himself rather than the service. He was a classic example of the old saying, the first to put up his umbrella when the shit hit the fan."

"You were close to him," said Eleanor.

"From the earliest days, Eleanor! The family were farming stock on the Welsh border, lived in the third of three villages on a tiny ribbon road – Bell End, Endaway and Twattsfield. Coming from the third, even Frank reckoned John should have been born in the first!"

"Frank was popular with the filing girls," said Eleanor, smiling. "They were devastated when the news came of his death."

"And John saw it as his opportunity," Davidson added.

"I remain to be convinced that he grieved," said Henderson, drinking a mouthful of whisky and looking toward the middle distance.

"Has a decision been made?" Eleanor looked at the two men, trying to detect some emotion.

"The whole purpose of dragging us here," replied Davidson. Henderson nodded.

"And you know, Katie only had half a tale," continued Davidson.

"So, I reckon, have we." Eleanor leant back in her chair, thus preventing a small tear falling on her cheek. "Were we total bastards, I wonder?"

Chapter Fourteen

A month passed by, circulating around the usual domestic terrors – car insurance, the varied home insurances, new terms for private health insurance and, of course, tax. Death can strike but once. Taxes come at all times, even posthumously. Jan had made little progress beyond making a start on drafting the material to hand. It was that awful realisation of how limited her story was that pushed her to renewed contact with Katie. She eventually persuaded her to head north for a few days, sending her an electronic contract for a joint enterprise focused on a life of Danny Hird. It proved sufficient for Katie to drive up to Manchester late on a Thursday evening to avoid traffic, but even then she found herself stuck for an hour while a spilled load was cleared from the carriageway near Stoke.

She arrived looking the shade of pale associated with airport holiday travel, desperate less for food than a decent cup of tea. The following morning saw them at

Jan's dining table, ignoring the panorama of east Manchester and placing in shared files on their portable systems the tenuous results of their effort so far. They exchanged anecdotes about Michael Davidson, Wes Rhodes and Ben Fokker. The ex-prison officer was a more intriguing matter. Could he be persuaded to meet with both of them and go through his story in detail, in a systematic way? Would he be able to provide names? The very notion of such a plan made them consider Ben Fokker's warning. Should they both see Davidson and sound him out on this issue? Katie had heard nothing from him since their meeting. Was he stalling or had he nothing to say?

They spent the afternoon driving in Wych Elm and Rovington, taking in the sites and locations that would form an inevitable part of their finished product. The building that had been *Danny's Place* – extended and re-roofed – was now the premises of an independent funeral director. Painted in a shade of white with darkened windows it looked far more attractive, as a building, than it had in Danny's time. Further up from the centre, off Bridge Street, the old quarry area was now landscaped and surrounded by recently built 'executive family homes,' though Katie dismissed them as aspiring Surrey council accommodation. The Hird family home remained, squat and square in grey stone, now surrounded by a wall and plain metal security gates. Two large four-wheel-drive vehicles were visible on the drive. An extension was ongoing behind the attached garage. The flat above sported new windows, with work continuing.

"Should we be getting permission to photograph these houses?" Katie was asking.

"Only if we choose to use them," came the reply. "For all the owners know, we could be getting shots of Angle Pike."

Their visit to Danny's cottage in Rovington brought a surprise of sorts. A large 'For Sale' sign adorned the front weedy lawn area and a 'Sold' sticker was angled across it with no indication of the sale being subject to contract. Jan was indignant that the solicitors had not informed her of the property being for sale.

"They probably thought you might buy it," laughed Katie. "You did buy Bernard Wood's place after the *Hess* book."

"Yes," she replied. "I kept it for three years and made £20,000 on it."

"That's what you would make in a week in Chelsea," Katie was laughing again.

The cottage had a pleasant location, not far from Wych Elm, but essentially isolated, and the trees gave it a dark aspect. The place was beginning to look unkempt but more than a simple decorative budget would be needed to bring the place up to standard. They drove off with Jan determined to make it her business to identify the buyer.

The evening was spent at a comedy show in the City Arena. The tickets had been bought for Jan months earlier by a journalist contact on a Manchester paper, a thank you for services rendered. She could have sold them at twice the face value but retained them, not because she was a fan of Peter Dodd and his local, northern observational humour but because, at the time, she thought a little Sunday magazine article could emanate from it. Katie did find this northern, taciturn clown on the right side of amusing. In the event, they shared more than a few raucous laughs.

The boisterous audience were close packed, howling with laughter at Peter Dodd's warm up lines and it was then, quite early on, that Katie bawled into Jan's ear that two girls on the end of their row were looking at them and engaging in conversation. Katie could lip read – "It is her" and "She's been on the telly and radio" – and concluded they were focused on Jan. Meanwhile the artiste continued his routine.

"Why do squirrels swim on their backs? To keep their nuts dry!"

"Why do elephants not have claws? So they don't scratch you when you pick 'em up!"

As the arena emptied at the end of the show the same two girls were hanging back, obviously wanting to speak to Jan. At first she thought they might have wanted an autograph, but that had rarely happened, even in the past. It wasn't until they were standing in a breeze outside the building that their ambulatory conversation established that Sophie Gerrard was originally from Wych Elm and was living with Kylie Jones, a politics student, at Manchester University. Katie placed Sophie in her mid-

30s. She was petite, dark-haired and attractive. Kylie was about 20, a bubbly blonde edging toward plump, with doe eyes and a permanent smile.

Sophie mentioned she had heard of Jan making enquiries about Danny Hird in Wych Elm. Her mother had mentioned it during a phone conversation. Did Jan know she and her mum were at school together? Jan's heart sank. Her memory of names from 50 years past was rather vague.

"What was her name? What years was she there?"

"Sheila Stevens," replied Sophie. "She was there from 63 to 70, did her A-Levels and joined Howcroft Chemicals, in the office."

Jan did remember her, and said so. She was the school hockey captain, pencil slim, dark haired and an all-round athlete.

"She worked in *Danny's Place* as part of the singing chorus on Friday nights, until the business was sold. She knew Danny in the two years she was there. He called her Shadow because of the way she danced."

"My grandad's brother knew him too," Kylie joined in. "Years ago mind you. Danny threatened him."

"Why was that?" Katie asked.

"He was an MP," Kylie responded with a laugh. "You were once, I think. Am I right?"

Katie nodded, saying it was 20 years ago.

"My grandad said Harry, his brother, was no good. He was Sir Harry Hylton Jones. Danny had gone to his office, up here, and threatened to smack him one. Mind you, that was 50 years ago. I didn't know Sir Harry well and he's dead now. My dad told me he was gay. Well, he didn't say that word, he just said he was a bender. Not that there's anything wrong in that. But my dad said he got up to all sorts. You know what I mean?"

Jan was intrigued enough to invite them back. Over white wine and coffee little more came from Kylie, but Sophie described a trip Danny had paid for. Her A-Level English class was sent on a day to Haworth in Yorkshire. The school budget was tight that year and Danny knew their teacher, Miss Manners, and had paid for a mini bus and driver to carry a group of eight girls and three boys plus Miss Manners up to West Yorkshire. On arrival they found Danny there, having driven ahead of them "in his old posh limo. It was a Sapphire, I think" and at lunchtime he ordered "13 Emily burgers, 13 Branwell juices and 13 large Wuthering Fries" to feed us all. This tale had everyone chuckling.

"He seemed to know the burger man. They were talking quietly as we stuffed our faces, chattering and sitting on the grass. I heard him say something about someone called Mead and how the burger man had done a good job on him. He had been a hoot all lunchtime, but this sounded, well, a bit off. They were speaking in low voices with head movements and moving eyebrows."

Both Katie and Jan sobered up and asked Sophie to go through the story again. She didn't know the burger man's name and could only recall the *Bronte Burgers* name emblazoned on the sides. They were left with this tantalising snippet from 10 years or so in the past. Miss Manners was no longer at Wych Elm High School. She had married and moved away. In any event Sophie had been closest to the van. No one else would have heard and she was the only one listening.

More drinks were poured and Jan asked about her mother's experience of Danny Hird. Sophie blushed a little and Kylie spoke for her, eyes sparkling. Her face adopted a leer as she told the tale.

"He was a perv!" Kylie giggled. "Her mum told me he was forever touching her up and saying what a lovely bum she had."

"Oh shut it, Kylie," said Sophie.

"I'm only saying what she said when we were at your cousin's wedding."

"Yeah, but my mother had sunk a few. She could have been winding us up."

"She was clear minded enough to say it was worth it for the five quid in hand!"

"That was her pay for the evening. You make her sound like the local pro."

Within a short time Jan called them a taxi and she and Katie were left to ponder on the random nature of an evening out. Katie would approach her former prison officer at the earliest. That was for sure.

She sent off an email as soon as she arrived home, late on the Sunday evening,

Jack – have info re Mead. Need to discuss. Meet next week? You say where and when.

KR.

An email went to Jan,

Have suggested meet the coming week with J. Will let you know when.

K.

It arrived some hours later missing '*with J*' and the week elapsed with no contact. Friday came and at 6pm Katie was about to send an urgent request for a reply when the following message arrived,

Sorry been away. Cannot meet here. Meet at corner of Hanover Gardens Kensington at four pm Sunday at the entrance to Glebe Park.

j.

The venue was not far from Katie's home and could be described as convenient. She sent a brief message to Jan simply saying the meeting was on. However, it reached Jan as follows,

Have arranged meeting Sunday at four. Will advise. K.

Saturday was spent with paint charts, planning a re-decoration project for the lounge and hallway, a tantalising desire which she had put off for a year, partly due to the disruption the work would involve and partly due to the appalling cost of such work in the capital. If it were to be done there was no room for error in terms either of the colour scheme or of the contractor appointed to do the work. Seven years before she had chosen 'pale pink' for her hallway and found herself living with a shade of screaming pink far deeper than the colour chart had shown. This time she bought five sample pots to try out before committing herself, looking at the five streaks on a piece of plaster board in daylight, shade and night. The choice eventually fell on 'Pelican Twilight' and, having made this small piece of progress, she listed four decorators, three from professional lists and one recommendation, to contact and organise some estimates for the following week.

Sunday lunch was restricted to a slice of ham and some leftover salad, washed down by a small glass of Pinot Grigio. She wore jeans, boots and a heavy coat for her walk to Hanover Gardens. Passing the flower shop on the main road, for some unaccountable reason, she found herself thinking in detail of the IRA bomb planted in a van at that very spot, which, some 30 years before, had dispatched the wife and family of her husband, Daniel Wade. He had been absorbed in the wares of a model shop, a few yards behind them. His wife and two young children had walked on, taking the full blast of a 70lb nail bomb. Five others had died and over 50 were left with horrendous injuries, yet Daniel was physically unscathed. His mental state was something else entirely. For days he was in a sort of catatonic silence. Jan had known him since her schooldays at Wych Elm Grammar

School, an earnest, hard-working and utterly reliable sort. He worked in housing finance and had just left a small branch office in Manchester to take over a large city regional office. He and the family were renting a flat in Chelsea while searching for a family home.

Katie had been introduced to him by Jan. The new, quieter personality that emerged became her husband a year later. By then he had his own firm, *Wade Associates*. Four years later she was an MP and her husband controlled the *Provincial Housing Group*. He had 200 salesmen selling mortgages, insurance and wholly unsuitable investment vehicles, which paid huge commissions. On paper, on one measure, it was worth in excess of seven million pounds. He scooped most of it and, worst of all, for no real reason. The murder of his family had given him a large sum in life assurance. It had, however, taken his personality and, more than once, she'd heard him say, in company and especially with his father, that his future was bound up with the Irish.

"Give me the chance and I'll sink their bloody island."

It is strange how past events can suddenly and without warning produce a gush of memories, clamouring for attention and making demands in no order or arrangement. Katie had walked this route any number of times and snippets of Daniel Wade had come and gone like a whimsical breeze. She could not recall a hurricane, like this one.

She could see the Prison Officers' Association building, the first of an elegant terrace on the left. It had a small car park, on this occasion, invariably full. The park gates to her right were open, tall green ironwork in need of a brisk hosing down. There was no one about and Katie trained her eyes on the prison officer building, waiting a few minutes and then glancing behind and into the park. If she had been asked to describe it, the call she heard was like a forced whisper.

"Down here!"

She turned and walked in the park area, trees of deep evergreen forming a canopy. She approached an empty wooden bench. A figure moved from the bushes to her right as she crept by. A ligature was flung around her throat and twisted in a fast movement. A second figure appeared pushing a large wheelie bin; they lifted the lid and the two of them hoisted her body inside. They walked to a small green van, its back doors open and a wooden ramp extending to the path. One figure ran the bin up the ramp and pulled the wood inside, the other closed the doors, spoke into a phone and reversed the van out of the park. It appeared minutes later to the rear of Katie's home. People in overalls were already there. No words were spoken. Her body was pulled inside. The van was driven away, slowly. Some 30 minutes later another vehicle appeared at the front, stopping just briefly in the street. Four people jumped in appearing to wave in the direction of the building they had left. The car drove off at speed.

Anne Luscombe was seated in her office, behind her desk. Sir John Bright was upright in a chair directly facing her.

"Found this morning, you say."

"It is going to plan," she replied. "At least as far as these things can be planned after the event."

"Keep a close eye and use every means at your disposal," he said, glancing toward the ceiling. "Madge Wells herself told me that the stuff Danny Hird extracted from France after the war would make Blunt's papers from Schloss Kronberg look like a chimps' tea party. Remember Hylton Jones can be blamed for anything, being safely dead. The palace and Danny must be corralled away from Mead and his activities."

"According to my reading," Anne fixed him with a meaningful stare. "Mead did some useful work for us in the 80s."

"Oh yes," Bright responded. "He did, but he himself never advanced beyond useful. He was another of those characters whom squalor follows around."

That morning, Tuesday, Katie's weekly cleaner, Julia, let herself in. The silence, such more so even when Katie wasn't at home, struck her with some force. The smells were unfamiliar. Was it ammonia? Then the sweeter, sickening aroma of death, hovering then ascending, invaded her nostrils. She had experienced this aroma regularly on her aunt's little farm outside Krakow where she had spent her summers as a young girl. She braced herself, entered Katie's bedroom and found an

291

unmade bed, jeans in a heap on the carpet and discarded underwear on top of the bed. Even without the smell she would have known something was not right. She looked behind the sliding wardrobe door. Hanging there, clothes pushed along the rail, was Katie's body and some residue. A leather ligature was tight around her throat, while her toes just touched the wooden panel below. Her hands were tied in front of her, with a soft leather belt.

Julia did not scream, she gulped some air, composed herself and from the house phone contacted the police.

In Manchester Jan had rung Katie's mobile twice on Sunday evening. It was switched off and Jan left a voicemail. There was no contact on Monday and Jan began to wonder what was up, but not to the extent of fearing something was seriously wrong. She had, however, rung again on Tuesday morning, at 7.30am, knowing Katie would be taking some breakfast and catching up on correspondence. It was then that Jan was taking the view something was amiss. The 1pm news bulletin confirmed her worst fears. The live pictures of police activity, then later, confirming the death of a 60-year-old former MP and a former wife of fugitive fraudster Daniel Wade led Jan to contact the Metropolitan Police and fly down to London to make a statement.

The months that followed gave Jan the impression she had walked into a collective asylum, an asylum for the insane but where the inmates had a key to an imposed reality beyond the grasp of those outside. Nothing was as it seemed. The police enquiry pointed toward a sex game gone wrong, possibly solo or maybe involving others. Jan protested at this idiocy but found herself floundering when the lead inspector pointed out that the prison officer she was supposed to be meeting wasn't even in the country. He was in the second week of a late holiday in Benidorm with three of his grandchildren. The fact that the three children were of school age and out of school without proper authorisation caused a news tangent and days of wasted time.

Then there was the issue of her flat. The police were certain it had undergone a deep clean, yet bits of DNA evidence were left where it was certain to be found. None of it was on any database. Analysis of her laptop showed evidence of a sophisticated hacking job, months in the making. Had she been a member of *Kinky Kats* contact group? Searches of property in mediocre suburbs west of London yielded nothing concrete other than screeching publicity from the site owner – a male transvestite, originally from Nigeria, living illegally in the UK for the past 10 years.

One witness thought she had seen her leave the flat on the Sunday in question, but details were scarce. One local resident, in his 80s, thought he had seen someone like Katie standing by the park gates but felt he could not be absolutely sure. Detective Inspector Philip Handley, a quiet Londoner, with six years' experience, did listen to Jan. The clean flat and intense forensic scrutiny of the body seemed to give a series of contradictory results and he acknowledged to Jan, early on, that he trusted her back story of Katie rather more than the information he was getting elsewhere. The body had undergone three autopsies – well-nourished, healthy traces of cocaine in the nostrils but no evidence of past or frequent use. The decomposition of the body had made the speed of death problematical, but not the cause. There was evidence of sexual activity, but even this particular event appeared to be very recent rather than at all frequent. Sperm traces on the underwear did not match that found near the anus.

"I feel *someone* is painting pictures for me to look at," Handley had said to Jan, only repeating what he told his team. "There must be an original, but I'm just seeing layers of recent paint." He was aware of Katie's plans to re-decorate the flat. Not the sort of thing a potential suicide would organise, especially in the depth of detail evidenced here.

Every lead, initially promising, seemed to dry up or finish in an uneventful cul-de-sac and go no further. The internet speculation was less than helpful. The fact she had owned a Fiat Panda in 1997 allowed a story to develop that she was somehow involved in Princess Diana's death. Another narrative placed her in Brighton at the time of the Grand Hotel bombing while a reporter in Scotland questioned whether the body was really hers. Someone very like her had been seen days later in a Dumfries hotel and, later, walking around Sweetheart Abbey discussing Scottish independence with a local councillor.

The obituaries tended to follow that of *The Sentinel* newspaper, which combined a certain level of accuracy with the sensationalism of yesteryear,

The former MP Katie Ross, former wife of runaway fraudster Daniel Wade was recently found dead in her home in circumstances that remain unexplained. The case is still under investigation by the Metropolitan Police.

Katherine Mary Taylor Ross was born in London on 1st February 1951, the only daughter of the late Henry Ross and former dancer, Dora Taylor. She was educated privately at Ponds Wood Day School and University College, London, graduating with a first in French in 1974. She taught French and Latin at St Philomena's School for Girls for some years and later worked in advertising, translating in the offices of Cheyne Productions. She married Conservative MP Ivan Beevers, member for Suffolk West in 1977, divorcing within two years.

In 1985 she married Daniel Wade, a widower due to an IRA bomb in Chelsea killing his wife and two children. They parted in 1990, divorcing in 1992, while he was living abroad evading arrest for a £4 million fraud at the Provincial Homes Corporation.

She had been elected in 1987, much to her own and her husband's surprise, to the House of Commons as member for Purley South, overturning a 6,000 majority of the sitting Labour MP. She held the seat in 1992 by

600 votes, despite the adverse publicity surrounding her husband's financial activities, only losing in 1997 by 10,000, in the Labour landslide.

Her friend Jan Dale had published in 1983 her infamous book Hess & the Hamilton Story, which ran to eight editions and high sales in Europe and America. Katie had done a good deal of the research on this book over a four-year period and provided the French translation. She was rumoured to be working with Jan Dale on another project at the time of her death.

She had lived in Madrid in the 90s, owning a large hotel in the city. She shared her life for some years with the science fiction writer Lester Walton, 18 years her junior.

Her son, Anthony, survives her. He was born following a teenage pregnancy and raised in the family home by her mother in Hampstead. He lives in Singapore working as the chief executive of an international bank, registered in Hong Kong.

The accompanying photograph, a facial portrait from 1992, showed her to good effect. Jan had seen the photo before and it is the one she would have chosen. Her son came over from the east and stayed in a central London hotel to attend to the private affairs. He and his mother rarely saw each other but had corresponded regularly by email and, later, by more sophisticated means including Skype. He trusted the police handling of the case; like them, he was totally sceptical of the alleged evidence in view. He told Handley, while his mother did like men's company, she was never ever promiscuous. When young she might fall head over heels. Older, she was far more likely to dig in her heels and be more careful.

Jan spoke to him briefly on the telephone to discuss the funeral arrangements. It was three weeks before the body was released. Jan met him for coffee at the Dorchester and discovered a man of 48, a dark-haired version of his mother, smiling weakly and supported by his Oriental wife, of staggering beauty and deportment, dressed in a shade of red which set off a mane of jet black hair. He asked little although he made it clear he was aware she and Katie had been working "on some old disc jockey" which, by its very phraseology, gave an accurate impression of his disregard for the subject.

Telephone conversations with Ben Fokker were of a sharper tone. He was certain who had done it and, as he put it, "I will say so." Arrangements were made to meet in London once the funeral date was settled. Jan was acting in a haze of anger and self-doubt. The only positive thing she had done was obtain the name of the new owner of Danny's cottage. It was a newly married employee at his solicitors' Manchester office. Sheila Holt had put in an offer above the asking price and her builder husband, Barry, had plans for the cottage once a contract on a mill conversion was fully completed.

Karl Dodgson passed Tracey Brown in the main corridor. Unusually for him he stopped her with a fixed expression of concern. She looked at him enquiringly, asking if he was feeling unwell. Tracey had never ever seen Karl with anything other than an expression of technical curiosity and the transformation was quite striking.

"I'm fine. The Ross case is worrying me. I'm putting as much flak as I can online but it's having no effect. The Met are unimpressed, the story is flagging and the forensics are not going to sway the coroner. The inquest could turn into a shambles."

"Anne is very much aware, Karl. Just do what you can."

Sir John Bright suddenly found difficulties in getting appointments with Anne Luscombe and at the end of the month he found his security pass into the main complex no longer functioning. After a few days' working the system he was granted an audience with Tracey Brown. She sat behind a glass desk in a small meeting room, not even her office, receiving him in a manner he discerned as cold charity. In her white blouse, perfect make up, knee-length black skirt and sheer nylons she ought to have been a vision of male desirability. Instead she gave off an air of a roused cobra, aesthetically beautiful but potentially deadly.

"The operation is not going smoothly, the inquest may be a disaster and questions are being asked whether this could not have been done differently, or perhaps not at all."

"See here," replied Sir John, his composure already ruffled enough. "This operation would have gone like clockwork in my time and Anne need not throw the solids in my direction. You tell her that."

"The fact is," Tracey continued, eyes unblinking. "The old ways can't be controlled in the way it was done in the past. It's a new game today. The police are more difficult to lean on – they are busy enough clearing out skeletons of their own. A scientific examination of dead bodies yields far more, forensically speaking, than in the past. A clean-up, done too well, becomes suspicious in itself. There will be a case review, in depth, somewhere down the line. It isn't looking good."

"Is that why my X-pass no longer works?"

"That function has already been reviewed," she replied. "Reviewed for everyone - everyone on this case, certainly."

"I see," Sir John replied, sucking his teeth in order to maintain some equilibrium. "I take it my advice is no longer welcome."

"I can't be sure of that," replied Tracey. "Maybe not in this matter, but who knows what the future may bring?"

"Who indeed?"

He stalked from the building to a waiting taxi, accompanied to the door by a female security guard. Her quip, "Mind how you go, dearie," produced a glacial stare in return as he closed the car door, ordering the driver to take him to his club. He consumed four brandy and gingers that afternoon, still reflecting, at the end of it, on being called 'dearie' like a care-home resident being dropped off at the zoo. His conscience clear, he made his way home in a determined fashion, saying to himself,

"If this goes tits up, it's no fault of mine."

He did not sleep well.

Jan found sleep a greater issue than it had been for some time. She had a feminine tendency to water the weeds of conscience at night, pouring over what could have been done rather than what was done. Some days, there was much to do and consider. Others passed from breakfast coffee to evening tea without so much as a phone call. It was a relief when Wesley Rhodes rang on a Tuesday morning, complaining that his clerical contacts within 'the service' were no longer taking his calls. Jan confirmed that her own journalist and police avenues were meeting walls of silence or, worse, politically correct verbiage on the lines of,

"Let me say that our main concern is this poor woman's family."

Or, "Our main concern is catching those responsible for this crime."

"If she did it herself," grunted Wesley, down the phone, "there is no crime. I can remember when failed suicides were arrested for attempting to take their own life. That was in the days when the state purported to know the mind of God. That seems to be the preserve of the more noisy elements within the Muslim community these days or perhaps the more traditionally-minded Roman priest."

He ended the call by confirming Ben Fokker's view, but adding,

"Who will listen to us? Who listens to the old folk? Better we pass away."

The funeral was finally arranged for a Wednesday morning at the church Katie had attended as a child in Hampstead and afterwards at a municipal crematorium. Anthony felt he could take his mother's ashes to the east and deposit them "away from all this." The service was expected to be low key, yet in the event, electronic communication being what it is, over 200 people were in the church singing *Blest are the Pure in Heart. I Vow to Thee My Country and Jesus Shall Reign.* Her ex-husband Ivan Beevers asthmatic and using a stick to support himself on an arthritic knee, sang as lustily as the rest. Like many others he wore a black greatcoat over a black suit and tie. Lester Walton arrived in a parka-style jacket and open shirt, saying little, other than trying to interest Jan on his latest theory of time – "There are slits in it where things can pass through. Some places seem prone to this phenomenon, especially Wych Elm, where you come from. The stats don't lie."

Jan gave him short shrift.

"Neither time nor place. Grow up."

Wesley Rhodes arrived in a disabled taxi with a male nurse pushing his wheel chair. He did not attend the crematorium, having coughed his way through the church service. Jan had spoken with him outside the church. His nurse was concerned about his breathing. There were a couple of press photographers hovering around.

Jan sat with Ben Fokker. Near the back of the church, one row consisted of the former employees of Cheyne Productions, but the end aisle position was taken up by Michael Davidson, with Sir John Bright slightly adrift at the far end of the pew. Ben turned theatrically toward them, recognising Davidson and correctly identifying Bright from post-retirement press photos. He nudged Jan and said in a stage whisper that was heard along their pew,

"Ah Jan, it looks as though the undertakers have arrived."

Jan glanced back but made no comment. Neither Davidson nor Bright spoke to each other, but both eventually stood in the small crematorium chapel. In the chilled atmosphere outside Davidson passed Jan an envelope, making a perfunctory nod, whispering something like "sad times," while Bright strode off down the concrete path. The wake was a buffet and bar arrangement at the Savoy, dominated by serving and former MPs in a series of circles, barking comments on party matters and drinking copious quantities of gin. Ben ordered a taxi to take him to Liverpool Street and his train east. Jan took a taxi to her hotel, opening Davidson's envelope en-route. A slip of paper inside gave his address and contact numbers. She slipped the paper inside her handbag. Once in her room she stripped off her outer clothes and slept on the bed, lying in a deep sleep for seven hours, waking just before midnight.

Ignoring the list of messages on her phone, she ordered a large brandy from room service, donned her night attire and slept through till breakfast, rising still as if in a fog. Disorientated and in no position to make decisions, she booked an early flight back north, feeling dubious of all around her.

Chapter Fifteen

Nine weeks elapsed and Jan was in the lounge bar of her club. She paid the annual subscription, but only used its facilities on a working basis, at most three or four times a year. Its official title was the *City of Manchester Press and Writers' Club*, but the original Victorian premises had been blown away during the IRA bomb attack on Manchester city centre in 1996. Over time the centre had been rebuilt and in some instances reconstructed. The 1960s cheaply built centre was now more of a continental style, retaining the edge that Mancunians brought to everything. At the time of the explosion, comment had surrounded the fact that Manchester had been an Irish target and Liverpool had not. The reply from the security services featured the insinuation that there was nothing worth bombing in Liverpool anyway, later adding that the number of Irish families owning businesses in the old port city would render any terror attack the equivalent of the IRA shooting themselves in the foot.

The original brass plate was retained for the new club premises, though above it was a plastic sign providing the traditional name *The Scribblers*. It now served healthy bar meals and the smoking room had become a non-smoking lounge on the third floor giving a glass vista view of the cathedral. The oldest aspects of the club were most of its regular members, predominantly male, mostly working in local newspaper offices. There were a few experienced female reporters, mainly in their 40s, their attempts at femininity failing to hide their steelier extremities, as well as an assortment of aspiring soap actors building their local profile and maybe getting a drink or a free lunch.

Jan fell between both of those stools. She was basically a known author for many years, still into journalism and the occasional television appearance, nevertheless better known within the club as a 'user' of both people and their ideas. It would be difficult to pass judgement on that view, one way or the other. Most people have only their experiences or acquired experiences to work on. Jan regarded herself as lucky. Her luck was, by and large, an object of resentment among her peers and by those younger than her, especially men who felt themselves overlooked in the market stall of life. Women were wary of her, even those of her emotional persuasion. It tended toward conversation that was performance based or simply a strident attempt to live up to an agreed image. It may be useful to think of it as Shakespeare's world stage minus the laughs, essentially a stage play conducted around a series of unspoken rules. She was drinking coffee in the smoking room. A local newsman had just left. They had been swapping notes on Sir Harry Hylton Jones' work as a constituency MP, including his frequent visits to council managed boys' homes and an awkward incident at one of the city's main hotels in 1964 when he had been caught in bed with three boys, allegedly on a day trip from one of the homes. The police had been called but there was no arrest, no charges laid and a statement made by the hotel management referring to "an unfortunate misunderstanding." One of the boys had been traced. Now approaching 60 and living in a seaside flat in Blackpool, Jason Swire of *City News* had interviewed him. He said that Jones regularly took boys out on day trips, usually to hotels, where they were given a decent meal and then escorted to his room "to rest" in his bed, naked, while he molested them.

The other two boys were proving difficult to trace. One had joined the Merchant Navy and may have been lost 30 years back in a typhoon in the South China Sea. The other had apparently died of AIDS in 1987 and Swire had left to follow a lead on the seaman. Jan had given him Kylie Jones' name and he was arranging to see her at one of the university bars later in the week.

Her phone, on silent, vibrated in her bag. Jan moved into the corridor and read a message from Chris Babbage, the solicitor. He had only texted her once during their conversations about Danny Hird. For him to do so was unusual. Last time it was just to change the time of an appointment. This was clearly different.

Jan – when you get this, call at the office asap. Urgent.

Chris Babbage.

The previous morning, Barry Holt, builder and husband of Sheila Holt who was the secretary at *Babbage & Co.*, had called at Pike Cottage to view progress on their new home. Being in the trade he was able to call in favours from others to upgrade the plumbing, kitchen and electrics of their country abode. He and Sheila were still renting a small suburban flat while the work was ongoing. The interior had been completely re-plastered and, he noted, was drying nicely. He estimated six more weeks to finish the job, in good time to move in before Christmas. The garden areas had been cleared. The only outstanding problem was the separate brick garage. The slate roof was a good 60 years old and needed attention. The front and sides were built in red glazed Accrington brick, not pretty but durable; cleaned up and pointed properly, it should be good for another generation or two. The garage was not really wide enough for modern vehicles and, at best, two small cars could be squeezed in, nose to tail. He decided there and then to remove the back wall, ordinary brick, worn and patched at various times in several places. Adding roughly eight feet would produce an adequate tunnel garage, taking two decent sized vehicles, one of which would be his works' pick-up truck.

He was scratching around the back wall and suddenly realised something was not quite right. The outer corner had been extended in a rough fashion, in the shape of a low box. Inside he could see this area had been sealed with a thick smear of concrete, darkened and affected by damp. This had been barely visible when they first bought the house. The garage was full of old tools and junk. He and two of his regular labourers had cleared it one weekend and they had concentrated on the scrap value of some of the tools and several old bicycle frames.

He produced a masonry hammer from his van and began to hit the concrete. It was pretty solid, only the outside layers turning to dust as he hit the wall. He changed tack, went back outside and hit the extended brickwork in the motion of a bowls player. Three layers of brick fell away immediately. Behind, in what was effectively an oblong cavity, was a darkened red plastic box, sealed with textile tape around the lid, accompanied by an old thermos flask, still bearing a tartan design and a cream screw top.

"What the hell's this?" he spoke aloud. He then hesitated before proceeding to pull at the box lid. He had to cut the tape using a pen knife, working part of it loose and, in doing so, cracking the plastic. Inside, tightly packed, was a collection of bones, including what was clearly a human skull. At first he thought it might be artificial, plastic, a toy perhaps but hair strands, few in number, told him otherwise. Barry was not in any way frightened and while he thought he might call the police his instinct was to contact his wife, Sheila, at *Babbage & Co.* A call from Barry during working hours was a rare event. When he described what he had found she told him to open the flask. It could have been curiosity that made her do this, or the need to say something while she thought about this weird find. Inside the flask was a handwritten letter, signed by Danny Hird. He slowly read the contents aloud to her.

"Barry, listen. Place the letter flat on a dark surface. The pathway should provide a backdrop. Take a photo on your phone and send it to me."

Barry did as he was told. Sheila told him to wait. When Chris Babbage heard the tale and looked at the enlarged photo on his computer screen he found the content easy to read and quite disturbing. It was Danny's writing, blue ink, hardly faded, on white foolscap giving a precise narrative as to how the accompanying bones were secreted in his garage wall.

"Tell Barry to call the police now. Make sure he tells them he has opened the box and flask. They will need his prints. Tell him not to volunteer that he sent a photo here. Only say so if asked."

A train of events set in motion. He texted Jan on the basis of her interest in the Alan Thompson case and her ability to operate quickly and use her contacts to avoid the case being, as he told himself, twisted, skewed or buried. He still acted for the Hird estate and was determined to protect it.

Jan sat in Babbage's office looking at the large screen on the desk. Chris Babbage sat by her, reading the photographed sheet for the third time. Jan was rarely stuck for words, but her silence, as she read, was as deafening as a roar. She now knew the truth about Alan Thompson. The story was one of sheer horror. Danny had begun with a short paragraph, describing how, on Sunday 29th April 1979, he had driven up to Rovington Moor, behind Angle Pike, to collect the remains of a former client, Alan Thompson, originally buried there on Monday 3rd April 1967 "by Curtis Mead, under my direct supervision." He then gave the narrative supplied by British security officers, remarking it was an organisation he had worked for "on various matters for over 30 years." He then pointed out that subsequent information came his way, during an interview with Sir Harry Hylton Jones MP, that the details he had been initially given were untrue. Nathan Heim had aroused Danny's suspicions in the months following the original incident and the activities of Curtis Mead's organisation in the 70s had caused him to make a series of enquiries through some London contacts.

The interview with Sir Harry was given in a perfunctory manner. In reality Danny arrived at his constituency office on an overcast Saturday, early in 1979. He had driven into north Manchester from Wych Elm, using a hire car. The Sapphire was undergoing a complete service and, anyway, using such a vehicle would have drawn unwanted attention in the narrow streets of this essentially Victorian sprawl which Sir Harry represented in parliament. As usual his preparation had been careful and he had made the last appointment of the day in his own name.

He made slow progress as he passed Spring Street, Summer Street and Autumn Street on a cobbled road, before turning left into Winter Street and passing between 10 small terraced houses on each side. He pulled in to the left side at the far end, outside what had been a corner shop. The framed windows were cheaply painted in a gaudy red colour and the former display window was festooned with stickers, slogans mostly, with photos of Sir Harry in the middle at eye level.

Danny was very much aware how the MP had built up an image above that of his own and other rival political parties. He gave the impression of an avuncular, wise old uncle and performed well on television. Like any good actor, the image was at variance with the true personality. The obesity was more to do with greed than any supposed medical issues, but he was careful never to be seen actually enjoying a meal in public. He was seen regularly walking out around the constituency with a maiden aunt for company and sometimes his mother. She was into her 80s and less sprightly than her younger sister, whose previous claim to fame was a series of operatic recitals in the local Methodist chapel.

The office door from the street still sported its shop doorbell, clanging on entry. A young graduate type of boy – clean cut, fair hair and in a blue suit – was seated behind a desk where the shop counter had once been. He greeted Danny warmly.

"Hello," he began. "I'm James Naylor, Sir Harry's constituency secretary. I'm pleased to meet you, Mr Hird."

"Well, young James," Danny responded. "His Lordship is upstairs, I take it?"

"Yes, his suite is up the stairs. He is expecting you."

"Suite? That does sound sweet. How much does he pay you, James?" Danny asked. "What is the going rate as his local secretary?"

"Oh, I do this just for expenses. It's an honour to work for Sir Harry."

"I bet it is," Danny replied, barely suppressing a smile. "Here's a tenner. Buzz off for half an hour. We've a bit to discuss. It's a bit sensitive."

James took the note and made to say something but Danny ushered him out, clicking the lock catch behind him. He walked up the uneven stairs, on a carpet that should have been replaced 10 years earlier, and noticed an open lavatory door on the landing. The door to the right opened onto the panorama of Sir Harry himself, munching a slice of sponge cake, seated behind an oak desk which seemed too heavy for the floor it rested on.

Sir Harry jumped up, thought of retrieving his black suit jacket from behind his chair but then thought better of it, and held out his crumbed hand, spluttering as to why he hadn't been buzzed on the internal phone. Danny walked round the desk, grabbing his hand as if to shake it, but spun him hard, face into the wall. Sir Harry attempted to struggle but Danny's left forearm was hard across the back of his flabby neck.

"Let's cut the bullshit, eh?"

Danny used his right hand to pull a sharp carpet knife from his coat pocket, waved it briefly by Sir Harry's left eye and then in one movement cut his trouser belt and seam at the back. The voluminous garment slid round his ankles.

"What in heaven's name do you want? Is this a bloody joke? Where's the candid camera?"

"No cameras Harry, not for you just yet anyway. Just this!"

Danny had returned the knife to the pocket and produced his old revolver, the Webley *Bulldog*. He used the barrel to lower the white underwear and then stuck it firmly into the anal crevice.

"Jesus!" Sir Harry breathed out.

"He won't be helping today, Harry. It's his day off."

"What the hell to you want?"

"The truth about Alan Thompson, that's what. My potential business deal 12 years back was ruined by you and your arseholes in London. What happened? Who killed him?"

"I was as much shafted with that – eeeh!"

Danny pushed the barrel harder.

"Don't lie to me, Harry. The gun has a couple of dum-dum bullets, just for you. You will die slowly and your intestines will cover the floor of this office."

The words were delivered with quiet menace. Sir Harry knew that Danny meant it. Tears were in his eyes. He had become a pile of white, sweating blubber. If Danny's arm had not maintained its grip, he would have been shaking in sheer terror.

"You and me are on the same bloody side," he gasped. "That Curtis Mead supplied lads for us and we'd ordered something young, fresh and brown. He brought this drugged-up wreck to us and, well, I like 'um tight but he'd done him before any of us. The admiral used him a bit but we sent him back with Mead. We paid him nothing until he brought a scraggy specimen on the run from some care home an hour or so later. We told Mead not to give us soiled seconds again. I didn't know young Thompson or where he came from. If I had, I'd have sent him back. Even I've got to be careful on my own patch."

Danny recognised truth from fear.

"Listen, Harry mi' boy," Danny whispered. "If I find you are lying, you, your mother and your auntie are dead. Do you understand?"

"I'm telling you the truth. The people you and I know are using Mead now, trapping Russians, Czechs and even a bloody Yank. That's how the little shit is doing most of south London's drug business with the police nowhere near him. He's been blackmailing Heim's business to buy it cheap and legitimate himself."

Harry tried to draw breath, but only succeeded in frothing from his mouth.

"The bastard is riding roughshod, literally, over south London. He has gangs of Yardies, white scum and even an Irish outfit under his control. That lad found in the Thames last week, tied to a bloody fridge, it was his doing."

Danny kicked Sir Harry's legs away. He landed in a crumpled heap on the floor, instinctively putting his hands above his head.

"Pass it on to our friends," Danny said. "I'm after Mead."

Harry was able to gather his thoughts and looked at Danny from behind his fingers. His eyes were wild and fixed.

"They'll shit on you," Sir Harry replied, still shielding himself. "Do it by all means, but don't flaming well tell them. You and I are worth nothing to them now. We're too bloody old and past our best."

"Speak for yourself," was the arch reply.

Danny walked away, down the stairs, leaving Harry on the floor, grey and shaking. He brushed his lapels as he unlocked the door catch, wiped his pistol barrel on the hanging curtain and drove off, just as James Naylor returned, waving as he passed by. Danny reflected briefly, ever so briefly, on the price of honour.

When the security service did, eventually, become aware that Danny was out to eliminate Mead, they realised that he was aware of his importance to them. He was their principle agent in the capital. Danny had to be dissuaded or stopped. He had been visited at his London flat by John Bright to warn him off. At this point, to protect himself and the truth, he decided to remove the remains from the moor and secrete them and the flask as an insurance for himself against an organisation he could no longer trust. The coordinates he had given them were now useless. Sir Harry Hylton Jones had been right as far as the service was concerned.

The letter was dated 30th April 1979, and at the end of it a biro noted added "deposited in flask, Thursday 3rd May," signed Daniel Jacques Hird.

Jan immediately asked Babbage whether he had known of Danny's security status. He confirmed he was aware, but had been given no details.

"You realise, don't you, that it's a near certainty that Katie was murdered?" said Jan, speaking softly.

"We must make sure the police are fully informed," Babbage replied, acknowledging his agreement. "Fully informed, Jan. Use every means at your disposal."

"Damned right," said Jan.

The early meeting took all morning in a Berkshire country hotel. It was cheaper to use out–of-town hotels, more convenient and easily secured. Anne Luscombe arrived in her black VW sports job, accompanied by a plain clothes security man who, in another age, could have passed for a floor walker in one of the better London stores. The meeting lasted less than an hour and then she, two men in grey suits and one civil service type of woman, grey bushy hair, clipped tone and somewhat argumentative, retired to a private bar upstairs, which gave a view of the upper Thames and a distant golf course.

"We are relying on you to manage this your way, Anne," one man was saying, the others standing in silent agreement. "There will be a coroner's hearing. Any other type of public enquiry is unlikely to work. The best we can hope for is an open verdict. Murder by persons unknown would apply more pressure and, if it happens…"

"…Sir John carries the can."

"Not in full public view," said the bushy-haired female. "But enough will be released to keep the press happy. This has been his cock-up. I expect they'll give him something agricultural to chair, in due time."

"And me?" Anne asked.

"You are not under pressure, Anne. The meeting was to reassure you of that. Your real job is the overflow from the middle east in our suburban jungles," replied the second man, with a wave of his hand. "That's where we want you. Clear this lot up quickly, eh?"

Anne did not feel at all reassured. She drove home from the meeting with the distinct impression she was being set up for a fall. She refrained from saying so, in the office, all the while maintaining a confident front. But she felt she needed someone to whom she could confide. Her husband was a good listener, meticulous in his own skill of cabinet making, sound in judgement, careful in business. However, to make any worthwhile comment, he would need all the facts and, in this regard, in her position, she was unable to go beyond generalities. He had suggested she take a break during the next school holidays and drive the children to rural France or rent a small place in Tuscany. She, in turn, had been non-committal, saying she would think about it and talking of consulting diaries and colleagues. For him, this was usually a negative sign.

Jan had wasted no time in letting Ben Fokker know about the discovery. She had spoken to him after an initial conversation the detective leading the case, Julian Rathbone – an open, listening type, not so much out of his depth but more used to a different kind of pool. Outside involvement became apparent very quickly, but his chief constable was not one to roll over and he backed his man, accepting assistance from the Home Office, but not direction. Jan was clear in distinguishing what she knew and what she suspected – cooperation was established with the metropolitan force enquiry into Katie's death and Curtis Mead's name was being freely bandied around the electronic and print news. Ben had advised her to ensure this happened. Sir Harry Hylton Jones became headlines again as the story twisted and turned. Jan got an interview with Alan Thompson's elderly mother, an interview delayed only by yet another funeral. Wes Rhodes succumbed to a cardiac arrest, dying in his sleep.

His send off, organised by him, in the local parish church saw a gathering including Jan and Ben, his main carers, a couple of very distant nephews and a niece, plus those former colleagues capable of making the journey and standing unaided. More recent news acquaintances also tagged along. He had even written his own address, delivered by the local female vicar, with a dose of his characteristic innuendo that seemed to be lost on the earnest, entirely well-meaning lady who spoke with a solemnity wholly at odds with the content. The section beginning *'As for my wives'* caused her to raise an eyebrow, as she had read it in the singular the night before. When, by his pre-arrangement, six ladies in open black coats, short black skirts and sheer stockings, mounted on five-inch heels, suddenly appeared at the graveside to wave the casket into the earth, everyone was in a fit of convulsions, Ben declaring he had never seen a better last testament. He made a loud enquiry to one of the ladies as to how much they had been paid.

"A grand each, love, for 20 minutes' work. Better than a West-End run!"

The reception was one where the spirits flowed as of the old days. Wesley had kept his promise. It was a free bar. The service was represented, quietly, by Albert Henderson. Neither Ben nor Jan knew him, but a close observation of the man making small talk with them and others led Ben to remark that he had the air of an old spook about him. Jan approached him at the bar.

"Do you know a good friend of mine, Michael Davidson? Have you worked with him in the past?"

Henderson kept a straight face. He knew exactly who she was and thought it typical she would pose such a loaded question.

"Yes, I knew a man of that name. Mind you, I haven't worked with him for years."

Jan smiled and nodded, walked back to Ben and relayed the reply.

"He isn't lying, of course. He's using the truth to say bugger all."

Younger journalists, mostly freelance, were taking full advantage of the free facilities and voices were becoming raucous; laughter was competitively loud and at one stage someone fell over a table. It was at that point that Ben and Jan ordered a taxi that took them to their respective stations for swift departures home. In Jan's case it was after 11pm when she approached her Manchester foyer. Kylie Jones was standing by the piece of modern art outside.

"What are you doing here?"

"Waiting for you," Kylie answered, a little petulantly. "Why did you send Jason Swire to see me? Why didn't you come, yourself?"

"How long have you been waiting?"

"I was in the *Canal Bar* down the road and came out at half 10."

"Where's Sophie?"

"She's away with her Sixth-Form English group, all this week, in the US," Kylie drawled. "They're supposed to be studying Modern American literature. She goes every year. It's three days in New York and two in Washington DC. God knows what she's up to, or who with."

"Feeling abandoned?" replied Jan, sympathetically. "Come up for a drink."

Kylie wheeled Jan's overnight case along and they were soon in the flat, drinking vanilla coffee in the lounge. Kylie lost most of her spikiness as Jan explained she had been to a friend's funeral. It seemed that young Jason Swire had tried to hit on her during their chat and was reluctant to accept the rebuff, texting and emailing on a regular basis.

Jan could see how Kylie would attract boys, a bubbly blonde with a smile, openness and a ready wit. She was wearing cropped jeans and a tight t-shirt, emphasising her full but symmetrical figure. Jan was in the ubiquitous funereal little black dress, black patent heels and sheer hold-up stockings – a vision Wesley would have warmed to, even in old age. Uncertain at first, she quickly gleaned her persona was having a similar effect on Kylie. The young student had sat closer to her on the sofa and was exuding a need for sympathy.

"How are things between you and Sophie?"

Jan made the enquiry as neutral as possible, but Kylie turned her face straight to hers and sniffed a little before replying.

"We've been a pair for two years. We met in the *Canal Bar* and clicked," Kylie whispered. "The trouble is, I'm working my socks off doing my degree and not doing much socially. She is teaching at St Anne's, a school for posh girls, where results are everything. Sophie spends her time marking, sleeping or doing school stuff and gets upset when I do my own thing."

"Do you love her?"

Kylie actually blushed.

"Yes, I'm sure, but I need it to be more than just in my head."

At that juncture, she sank her head into Jan's shoulder. Jan began to stroke her hair. The temptation to use the phrase "I'm old enough to be your Mum" was avoided, but only just. The full-on kiss did not immediately follow. Kylie slid to her knees on the floor and raised Jan's dress to expose the top of her left leg. She began to kiss the older woman's skin with complete abandon. Jan had not been aroused like this for quite some time and her natural caution and calculation moved to the back of her emotional repertoire. They spent a night of passion, introspection and investigation, emerging from the bedroom at 10am the next day, both somewhat wary but Kylie showing her open appreciation, extolling her experience and then betraying her youth over a cup of breakfast tea with what could have been a lethal phrase.

"You won't tell anyone, will you?"

"Don't be silly. You have a lecture this morning. Get yourself sorted out. Do you want me to call a taxi?"

"No, it's ok. I'll walk to my – our – place. It isn't far if I walk fast. Will you call me?"

Jan reassured her, embracing her as she left, saying she would be in touch. She warned her about intimacies appearing on social media and what she'd do to *her* if anything slipped out in that way. Whether she could help Kylie with the politics of Argentina, her specialism this academic year, was open to question. But she could assist in other ways, convinced the young girl had hormonal problems which incorporated a need for a relationship based on respect, protection and security. Sophie seemed to be falling down on all three.

Their periods of respite in bed had seen Kylie ask extensively about Katie. Jan had discovered that her grandfather and his brother had both passed away in the previous 14 months. The brother, Uncle Joe, had confided in her father regarding Sir Harry, but she was able to add nothing new. Kylie had started her degree wanting to work for the UN but was now looking toward an internship in either the Commons or the Lords. She would start her final year next September and was already putting out feelers among the local MPs. Jan had said she may be able to help. In the meantime she could do ad-hoc work for her, paid, and she would provide a reference.

She took a call from Chris Babbage. The DNA extracted from one of the teeth in the skull matched a sample taken from Alan Thompson's mother. The local police had been digging behind Angle Pike, finding a shoe of some sort and a metal buckle. His sources were adamant that a report had already been prepared and a draft submitted to the Home Office. Jan told him she intended to do a book on the life and career of Danny Hird, neither a hatchet job nor a eulogy. Chris replied that he would consider letting her have access to the papers he held, subject to some editorial input on behalf of the estate. Jan said she would also consider his proposal, once her own work was complete. The only thing she would not compromise was the dedication. It would have its own page; to the memory of Katherine Ross, in affection and esteem.

Chapter Sixteen

Jan met Sheena Thompson in her neat stone terraced house in Wych Elm. In her 80s, small, thin but still active, she sat in a floral-themed lounge in a bulky easy chair in her spotless living room, pointing to framed photographs on the walls and the sideboard dedicated to Alan's memory. She gave Jan a couple of spare examples and allowed a photo of her, using Jan's latest electronic phone gadget.

"All this time, I wondered where he was and he was just a mile away on the moor."

It was difficult for Jan to comprehend her lack of criticism regarding Danny Hird. She kept pointing out how far he had known both what had happened and his own role in "this awful affair." Jan tried to show the worst side of Danny, dwelling on the fact that he had known what had happened all along.

Sheena was having none of it – Danny had made sure she was financially supported, had never raised any false hopes and had protected Alan's memory for her. There had been several false alarms and wild goose chases over the years, including one that Jan herself had instigated – Sheena made a point of it – but he had supported her throughout.

"The London agency paid me money, Danny gave me £2,000. He said it was from insurance but the cheque was his own. He was protecting me and looking after my interests. He did a lot for people in Wych Elm."

Sheena's take on Danny Hird was interesting. At times, Jan felt it could have been her own mother talking. At others she introduced novel insights into his family and attitude to people around him. The Hirds were described as solid, dependable and fair. Danny's father was straight with no side. On his mother, Sheena was more circumspect, not for her continental ways but for an increasing dominance in the family circle.

"When his dad was killed, any check on her disappeared. All her children spent their time at home trying to keep her happy. The others went away. Danny was left with that job. My husband used to say she could be hard work. She demanded a lot. I doubt whether Danny knew himself properly until the day she died. All his work on television, the music, the old dance place – it was his way of getting some time away from her."

"Are you saying his mother dominated him?"

"No, I'm going almost as far as that but not quite to that extent. It was more a case of her keeping control, clinging if you will, and living her life through him."

Jan was surprised to hear her concur with some of the traits she had uncovered from his past, agreeing he liked girls but never showed any commitment.

"They used to say the back seat of the green Ford he drove had reinforced springs, given the number of girls he drove up Rovington way. I daresay he deflowered more than a few. They did let him, though, didn't they?"

Jan asked about his handling of girls in *Danny's Place* and Sheena readily agreed he was someone with his hands everywhere. She referred to his religion, not with disapproval, but to make what she considered a salient point.

"He did little more than the old priest got up to. What was his name? Mellor? No, Mallon. He spent more time at that girls' home outside Bolton than he did in his parish and even in the chapel he was always giving advice to young married women. He only saw their husbands at Sunday Mass or in the bar at the Catholic Club. The advice he gave the younger women was always hands on."

An official interment of Alan's remains was planned in the churchyard. No date had yet been fixed but Sheena promised to pass it on as soon as she knew. Jan said she would definitely come.

A few days later Jan drove along the M62 into a suburb of Leeds. This was a city she knew little about and had only studied the geography nearly 30 years before at the height of the Yorkshire Ripper terror. It was the type of serial murder case that she would have investigated with aplomb, but, at the time, she was actively involved in the Hess business and unable to devote any time to the six years of semi-chaotic police work, which in the end was of more interest and more lasting than the personality of the Ripper himself. She regarded the matter as a monument to badly implemented police force amalgamations, ghastly bad luck and the limitations of regional police procedure.

Myra Griggs lived in a rented low-rise flat with a view of a rugby training ground and a distribution depot. She had been reluctant to see Jan, having dropped out of the group action against Danny Hird and leaving the national law firm to subsequently inform the others that without her testimony the chances of a successful claim against the estate were remote. Jan already had statements from the others and had to concur that without Myra, it amounted to very little.

She was met at the glass front door by a woman approaching 70 with dyed black hair and a lined, sallow complexion. Put her and Sheena together, it would have been difficult to decide which of the two was the elder. Myra's voice had the gravelly quality of someone smoking at least 20 cigarettes per day, and her movement was decidedly slow. Her home was clean, but sparsely furnished and there was a decided lack of personal possessions – photos, ornaments and the like. Jan immediately recognised the signs of a life hard lived.

Myra's back story would have made a tragedy in itself. Born in May 1946 her father had evacuated from Dunkirk and served in North Africa, only to be drowned when the boat ferrying him and 16 others capsized in the swell alongside a larger ship off Gibraltar. Her mother contracted peritonitis, undergoing an operation and dying when Myra was four. Three grandparents took the view she would be best looked after "by the church" and she moved from a convent orphanage to St Jude's in Bolton at the age of 11. None of her older relatives visited her and she was altogether abandoned to what she described as "a grey existence of hard work, poor food, cold beds and colder people."

She vividly described *Danny's Place* and how much it was a light in her life and, furthermore, how far Danny himself had looked after her. He had given her five shillings, bought her a pair of new shoes and tried to get her some work in one of the Wych Elm mills.,

"When he and Sister Monica punished me that night, it was nothing compared to what Mother Superior would have done, had she known. Runaways were always caned in a morning assembly, in front of everyone, and while Sister Monica didn't approve of that, she did believe in corporal punishment done appropriately, in private. Those were her very words. She spent a lot of time with me, discussing family life and the successful rearing of children and how we were all discovering, little by little, God's plan for the world."

Myra went on to describe her subsequent life, married at 18, two miscarriages and an abusive alcoholic for a husband who left her penniless at the age of 40. She had survived a nervous breakdown and worked for nearly 20 years in a draughty converted cotton mill, packing bolts in greaseproof paper, boxing them in sixes and stacking the boxes on pallets for eventual export to Africa.

"The solicitor wrote to me at the end of last week to say Sister Monica had died. She lived in a care home in York. Both of them are gone now."

Jan had difficulty with Myra's story. *Why had she been prepared to sue the church and gain redress? Were Danny's motives honourable and what were Sister Monica's Jungian experiments all about?*

"I had nothing against Danny or Sister. My problem was Mother Superior, a hard bitch if ever there was one, and the priest, Father Mallon."

Jan's ears pricked up at the mention of this name. What had he been doing?

"It's more a case of what he didn't do. He saw all of us for confession, alone, once a week – just another groper!"

"Did Sister Monica know what was going on?" Jan asked, quickly.

"Mother Superior did. She was told often enough. We got the cane, he carried on. He died in a fire." Myra smiled. "That was his preparation for hell. He should burn for all eternity."

"Your married name is Griggs. Was he the boy you met in Wych Elm?"

"My name was Kearns and I'm told it's an Irish name. No, I didn't marry Mervyn. I married his older brother. None of them were any good, including their mother."

"You never remarried?"

"For once I learnt from experience. The state I was in, who in heaven's name would want me? I'm being treated for lung cancer now and despite what the specialist says, I reckon I'm on my way."

Myra gave a slightly hysterical laugh and then reverted to a benign smile. She had to be persuaded to have a photo taken. She did provide a faded black and white image of her, taken on her fourteenth birthday at St Jude's. It showed a camera-shy, slim girl with dark hair held back in an Alice band and appearing much younger than her age.

"Life's rich tapestry proved a bit threadbare in my case. Luckily, there was no one to disappoint. Things just happened and I just had to get on."

Myra was detailed in her description of Wych Elm and Danny in 1958 – the club, the prices and the customers. Her memory was pinpoint sharp. All of this was useful for the book. She was able to remember staff names, the local policeman and the name of a popular chip shop. At the end of their discussion, it was apparent Myra was getting visibly tired. Jan had no wish to offend. She did not want to belittle Myra. Neither did she just want to say sorry in the emotionless way promoted in media circles. As she left, she slipped two £20 notes from her purse and into her hand. Myra sighed and accepted the notes without protest, nor a word.

It was more difficult to arrange a meeting with Father Stannard, the local Catholic priest. He finally met her in Chris Babbage's office, with Chris present taking notes. There was nothing he was prepared to say on Father Mallon as he hadn't known him and had never met him. Regarding the two St Jude institutions, he had nothing to say. On Danny he was more forthcoming, describing him as a "continental Catholic" who believed much of what the church taught, "except when it contradicted his own direct experience." His charitable work was the true measure of the man. While he was not widely read, he did pursue some matters in depth. Over the years he had come to doubt Britain's position in the war. At this point, even Chris Babbage raised an eyebrow, asking him to elaborate. Jan simply asked whether he had become pro-Nazi.

"Don't be silly," Stannard retorted, giving Jan a look of utter disdain. "He was proud of his army service and his work with the resistance in France. His view was a considered one. The country bankrupted itself on a fight it could never win alone. The major contribution had been that of the USSR, a country and people he respected while finding communism risible. Danny reckoned human nature flawed and showed itself either at the public level, the private level or, in some cases, both. But there were no heroes. There were only those who either achieved much or saved themselves from themselves."

"On that basis," replied Jan, as a historian rather than a journalist, "he would have made an armistice with the Nazis after the Battle of Britain, maintained the Royal Navy, built up the RAF and taken on the Japanese in the east, protecting Malaya, India and Burma. It's like a war version of Chamberlain's Empire and Free Trade."

"Something along those lines, yes."

"While Russia did all the heavy lifting in Europe?"

"They did anyway," Stannard replied dismissively.

"It's just a theory," Chris Babbage intervened. "How could he or anyone else know what Europe would have been like in those circumstances?"

"He couldn't," said Jan. "With no American intervention the USSR would have incorporated all of Germany. What then?"

"First manned orbit of the Earth, five years earlier," said Stannard. "That's not me speaking, Danny believed it. Only last year he mused we should have been commuting to the Moon by now. Yuri Gagarin was one of his heroes."

The priest left, saying that while he was in Manchester he would be paying a visit to the Ryland's museum and looking in on a building site in Salford which had unearthed what appeared to be the outline of Iron-Age roundhouses. He ignored Chris Babbage's quip that most of Salford would welcome Iron-Age houses today, given the state of most of their modern counterparts. Jan left for a pre-arranged meeting with Kylie Jones in a nearby coffee shop.

Kylie had tried to persuade Jan to meet more regularly in the *Canal Bar*. Jan did not want to be seen too often in such an obviously gay venue, having kept her sexuality private for many years. She also wanted to avoid any confrontation with Sophie. While this was unsaid between them, she felt Kylie's views on the world were often interesting and enjoyed her company. Her IT skills were excellent and her ability to type dialogue from Jan's old battery recorder was admirable in terms of both accuracy and speed. They returned to Jan's apartment so that Kylie could earn her monthly retainer, dealing with the latest interviews and tidying the chapter files which would eventually become *Danny, A Life in Guises.*

Sophie was aware of the arrangements and thought it good for Kylie's prospects. Jan was concerned that her young assistant might clamour for a more permanent arrangement. Kylie had only hinted at it once. Jan had said she had no intention of being the lead in *The Killing of Sister George*, a reference lost on the youngster. However, Kylie looked it up on her IT handset and phone and at their next meeting, having watched the film version, told Jan she had no intention of eating her cigar. This became an in-joke between them.

On this particular evening, while Jan was giving Kylie her version of a deep tissue massage, she found herself discussing Danny's view of World War II and, in his scenario, how things may have turned out. Kylie, face down on the bed, murmured into the pillow that any peace agreement with Hitler would have been "peace on your knees" and that the Nazis may well have succeeded in eliminating European Jewry. She felt the real enigma would have been the United States. They may have defeated Japan much quicker, Britain may have saved its eastern possessions, but would India have been happy as a dominion? Almost certainly not – and did the British have the will to keep it? She thought not.

Kylie stayed an extra hour. It was as well that Sophie was involved in a school parents' evening. Jan had thought of taking Kylie on her final group of interviews, but thought again, deciding it was a distraction best avoided and, besides which, Sophie's family were in Wych Elm. One unguarded piece of body language, accidentally seen, may cause an issue or two. Better to go alone.

The interview with Mary Hobson in the care home was essentially a battle, as Mary constantly tried to turn any question about Danny into one about herself. Then she would try to get information about Jan's late parents, nibbling away about her father and questioning her mother's decision to move away.

"Your father, Jack, died in the police station didn't he? Was it a heart attack? Why did your mother move to your house in Essex afterwards? At least you looked after her. My family are selfish. They have dumped me here. Selfish, that's what it is! I'm not ill and could well do without all these old people around me. I no sooner get to know one and they die! Selfish, that's what it is. Do you know my son, Henry? He's a banker. You may know my daughter, Lucinda. Her husband is a dentist. You live alone. Do you have a spare room for me? I'd be no trouble."

Her take on Danny focused on his war service. She knew he had been in France. Her nostalgia for the war years became a subtext. The war was about "getting away from here" and meeting "more polished" people. She made the point that medals were not given away and had noticed the array worn by Danny at the Armistice Day services over the years. "He very rarely missed" and he stood "ramrod straight," often accompanied by his mother.

An interview with Sandra was arranged at her home and then cancelled. It was rearranged to meet at a country hotel outside Bolton. Sandra was careful in what she said, but patiently reiterated all that Danny had told her when she had nursed him in his latter days. There were signs of emotion in her face as she described what had happened on the day he died. His war references were few, except that he wondered about his role in it, saying his service in occupied France only sounded good in retrospect. He wondered whether "anything had really been achieved, by him or any of the others."

"His mind was sharp when he was fully awake. You know the London Olympics, next year? He mentioned the cycling events and was certain we'd do well in 2012. He talked about the new designs in cycles."

Sandra said he "liked the ladies" and emphasised this was a view her own mother had held. Jan listened, but made no comment. She did not mention his will and Sandra benefitting from it but she did ask about Andrea.

"She was miffed by Danny. I think she was, is, so used to boys chasing after her with their tongues hanging out, she couldn't understand Danny standing off her. She was just interested in him because he was famous. Otherwise he was another demanding, smelly old man. She isn't a kind person and as much for number one as Mary Hobson. Is she still with us?"

"Yes," Jan responded. "She's much the same, still having her weekly hairdo, still causing mayhem in her family."

"Danny used to call her the great survivor," Sandra said wistfully. "He said her utter discontent and flashes of anger kept her alive."

When Jan left, she was wondering in which section Sandra's narrative should appear. She could ask Kylie to incorporate it with Myra's interview but placing it there, alongside the older interviews with Linda Haslam (Mrs Smith) and Janice Johnson, as well as the first, Liz Layne (Mrs Grant), would upset the theme. Sandra may merit a chapter on her own. There was the thorny question of interviewing the current musical establishment, the members of his super groups, *Hot Wind* and *Poke Me Quietly*. Jan had relied on her literary agent to negotiate with their agents some suitable dates, venues, times. This had proved difficult. Currently it was well into the following month and would have been tagged onto a UK tour in the one case and a tour of Ireland in the other.

It was all the more surprising to receive a call from Carla Wayne who had been following Jan's work from California and had attended Danny's funeral under her real name, Carole Ortega, accompanied by her eldest son who worked for an American bank's London office. The former Carole Entwhistle had severed all connections with her home city, Bradford, but had owned a London mews house in Kensington for 20 years. Jan drove down to see her. She was in London to do an interview for a pop history programme and to see her two grandchildren. She had taken the opportunity to be helpful as far as Danny's memory was concerned.

Carla Wayne did not resemble her media photographs. She was 67 and looked it, probably from too much Californian sun. She spoke from the front of her mouth in a faux American accent, which descended into Yorkshire vowels when she became excited. While she sang some of her old numbers on occasional television specials, her voice carried a smoker's descant and the whole vocal ensemble served to make Jan quietly amused. However, once the sound effects were discounted, what she had to say was highly significant.

Danny had picked her out from the northern club circuit right under the nose of a rival Leeds impresario, a flamboyant character into young girls for oral purposes beyond singing. Danny had nurtured her talent in Manchester venues; she would stay overnight in one of his mother's spare rooms and be driven around either by Danny himself or Cliff Hindle. Eventually signed up to the Heim agency, her first record release reached number six in the charts, followed rapidly by two number twos and a three.

"I was never quite number one over here, but my last two made it in the States. Nathan Heim put together an American tour, and the rest, as they say, is history. I met Mike, my husband and went the family way. Heim was displeased, Danny was virtually atomic. He called me a ruined talent."

If the truth be known, Danny was more concerned about his commission – Jan was thinking this as Carla confirmed it. Then Carla's tone changed. She described the early 60s as a man's world, the last such world, and not a boy's world. From 1960 to 1964 was the last time men in their 30s or 40s, with money and preferably looks, could draw on residual feelings of paternalism, loyalty and above all deference to control women. Danny was a classic case insomuch "he ticked every box" and was not in any way "what we called a Nancy Boy" in the way Heim and many of the others were – a silent group of talent around Heim, close-knit and in fear of public exposure as well as the law.

"Most girls then were working at 15, married by the time they were 20 and raising three kids in their 30s on little dough. There was next to no chance of escape from a life of domestic bliss. A chance came rarely and was usually out of reach."

"Danny was your chance? Is that what you mean?" asked Jan.

"No. My husband was the chance. Danny was my means of getting there. Other girls saw Danny and similar guys as a means. They, the guys and the girls, took their opportunities. The guy in Leeds, Jimmy, tried every way to get me in bed and I know for sure he arranged three abortions for under-aged girls he'd used like playthings. Danny was careful, used rubbers and rarely went all the way."

"Did he…?"

"No. He didn't screw me. He did kiss me affectionately, a lot. He tanned my ass when I was difficult. That was him. He was good to me, all in all. He lived in the shadow of Madame Hird, calling her Maman or La Dauphine. She exerted a pall over him, a sort of invisible control. That's why Cliff Hindle was in the garage flat and Danny used the bedsit at the club. He wrote to me when he moved to his cottage, calling it "the place I can live in and be my real self.""

Carla gave a full picture of his mother without rancour or direct criticism. She was smart, a real lady, a good cook and an amusing personality but, in her presence, Danny diminished a little and to the extent people deferred to him he, in his turn, deferred to her. Cliff Hindle had once said to Carla, in an unguarded moment while driving to a performance in a seaside club near Blackpool, that it was as though Madam had a photograph of Danny in a compromising position and her possession of it gave her power; it was hidden somewhere in a secret place, known only to her and no one else. The photograph could have been a metaphor for anything. Walk into a room and find a man on his knees praying – he and you would be embarrassed.

Jan was almost gushing at the end of their chat. She had never cared much for her music. Carla Wayne was too much an early 60s performer, her songs moved quickly out of the mood of the time and only bounced back again in the 90s when two of them were used in television adverts. Yet over an hour of incredibly relevant material was provided, the gist of which brought much else into focus and, though it did not tie up the loose ends it put the threads into a coherent pattern. This suntanned woman, of peculiar vocalisation and mixed motives, had provided a template which, until then, Jan's narrative and theme had lacked. 'When Kylie puts this together,' Jan was musing to herself, 'I'll have to provide some samples of Carla Wayne's musical talent.' When Jan asked to take a photo, Carla provided a studio shot of dubious age and parentage.

"No one wants to see me as I am," Carla explained. "That is Carla Wayne. Mrs Ortega is something else altogether."

"Do you have an earlier one, from your 60s heyday? I could get one off the net but would prefer to use one you like."

Carla rummaged in a desk drawer and produced a full-length black and white shot from 1963. She studied the image herself for a second and then handed it over, creating an arc with her manicured hand.

"Is that to your taste?"

"Oh yes, very much so."

"I thought it might be."

Jan walked back to the car park reflecting on one of her better days. She called Dora, her agent, saying much the same.

The eventual meetings with the super groups were rather more prosaic. She spoke to the four members of *Hot Wind* at a spa hotel in Yorkshire. The four held university degrees, but betrayed little by way of intelligence or culture. This was due to the presence of their management team who insisted on an essentially corporate message. Danny had their gratitude and respect. That was basically the theme. Jan was left wondering how far the fear of litigation was conspiring to suppress free speech. *Poke Me Quietly* had a less corporate approach and went into some detail as to how Danny secured their contracts, protecting their earnings as well as his own. Their lead singer, approaching 50 and wearing a broad black belt to hold in his encroaching corpulence, expressed his opinion very clearly.

"Danny was as tight as a duck's arse. I'm from Yorkshire and he was one of us as far as money was concerned. He'd have split a ha'penny. But what he did for himself, he did for us. One of the Americans he dealt with always, to this day, speaks of him as the guy who knew the value of a cent."

The group were preparing in a hotel on the Isle of Man for a tour of the whole island of Ireland. They had a cost-effective deal giving them "proximity with privacy," a phrase they associated with Danny from their earliest days.

Kylie worked hard on the structure of the new material and thoroughly enjoyed anything associated with the two super groups. Jan managed to get autographed serviettes from all of them, even though the agent for *Hot Wind* tried to impose a charge "for the service." Jan was on the verge of telling him where to put his service before two of the group persuaded him "not to push it."

Back on the mainland, on the same day, Anne Luscombe received a call from her senior Home Office contact, informing her that Northumbria Police had arrested and subsequently charged a prisoner in Wakefield prison for the murder of Nigel Beveridge Mitchell some 20 years earlier. The arrested man, a longstanding drug dealer and user, was 45-year-old Shawn Todd, currently serving a 10-year sentence for ABH and drug dealing to minors. Anne was pleased, being told his arrest was a result of a local television programme reconstructing the murder eight months before. Todd's name had been given to the police and, coupled with evidence already in their possession, they felt confident of success. Todd admitted shooting at Bev Mitchell and was able to tell them where, after all these years, he had kept the gun. He could not account for the subsonic bullet found in Mitchell's back, one that could not have been fired by his pistol. It could be plausibly argued that the bullet that killed Mitchell was not fired by Todd. A further televised reconstruction took place, with an appeal for evidence. Anne responded tersely, wanting to be kept fully informed.

Jan was trying to contact one of Danny's old *protégées* from the same era as Carla Wayne. Eddie Wise had been a plasterer from Daisy Hill. Starting on the club circuit, copying popular ballads of the time, Danny took him under his wing and he eventually recorded two of his own songs for the Heim agency. The record charted at number 40 in 1966 but as far as chart success was concerned, that was the peak. He had continued club work for another 20 years. Jan traced him to Darwin, Australia. She spoke to him, white–haired and in his 70s, on an internet link, finding he was still involved in entertainment on a local scale. He was unable to add anything to what she already knew, saying he was supportive but primarily concerned with contracts and money.

For much of the Easter vacation Jan utilised Kylie's IT skills and emailed the finished product to her agent in the final week of the holiday. Publication went ahead for the summer holiday season. Chris Babbage had allowed photos from the family archive as well as a selection of personal letters. The book was heavily publicised and trailed. The initial print run was sold in less than a fortnight. The section on France, taken substantially from the CDs found in the old book collection, engendered a French interest. A translation was being prepared. Katie would have been in her element. The dedication did not go unnoticed. The final chapter, drawing attention to her demise, kept to the known facts but in a way that implications could easily be drawn. It was during this time that Sir John Arnold Bright was appointed part-time Chairman of the Pesticides (Agricultural Uses) Commission.

Kylie was approaching her finals. She revised a lot with Jan. Sophie had begun to notice. Jan's tenant in her Camden flat gave notice and it was kept for Kylie's use, pending an internship with a local MP in his parliamentary office. The MP was suitably male and gay, and much flattered by Jan's approach to him on "this first-class student's behalf." Who could begin to guess where this may lead? Who indeed!

Chapter Seventeen

The drizzle was unrelenting, the sky moving eastward in a variety of shades of grey. The streets were quiet, even the traffic was rather less in frequency than usual and any passing cars or vans tended to splash the pavements as they trundled along. A figure walked ungainly on the uneven footpath. He was wearing a flat grey cap and he looked up occasionally from beneath the brim, silently cursing the weather as yet another factor in his less than positive life. An elderly Barbour jacket enveloped his upper body, but his grey flannels and light shoes were soaking. He pushed the security button by the glass doors of High Percy police station, once a hub of activity with its own set of cells on the premises. It was now a neighbourhood station, with just two policemen on duty at any one time and a shift of traffic wardens, in their yellow banded caps, universally hated by most of the driving populace as they squinted at each other when they passed by in the streets.

The man removed his cap, folded it into his pocket and tried to flatten his strands of grey-streaked hair in an attempt to cover his balding pate. The wet ends of his straggling locks made the task nigh impossible. He gave up and approached the female officer at the desk. He noticed immediately that she was a little overweight and she had dyed blonde streaks in her hair. In the past he would have labelled her "a typical peroxide blonde." Drawing breath, he tried not to show that he would have much preferred to speak to a man.

She greeted him politely and he stated his business in an efficient fashion. He had seen the recent television programme on the Bev Mitchell case, re-constructing the chain of events. He told her that he and his friend John Laws, "known as Jack," had each given statements at the time of the shooting and had each referred to a stranger, Jacky Brown, allegedly from Leeds, who was in the bar at the time and who had briefly spoken to them.

"For years I've wondered about that man. At the time, I said he looked like that disc jockey on the box, Danny Hird. My friend Jack disagreed, both then and later. The poor bugger is in no position to say anything now. He was cremated last month."

He opened his jacket, fumbling in one of the inside pockets, producing Jan's book, borrowed from the local library. The later photosets had made him convinced that Danny Hird was the man in the pub.

"His hair was black, either dyed or possibly a wig. But I am sure it was him."

The officer asked for his name – Keith Shields – and for an address and telephone number, then asked him to wait while she made a call. Keith sat on a plastic chair, still dripping, as traffic wardens moved in and out of the building. Keith looked them up and down as they strutted by. The policewoman emerged from the back office and said he would be contacted at home, the same evening, to complete a statement. Keith wondered why it couldn't be done there and then, but felt reassured when she told him one of the detectives in charge would want to be present and clarify his statement.

"Fine," he replied. "I'll wait for the call. I won't be out and I'm not working anymore. I've got a bad back from lifting – a bit of a cripple these days."

He readjusted his coat, donned his cap and walked out into the damp gloom. His sparse flat was just 300 yards from the station. As he moved gingerly along he laughed to himself. Only one of Mitchell's old bars remained open, and that was an Indian restaurant. The others were demolished, and rot-infested shops occupied by flats similar to the one he rented – bleak, basic and frugally fitted out, but situated in open green spaces with cycleways and what had been flower beds.

Tarquin Trott was irritated. Sent to open the Manchester office of Media XL5 with his wife and stepdaughter, his bonus had not covered the type of house they had desired in rural Cheshire. His earnings were substantial but the commissions for hiring staff in the northwest did not approach those of Surrey. He was pleased they had not sold their relatively modest house in Weybridge. The rental income supported his daughter, Tamsin, in her efforts to open a dance studio. The substantial stone house they had bought in Wych Elm at least looked rural, and the flat, of sorts, above the double garage had provided Tamsin with a practise studio, where she took local private pupils at £80 per session, usually for a half hour, with a printed 'exercise folder' which built up over a six-week course.

His irritation had come from the necessity to spend money rewiring this 60s conversion so as to allow Tamsin to engage in modern electronic pyrotechnics during the fevered dance routines and to use an up-to-date sound system. Bernice, his second wife of five years, had persuaded him to pay for this work; he would have preferred to hire somewhere bigger and ready-made. The end result found him standing over ripped-out floorboards and rolls of new cable with two contractors pointing to a canvas package hard against the wall. A quick perusal had indicated a rifle of some kind, in good condition, with a box of ammunition. The call to the police caused them some excitement and a specialist firearms officer confirmed this was "a genuine De Lisle silenced carbine of second world war vintage" and he added, just after informing Tarquin he would need to provide his fingerprints having touched the weapon, that "copies of this gun have been made, especially for use in American rifle clubs," but this was the genuine article. It would be checked against any outstanding gun crime cases in the whole of the UK.

Jan was in bed with Kylie, in the Camden flat, both naked and in a semi sleep-like state. Sophie had been speaking on Kylie's phone, asking how the work was going with her gay MP. She had said it had been a quiet start and he seemed to have an interest in the scouting movement and was indicating a need for some research on those lines.

"Can you imagine anything more mind numbing? Me, with a first in politics having, to spend my time on scouting for boys?"

Sophie had asked about Jan and Kylie had made some remark about not seeing much of her "seeing as she is luxuriating in her book sales." She talked of her agent constantly phoning the flat trying to reach her. Hopefully, Sophie might be reassured by that. Jan's phone began to buzz. It was very much a case of being careful what you wish for. Dora, her agent, had picked up the breaking news of a gun find in Danny Hird's family home. It was a case of heading back to Manchester and trawling around Wych Elm. Chris Babbage contacted her, giving the same news, adding,

"We're in luck. It looks as though Rathbone is in charge. It makes sense, really, as he dealt with the bones."

The security officers through the Home Office were also privy to the news. Meetings were infrequent, calls and emails abounded. A month passed and Tracey Brown was transferred to an office in Cheltenham "assessing foreign intelligence." Anne Luscombe was moved to the Home Office in an internal security post. The older members of the service waited and watched. The Metropolitan Police began to re-examine the Katie Ross case. Sir John retained his chairmanship, but Anne added, in a call to Tracey, "for now."

Jan was preparing an appendix for the next edition of her book. When she mentioned this to Ben Fokker during a phone call he chuckled saying he "hadn't laughed so much in years." He judged that the new edition would sell even better than the current one. Her agent fully concurred. Articles appeared in news magazines, newsreels and on the net. Jan was being lauded, yet again, for her prescience and courage.

Sophie was considering the contractual terms of a private enquiry agency. It was expensive. Might it be better to simply confront Kylie? She was unsure whether it would have the desired effect. The row last time she broached the subject had taken weeks to heal. But she was certain something was amiss and things could not continue as they were. Something or someone had to give.